The Grey Woman & Other Tales by Elizabeth Gaskell

Elizabeth Gaskell is equally well known as Mrs Gaskell. When her mother died, she was three months old and she was sent to live in Knutsford, Cheshire with her Aunt Hannah, this setting would become the basis for her novel Cranford. At 22 she married and settled in Manchester to raise her family. Friends with Charlotte Bronte she went on to write her biography and was also highly regarded by a certain Charles Dickens who published her ghost stories in his magazine. Much of her work views the emerging industrial society of Victorian England through her own moral and religious values and has an uncanny ability to look at and report on the many strata of society.

Index of Contents

THE GREY WOMAN

PORTION I

There is a mill by the Neckar-side, to which many people resort for coffee, according to the fashion which is almost national in Germany. There is nothing particularly attractive in the situation of this mill; it is on the Mannheim (the flat and unromantic) side of Heidelberg. The river turns the mill-wheel with a plenteous gushing sound; the out-buildings and the dwelling-house of the miller form a well-kept dusty quadrangle. Again, further from the river, there is a garden full of willows, and arbours, and flower-beds not well kept, but very profuse in flowers and luxuriant creepers, knotting and looping the arbours together. In each of these arbours is a stationary table of white painted wood, and light moveable chairs of the same colour and material.

I went to drink coffee there with some friends in 184—. The stately old miller came out to greet us, as some of the party were known to him of old. He was of a grand build of a man, and his loud musical voice, with its tone friendly and familiar, his rolling laugh of welcome, went well with the keen bright eye, the fine cloth of his coat, and the general look of substance about the place. Poultry of all kinds abounded in the mill-yard, where there were ample means of livelihood for them strewed on the ground; but not content with this, the miller took out handfuls of corn from the sacks, and threw liberally to the cocks and hens that ran almost under his feet in their eagerness. And all the time he was doing this, as it were habitually, he was talking to us, and ever and anon calling to his daughter and the serving-maids, to bid them hasten the coffee we had ordered. He followed us to an arbour, and saw us served to his satisfaction with the best of everything we could ask for; and then left us to go round to the different arbours and see that each party was properly attended to; and, as he went, this great, prosperous, happy-looking man whistled softly one of the most plaintive airs I ever heard.

"His family have held this mill ever since the old Palatinate days; or rather, I should say, have possessed the ground ever since then, for two successive mills of theirs have been burnt down by the French. If you want to see Scherer in a passion, just talk to him of the possibility of a French invasion."

But at this moment, still whistling that mournful air, we saw the miller going down the steps that led from the somewhat raised garden into the mill-yard; and so I seemed to have lost my chance of putting him in a passion.

We had nearly finished our coffee, and our "kucken," and our cinnamon cake, when heavy splashes fell on our thick leafy covering; quicker and quicker they came, coming through the tender leaves as if they were tearing them asunder; all the people in the garden were hurrying under shelter, or seeking for their carriages standing outside. Up the steps the miller came hastening, with a crimson umbrella, fit to cover every one left in the garden, and followed by his daughter, and one or two maidens, each bearing an umbrella.

"Come into the house—come in, I say. It is a summer-storm, and will flood the place for an hour or two, till the river carries it away. Here, here."

And we followed him back into his own house. We went into the kitchen first. Such an array of bright copper and tin vessels I never saw; and all the wooden things were as thoroughly scoured. The red tile floor was spotless when we went in, but in two minutes it was all over slop and dirt with the tread of many feet; for the kitchen was filled, and still the worthy miller kept bringing in more people under his great crimson umbrella. He even called the dogs in, and made them lie down under the tables.

His daughter said something to him in German, and he shook his head merrily at her. Everybody laughed.

"What did she say?" I asked.

"She told him to bring the ducks in next; but indeed if more people come we shall be suffocated. What with the thundery weather, and the stove, and all these steaming clothes, I really think we must ask leave to pass on. Perhaps we might go in and see Frau Scherer."

My friend asked the daughter of the house for permission to go into an inner chamber and see her mother. It was granted, and we went into a sort of saloon, overlooking the Neckar; very small, very bright, and very close. The floor was slippery with polish; long narrow pieces of looking-glass against the walls reflected the perpetual motion of the river opposite; a white porcelain stove, with some old-fashioned ornaments of brass about it; a sofa, covered with Utrecht velvet, a table before it, and a piece of worsted-worked carpet under it; a vase of artificial flowers; and, lastly, an alcove with a bed in it, on which lay the paralysed wife of the good miller, knitting busily, formed the furniture. I spoke as if this was all that was to be seen in the room; but, sitting quietly, while my friend kept up a brisk conversation in a language which I but half understood, my eye was caught by a picture in a dark corner of the room, and I got up to examine it more nearly.

It was that of a young girl of extreme beauty; evidently of middle rank. There was a sensitive refinement in her face, as if she almost shrank from the gaze which, of necessity, the painter must have fixed upon her. It was not over-well painted, but I felt that it must have been a good likeness, from this strong impress of peculiar character which I have tried to describe. From the dress, I should guess it to have been painted in the latter half of the last century. And I afterwards heard that I was right.

There was a little pause in the conversation.

"Will you ask Frau Scherer who this is?"

My friend repeated my question, and received a long reply in German. Then she turned round and translated it to me.

"It is the likeness of a great-aunt of her husband's." (My friend was standing by me, and looking at the picture with sympathetic curiosity.) "See! here is the name on the open page of this Bible, 'Anna Scherer, 1778.' Frau Scherer says there is a tradition in the family that this pretty girl, with her complexion of lilies and roses, lost her colour so entirely through fright, that she was known by the name of the Grey Woman. She speaks as if this Anna Scherer lived in some state of life-long terror. But she does not know details; refers me to her husband for them. She thinks he has some papers which were written by the original of that picture for her daughter, who died in this very house not long after our friend there was married. We can ask Herr Scherer for the whole story if you like."

"Oh yes, pray do!" said I. And, as our host came in at this moment to ask how we were faring, and to tell us that he had sent to Heidelberg for carriages to convey us home, seeing no chance of the heavy rain abating, my friend, after thanking him, passed on to my request.

"Ah!" said he, his face changing, "the aunt Anna had a sad history. It was all owing to one of those hellish Frenchmen; and her daughter suffered for it—the cousin Ursula, as we all called her when I was a child. To be sure, the good cousin Ursula was his child as well. The sins of the fathers are visited on their children. The lady would like to know all about it, would she? Well, there are papers—a kind of apology the aunt Anna wrote for putting an end to her daughter's engagement—or rather facts which she revealed, that prevented cousin Ursula from marrying the man she loved; and so she would never have any other good fellow, else I have heard say my father would have been thankful to have made her his wife." All this time he was rummaging in the drawer of an old-fashioned bureau, and now he turned round, with a bundle of yellow MSS. in his hand, which he gave to my friend, saying, "Take it home, take it home, and if you care to make out our crabbed German writing, you may keep it as long as you like, and read it at your leisure. Only I must have it back again when you have done with it, that's all."

And so we became possessed of the manuscript of the following letter, which it was our employment, during many a long evening that ensuing winter, to translate, and in some parts to abbreviate. The letter began with some reference to the pain which she had already inflicted upon her daughter by some unexplained opposition to a project of marriage; but I doubt if, without the clue with which the good miller had furnished us, we could have made out even this much from the passionate, broken sentences that made us fancy that some scene between the mother and daughter—and possibly a third person— had occurred just before the mother had begun to write.

"Thou dost not love thy child, mother! Thou dost not care if her heart is broken!" Ah, God! and these words of my heart-beloved Ursula ring in my ears as if the sound of them would fill them when I lie a-dying. And her poor tear-stained face comes between me and everything else. Child! hearts do not break; life is very tough as well as very terrible. But I will not decide for thee. I will tell thee all; and thou shalt bear the burden of choice. I may be wrong; I have little wit left, and never had much, I think; but an instinct serves me in place of judgment, and that instinct tells me that thou and thy Henri must never be married. Yet I may be in error. I would fain make my child happy. Lay this paper before the good priest Schriesheim; if, after reading it, thou hast doubts which make thee uncertain. Only I will tell thee all now, on condition that no spoken word ever passes between us on the subject. It would kill me to be questioned. I should have to see all present again.

My father held, as thou knowest, the mill on the Neckar, where thy new-found uncle, Scherer, now lives. Thou rememberest the surprise with which we were received there last vintage twelvemonth. How my uncle disbelieved me when I said that I was his sister Anna, whom he had long believed to be dead, and how I had to lead thee underneath the picture, painted of me long ago, and point out, feature by feature, the likeness between it and thee; and how, as I spoke, I recalled first to my own mind, and then by speech to his, the details of the time when it was painted; the merry words that passed between us then, a happy boy and girl; the position of the articles of furniture in the room; our father's habits; the cherry-tree, now cut down, that shaded the window of my bedroom, through which my brother was wont to squeeze himself, in order to spring on to the topmost bough that would bear his weight; and thence would pass me back his cap laden with fruit to where I sat on the window-sill, too sick with fright for him to care much for eating the cherries.

And at length Fritz gave way, and believed me to be his sister Anna, even as though I were risen from the dead. And thou rememberest how he fetched in his wife, and told her that I was not dead, but was come back to the old home once more, changed as I was. And she would scarce believe him, and scanned me with a cold, distrustful eye, till at length—for I knew her of old as Babette Müller—I said that I was well-to-do, and needed not to seek out friends for what they had to give. And then she asked—not me, but her husband—why I had kept silent so long, leading all—father, brother, every one that loved me in my own dear home—to esteem me dead. And then thine uncle (thou rememberest?) said he cared not to know more than I cared to tell; that I was his Anna, found again, to be a blessing to him in his old age, as I had been in his boyhood. I thanked him in my heart for his trust; for were the need for telling all less than it seems to me now I could not speak of my past life. But she, who was my sister-in-law still, held back her welcome, and, for want of that, I did not go to live in Heidelberg as I had planned beforehand, in order to be near my brother Fritz, but contented myself with his promise to be a father to my Ursula when I should die and leave this weary world.

That Babette Müller was, as I may say, the cause of all my life's suffering. She was a baker's daughter in Heidelberg—a great beauty, as people said, and, indeed, as I could see for myself. I, too—thou sawest my picture—was reckoned a beauty, and I believe I was so. Babette Müller looked upon me as a rival. She liked to be admired, and had no one much to love her. I had several people to love me—thy grandfather, Fritz, the old servant Kätchen, Karl, the head apprentice at the mill—and I feared admiration and notice, and the being stared at as the "Schöne Müllerin," whenever I went to make my purchases in Heidelberg.

Those were happy, peaceful days. I had Kätchen to help me in the housework, and whatever we did pleased my brave old father, who was always gentle and indulgent towards us women, though he was stern enough with the apprentices in the mill. Karl, the oldest of these, was his favourite; and I can see now that my father wished him to marry me, and that Karl himself was desirous to do so. But Karl was rough-spoken, and passionate—not with me, but with the others—and I shrank from him in a way which, I fear, gave him pain. And then came thy uncle Fritz's marriage; and Babette was brought to the mill to be its mistress. Not that I cared much for giving up my post, for, in spite of my father's great kindness, I always feared that I did not manage well for so large a family (with the men, and a girl under Kätchen, we sat down eleven each night to supper). But when Babette began to find fault with Kätchen, I was unhappy at the blame that fell on faithful servants; and by-and-by I began to see that Babette was egging on Karl to make more open love to me, and, as she once said, to get done with it, and take me off to a home of my own. My father was growing old, and did not perceive all my daily discomfort. The more Karl advanced, the more I disliked him. He was good in the main, but I had no notion of being married, and could not bear any one who talked to me about it.

Things were in this way when I had an invitation to go to Carlsruhe to visit a schoolfellow, of whom I had been very fond. Babette was all for my going; I don't think I wanted to leave home, and yet I had been very fond of Sophie Rupprecht. But I was always shy among strangers. Somehow the affair was settled for me, but not until both Fritz and my father had made inquiries as to the character and position of the Rupprechts. They learned that the father had held some kind of inferior position about the Grand-duke's court, and was now dead, leaving a widow, a noble lady, and two daughters, the elder of whom was Sophie, my friend. Madame Rupprecht was not rich, but more than respectable—genteel. When this was ascertained, my father made no opposition to my going; Babette forwarded it by all the means in her power, and even my dear Fritz had his word to say in its favour. Only Kätchen was against it— Kätchen and Karl. The opposition of Karl did more to send me to Carlsruhe than anything. For I could have objected to go; but when he took upon himself to ask what was the good of going a-gadding, visiting strangers of whom no one knew anything, I yielded to circumstances—to the pulling of Sophie and the pushing of Babette. I was silently vexed, I remember, at Babette's inspection of my clothes; at the way in which she settled that this gown was too old-fashioned, or that too common, to go with me on my visit to a noble lady; and at the way in which she took upon herself to spend the money my father had given me to buy what was requisite for the occasion. And yet I blamed myself, for every one else thought her so kind for doing all this; and she herself meant kindly, too.

At last I quitted the mill by the Neckar-side. It was a long day's journey, and Fritz went with me to Carlsruhe. The Rupprechts lived on the third floor of a house a little behind one of the principal streets, in a cramped-up court, to which we gained admittance through a doorway in the street. I remember how pinched their rooms looked after the large space we had at the mill, and yet they had an air of grandeur about them which was new to me, and which gave me pleasure, faded as some of it was. Madame Rupprecht was too formal a lady for me; I was never at my ease with her; but Sophie was all that I had recollected her at school: kind, affectionate, and only rather too ready with her expressions of admiration and regard. The little sister kept out of our way; and that was all we needed, in the first enthusiastic renewal of our early friendship. The one great object of Madame Rupprecht's life was to retain her position in society; and as her means were much diminished since her husband's death, there was not much comfort, though there was a great deal of show, in their way of living; just the opposite of what it was at my father's house. I believe that my coming was not too much desired by Madame Rupprecht, as I brought with me another mouth to be fed; but Sophie had spent a year or more in entreating for permission to invite me, and her mother, having once consented, was too well bred not to give me a stately welcome.

The life in Carlsruhe was very different from what it was at home. The hours were later, the coffee was weaker in the morning, the pottage was weaker, the boiled beef less relieved by other diet, the dresses finer, the evening engagements constant. I did not find these visits pleasant. We might not knit, which would have relieved the tedium a little; but we sat in a circle, talking together, only interrupted occasionally by a gentleman, who, breaking out of the knot of men who stood near the door, talking eagerly together, stole across the room on tiptoe, his hat under his arm, and, bringing his feet together in the position we called the first at the dancing-school, made a low bow to the lady he was going to address. The first time I saw these manners I could not help smiling; but Madame Rupprecht saw me, and spoke to me next morning rather severely, telling me that, of course, in my country breeding I could have seen nothing of court manners, or French fashions, but that that was no reason for my laughing at them. Of course I tried never to smile again in company. This visit to Carlsruhe took place in '89, just when every one was full of the events taking place at Paris; and yet at Carlsruhe French fashions were more talked of than French politics. Madame Rupprecht, especially, thought a great deal of all French people. And this again was quite different to us at home. Fritz could hardly bear the name of a Frenchman; and it had nearly been an obstacle to my visit to Sophie that her mother preferred being called Madame to her proper title of Frau.

[Illustration p. 17: Monsieur de la Tourelle.]

One night I was sitting next to Sophie, and longing for the time when we might have supper and go home, so as to be able to speak together, a thing forbidden by Madame Rupprecht's rules of etiquette, which strictly prohibited any but the most necessary conversation passing between members of the same family when in society. I was sitting, I say, scarcely keeping back my inclination to yawn, when two gentlemen came in, one of whom was evidently a stranger to the whole party, from the formal manner in which the host led him up, and presented him to the hostess. I thought I had never seen any one so handsome or so elegant. His hair was powdered, of course, but one could see from his complexion that it was fair in its natural state. His features were as delicate as a girl's, and set off by two little "mouches," as we called patches in those days, one at the left corner of his mouth, the other prolonging, as it were, the right eye. His dress was blue and silver. I was so lost in admiration of this beautiful young man, that I was as much surprised as if the angel Gabriel had spoken to me, when the lady of the house brought him forward to present him to me. She called him Monsieur de la Tourelle, and he began to speak to me in French; but though I understood him perfectly, I dared not trust myself to reply to him in that language. Then he tried German, speaking it with a kind of soft lisp that I thought charming. But, before the end of the evening, I became a little tired of the affected softness and effeminacy of his manners, and the exaggerated compliments he paid me, which had the effect of making all the company turn round and look at me. Madame Rupprecht was, however, pleased with the precise thing that displeased me. She liked either Sophie or me to create a sensation; of course she would have preferred that it should have been her daughter, but her daughter's friend was next best. As we went away, I heard Madame Rupprecht and Monsieur de la Tourelle reciprocating civil speeches with might and main, from which I found out that the French gentleman was coming to call on us the next day. I do not know whether I was more glad or frightened, for I had been kept upon stilts of good manners all the evening. But still I was flattered when Madame Rupprecht spoke as if she had invited him, because he had shown pleasure in my society, and even more gratified by Sophie's ungrudging delight at the evident interest I had excited in so fine and agreeable a gentleman. Yet, with all this, they had hard work to keep me from running out of the salon the next day, when we heard his voice inquiring at the gate on the stairs for Madame Rupprecht. They had made me put on my Sunday gown, and they themselves were dressed as for a reception.

When he was gone away, Madame Rupprecht congratulated me on the conquest I had made; for, indeed, he had scarcely spoken to any one else, beyond what mere civility required, and had almost invited himself to come in the evening to bring some new song, which was all the fashion in Paris, he said. Madame Rupprecht had been out all morning, as she told me, to glean information about

Monsieur de la Tourelle. He was a propriétaire, had a small château on the Vosges mountains; he owned land there, but had a large income from some sources quite independent of this property. Altogether, he was a good match, as she emphatically observed. She never seemed to think that I could refuse him after this account of his wealth, nor do I believe she would have allowed Sophie a choice, even had he been as old and ugly as he was young and handsome. I do not quite know—so many events have come to pass since then, and blurred the clearness of my recollections—if I loved him or not. He was very much devoted to me; he almost frightened me by the excess of his demonstrations of love. And he was very charming to everybody around me, who all spoke of him as the most fascinating of men, and of me as the most fortunate of girls. And yet I never felt quite at my ease with him. I was always relieved when his visits were over, although I missed his presence when he did not come. He prolonged his visit to the friend with whom he was staying at Carlsruhe, on purpose to woo me. He loaded me with presents, which I was unwilling to take, only Madame Rupprecht seemed to consider me an affected prude if I refused them. Many of these presents consisted of articles of valuable old jewellery, evidently belonging to his family; by accepting these I doubled the ties which were formed around me by circumstances even more than by my own consent. In those days we did not write letters to absent friends as frequently as is done now, and I had been unwilling to name him in the few letters that I wrote home. At length, however, I learned from Madame Rupprecht that she had written to my father to announce the splendid conquest I had made, and to request his presence at my betrothal. I started with astonishment. I had not realized that affairs had gone so far as this. But when she asked me, in a stern, offended manner, what I had meant by my conduct if I did not intend to marry Monsieur de la Tourelle—I had received his visits, his presents, all his various advances without showing any unwillingness or repugnance—(and it was all true; I had shown no repugnance, though I did not wish to be married to him,—at least, not so soon)—what could I do but hang my head, and silently consent to the rapid enunciation of the only course which now remained for me if I would not be esteemed a heartless coquette all the rest of my days?

There was some difficulty, which I afterwards learnt that my sister-in-law had obviated, about my betrothal taking place from home. My father, and Fritz especially, were for having me return to the mill, and there be betrothed, and from thence be married. But the Rupprechts and Monsieur de la Tourelle were equally urgent on the other side; and Babette was unwilling to have the trouble of the commotion at the mill; and also, I think, a little disliked the idea of the contrast of my grander marriage with her own.

So my father and Fritz came over to the betrothal. They were to stay at an inn in Carlsruhe for a fortnight, at the end of which time the marriage was to take place. Monsieur de la Tourelle told me he had business at home, which would oblige him to be absent during the interval between the two events; and I was very glad of it, for I did not think that he valued my father and my brother as I could have wished him to do. He was very polite to them; put on all the soft, grand manner, which he had rather dropped with me; and complimented us all round, beginning with my father and Madame Rupprecht, and ending with little Alwina. But he a little scoffed at the old-fashioned church ceremonies which my father insisted on; and I fancy Fritz must have taken some of his compliments as satire, for I saw certain signs of manner by which I knew that my future husband, for all his civil words, had irritated and annoyed my brother. But all the money arrangements were liberal in the extreme, and more than satisfied, almost surprised, my father. Even Fritz lifted up his eyebrows and whistled. I alone did not care about anything. I was bewitched,—in a dream,—a kind of despair. I had got into a net through my own timidity and weakness, and I did not see how to get out of it. I clung to my own home-people that fortnight as I had never done before. Their voices, their ways were all so pleasant and familiar to me, after the constraint in which I had been living. I might speak and do as I liked without being corrected by

Madame Rupprecht, or reproved in a delicate, complimentary way by Monsieur de la Tourelle. One day I said to my father that I did not want to be married, that I would rather go back to the dear old mill; but he seemed to feel this speech of mine as a dereliction of duty as great as if I had committed perjury; as if, after the ceremony of betrothal, no one had any right over me but my future husband. And yet he asked me some solemn questions; but my answers were not such as to do me any good.

"Dost thou know any fault or crime in this man that should prevent God's blessing from resting on thy marriage with him? Dost thou feel aversion or repugnance to him in any way?"

And to all this what could I say? I could only stammer out that I did not think I loved him enough; and my poor old father saw in this reluctance only the fancy of a silly girl who did not know her own mind, but who had now gone too far to recede.

So we were married, in the Court chapel, a privilege which Madame Rupprecht had used no end of efforts to obtain for us, and which she must have thought was to secure us all possible happiness, both at the time and in recollection afterwards.

We were married; and after two days spent in festivity at Carlsruhe, among all our new fashionable friends there, I bade good-by for ever to my dear old father. I had begged my husband to take me by way of Heidelberg to his old castle in the Vosges; but I found an amount of determination, under that effeminate appearance and manner, for which I was not prepared, and he refused my first request so decidedly that I dared not urge it. "Henceforth, Anna," said he, "you will move in a different sphere of life; and though it is possible that you may have the power of showing favour to your relations from time to time, yet much or familiar intercourse will be undesirable, and is what I cannot allow." I felt almost afraid, after this formal speech, of asking my father and Fritz to come and see me; but, when the agony of bidding them farewell overcame all my prudence, I did beg them to pay me a visit ere long. But they shook their heads, and spoke of business at home, of different kinds of life, of my being a Frenchwoman now. Only my father broke out at last with a blessing, and said, "If my child is unhappy—which God forbid—let her remember that her father's house is ever open to her." I was on the point of crying out, "Oh! take me back then now, my father! oh, my father!" when I felt, rather than saw, my husband present near me. He looked on with a slightly contemptuous air; and, taking my hand in his, he led me weeping away, saying that short farewells were always the best when they were inevitable.

It took us two days to reach his château in the Vosges, for the roads were bad and the way difficult to ascertain. Nothing could be more devoted than he was all the time of the journey. It seemed as if he were trying in every way to make up for the separation which every hour made me feel the more complete between my present and my former life. I seemed as if I were only now wakening up to a full sense of what marriage was, and I dare say I was not a cheerful companion on the tedious journey. At length, jealousy of my regret for my father and brother got the better of M. de la Tourelle, and he became so much displeased with me that I thought my heart would break with the sense of desolation. So it was in no cheerful frame of mind that we approached Les Rochers, and I thought that perhaps it was because I was so unhappy that the place looked so dreary. On one side, the château looked like a raw new building, hastily run up for some immediate purpose, without any growth of trees or underwood near it, only the remains of the stone used for building, not yet cleared away from the immediate neighbourhood, although weeds and lichens had been suffered to grow near and over the heaps of rubbish; on the other, were the great rocks from which the place took its name, and rising close against them, as if almost a natural formation, was the old castle, whose building dated many centuries back.

It was not large nor grand, but it was strong and picturesque, and I used to wish that we lived in it rather than in the smart, half-furnished apartment in the new edifice, which had been hastily got ready for my reception. Incongruous as the two parts were, they were joined into a whole by means of intricate passages and unexpected doors, the exact positions of which I never fully understood. M. de la Tourelle led me to a suite of rooms set apart for me, and formally installed me in them, as in a domain of which I was sovereign. He apologised for the hasty preparation which was all he had been able to make for me, but promised, before I asked, or even thought of complaining, that they should be made as luxurious as heart could wish before many weeks had elapsed. But when, in the gloom of an autumnal evening, I caught my own face and figure reflected in all the mirrors, which showed only a mysterious background in the dim light of the many candles which failed to illuminate the great proportions of the half-furnished salon, I clung to M. de la Tourelle, and begged to be taken to the rooms he had occupied before his marriage, he seemed angry with me, although he affected to laugh, and so decidedly put aside the notion of my having any other rooms but these, that I trembled in silence at the fantastic figures and shapes which my imagination called up as peopling the background of those gloomy mirrors. There was my boudoir, a little less dreary—my bedroom, with its grand and tarnished furniture, which I commonly made into my sitting-room, locking up the various doors which led into the boudoir, the salon, the passages—all but one, through which M. de la Tourelle always entered from his own apartments in the older part of the castle. But this preference of mine for occupying my bedroom annoyed M. de la Tourelle, I am sure, though he did not care to express his displeasure. He would always allure me back into the salon, which I disliked more and more from its complete separation from the rest of the building by the long passage into which all the doors of my apartment opened. This passage was closed by heavy doors and portières, through which I could not hear a sound from the other parts of the house, and, of course, the servants could not hear any movement or cry of mine unless expressly summoned. To a girl brought up as I had been in a household where every individual lived all day in the sight of every other member of the family, never wanted either cheerful words or the sense of silent companionship, this grand isolation of mine was very formidable; and the more so, because M. de la Tourelle, as landed proprietor, sportsman, and what not, was generally out of doors the greater part of every day, and sometimes for two or three days at a time. I had no pride to keep me from associating with the domestics; it would have been natural to me in many ways to have sought them out for a word of sympathy in those dreary days when I was left so entirely to myself, had they been like our kindly German servants. But I disliked them, one and all; I could not tell why. Some were civil, but there was a familiarity in their civility which repelled me; others were rude, and treated me more as if I were an intruder than their master's chosen wife; and yet of the two sets I liked these last the best.

The principal male servant belonged to this latter class. I was very much afraid of him, he had such an air of suspicious surliness about him in all he did for me; and yet M. de la Tourelle spoke of him as most valuable and faithful. Indeed, it sometimes struck me that Lefebvre ruled his master in some things; and this I could not make out. For, while M. de la Tourelle behaved towards me as if I were some precious toy or idol, to be cherished, and fostered, and petted, and indulged, I soon found out how little I, or, apparently, any one else, could bend the terrible will of the man who had on first acquaintance appeared to me too effeminate and languid to exert his will in the slightest particular. I had learnt to know his face better now; and to see that some vehement depth of feeling, the cause of which I could not fathom, made his grey eye glitter with pale light, and his lips contract, and his delicate cheek whiten on certain occasions. But all had been so open and above board at home, that I had no experience to help me to unravel any mysteries among those who lived under the same roof. I understood that I had made what Madame Rupprecht and her set would have called a great marriage, because I lived in a château with many servants, bound ostensibly to obey me as a mistress. I understood that M. de la

Tourelle was fond enough of me in his way—proud of my beauty, I dare say (for he often enough spoke about it to me)—but he was also jealous, and suspicious, and uninfluenced by my wishes, unless they tallied with his own. I felt at this time as if I could have been fond of him too, if he would have let me; but I was timid from my childhood, and before long my dread of his displeasure (coming down like thunder into the midst of his love, for such slight causes as a hesitation in reply, a wrong word, or a sigh for my father), conquered my humorous inclination to love one who was so handsome, so accomplished, so indulgent and devoted. But if I could not please him when indeed I loved him, you may imagine how often I did wrong when I was so much afraid of him as to quietly avoid his company for fear of his outbursts of passion. One thing I remember noticing, that the more M. de la Tourelle was displeased with me, the more Lefebvre seemed to chuckle; and when I was restored to favour, sometimes on as sudden an impulse as that which occasioned my disgrace, Lefebvre would look askance at me with his cold, malicious eyes, and once or twice at such times he spoke most disrespectfully to M. de la Tourelle.

I have almost forgotten to say that, in the early days of my life at Les Rochers, M. de la Tourelle, in contemptuous indulgent pity at my weakness in disliking the dreary grandeur of the salon, wrote up to the milliner in Paris from whom my corbeille de mariage had come, to desire her to look out for me a maid of middle age, experienced in the toilette, and with so much refinement that she might on occasion serve as companion to me.

PORTION II

A Norman woman, Amante by name, was sent to Les Rochers by the Paris milliner, to become my maid. She was tall and handsome, though upwards of forty, and somewhat gaunt. But, on first seeing her, I liked her; she was neither rude nor familiar in her manners, and had a pleasant look of straightforwardness about her that I had missed in all the inhabitants of the château, and had foolishly set down in my own mind as a national want. Amante was directed by M. de la Tourelle to sit in my boudoir, and to be always within call. He also gave her many instructions as to her duties in matters which, perhaps, strictly belonged to my department of management. But I was young and inexperienced, and thankful to be spared any responsibility.

I daresay it was true what M. de la Tourelle said—before many weeks had elapsed—that, for a great lady, a lady of a castle, I became sadly too familiar with my Norman waiting-maid. But you know that by birth we were not very far apart in rank: Amante was the daughter of a Norman farmer, I of a German miller; and besides that, my life was so lonely! It almost seemed as if I could not please my husband. He had written for some one capable of being my companion at times, and now he was jealous of my free regard for her—angry because I could sometimes laugh at her original tunes and amusing proverbs, while when with him I was too much frightened to smile.

From time to time families from a distance of some leagues drove through the bad roads in their heavy carriages to pay us a visit, and there was an occasional talk of our going to Paris when public affairs should be a little more settled. These little events and plans were the only variations in my life for the first twelve months, if I except the alternations in M. de la Tourelle's temper, his unreasonable anger, and his passionate fondness.

Perhaps one of the reasons that made me take pleasure and comfort in Amante's society was, that whereas I was afraid of everybody (I do not think I was half as much afraid of things as of persons), Amante feared no one. She would quietly beard Lefebvre, and he respected her all the more for it; she had a knack of putting questions to M. de la Tourelle, which respectfully informed him that she had detected the weak point, but forebore to press him too closely upon it out of deference to his position as her master. And with all her shrewdness to others, she had quite tender ways with me; all the more so at this time because she knew, what I had not yet ventured to tell M. de la Tourelle, that by-and-by I might become a mother—that wonderful object of mysterious interest to single women, who no longer hope to enjoy such blessedness themselves.

It was once more autumn; late in October. But I was reconciled to my habitation; the walls of the new part of the building no longer looked bare and desolate; the débris had been so far cleared away by M. de la Tourelle's desire as to make me a little flower-garden, in which I tried to cultivate those plants that I remembered as growing at home. Amante and I had moved the furniture in the rooms, and adjusted it to our liking; my husband had ordered many an article from time to time that he thought would give me pleasure, and I was becoming tame to my apparent imprisonment in a certain part of the great building, the whole of which I had never yet explored. It was October, as I say, once more. The days were lovely, though short in duration, and M. de la Tourelle had occasion, so he said, to go to that distant estate the superintendence of which so frequently took him away from home. He took Lefebvre with him, and possibly some more of the lacqueys; he often did. And my spirits rose a little at the thought of his absence; and then the new sensation that he was the father of my unborn babe came over me, and I tried to invest him with this fresh character. I tried to believe that it was his passionate love for me that made him so jealous and tyrannical, imposing, as he did, restrictions on my very intercourse with my dear father, from whom I was so entirely separated, as far as personal intercourse was concerned.

I had, it is true, let myself go into a sorrowful review of all the troubles which lay hidden beneath the seeming luxury of my life. I knew that no one cared for me except my husband and Amante; for it was clear enough to see that I, as his wife, and also as a parvenue, was not popular among the few neighbours who surrounded us; and as for the servants, the women were all hard and impudent-looking, treating me with a semblance of respect that had more of mockery than reality in it; while the men had a lurking kind of fierceness about them, sometimes displayed even to M. de la Tourelle, who on his part, it must be confessed, was often severe even to cruelty in his management of them. My husband loved me, I said to myself, but I said it almost in the form of a question. His love was shown fitfully, and more in ways calculated to please himself than to please me. I felt that for no wish of mine would he deviate one tittle from any predetermined course of action. I had learnt the inflexibility of those thin, delicate lips; I knew how anger would turn his fair complexion to deadly white, and bring the cruel light into his pale blue eyes. The love I bore to any one seemed to be a reason for his hating them, and so I went on pitying myself one long dreary afternoon during that absence of his of which I have spoken, only sometimes remembering to check myself in my murmurings by thinking of the new unseen link between us, and then crying afresh to think how wicked I was. Oh, how well I remember that long October evening! Amante came in from time to time, talking away to cheer me—talking about dress and Paris, and I hardly know what, but from time to time looking at me keenly with her friendly dark eyes, and with serious interest, too, though all her words were about frivolity. At length she heaped the fire with wood, drew the heavy silken curtains close; for I had been anxious hitherto to keep them open, so that I might see the pale moon mounting the skies, as I used to see her—the same moon—rise from behind the Kaiser Stuhl at Heidelberg; but the sight made me cry, so Amante shut it out. She dictated to me as a nurse does to a child.

"Now, madame must have the little kitten to keep her company," she said, "while I go and ask Marthon for a cup of coffee." I remember that speech, and the way it roused me, for I did not like Amante to think I wanted amusing by a kitten. It might be my petulance, but this speech—such as she might have made to a child—annoyed me, and I said that I had reason for my lowness of spirits—meaning that they were not of so imaginary a nature that I could be diverted from them by the gambols of a kitten. So, though I did not choose to tell her all, I told her a part; and as I spoke, I began to suspect that the good creature knew much of what I withheld, and that the little speech about the kitten was more thoughtfully kind than it had seemed at first. I said that it was so long since I had heard from my father; that he was an old man, and so many things might happen—I might never see him again—and I so seldom heard from him or my brother. It was a more complete and total separation than I had ever anticipated when I married, and something of my home and of my life previous to my marriage I told the good Amante; for I had not been brought up as a great lady, and the sympathy of any human being was precious to me.

Amante listened with interest, and in return told me some of the events and sorrows of her own life. Then, remembering her purpose, she set out in search of the coffee, which ought to have been brought to me an hour before; but, in my husband's absence, my wishes were but seldom attended to, and I never dared to give orders.

Presently she returned, bringing the coffee and a great large cake.

"See!" said she, setting it down. "Look at my plunder. Madame must eat. Those who eat always laugh. And, besides, I have a little news that will please madame." Then she told me that, lying on a table in the great kitchen, was a bundle of letters, come by the courier from Strasburg that very afternoon: then, fresh from her conversation with me, she had hastily untied the string that bound them, but had only just traced out one that she thought was from Germany, when a servant-man came in, and, with the start he gave her, she dropped the letters, which he picked up, swearing at her for having untied and disarranged them. She told him that she believed there was a letter there for her mistress; but he only swore the more, saying, that if there was it was no business of hers, or of his either, for that he had the strictest orders always to take all letters that arrived during his master's absence into the private sitting-room of the latter—a room into which I had never entered, although it opened out of my husband's dressing-room.

I asked Amante if she had not conquered and brought me this letter. No, indeed, she replied, it was almost as much as her life was worth to live among such a set of servants: it was only a month ago that Jacques had stabbed Valentin for some jesting talk. Had I never missed Valentin—that handsome young lad who carried up the wood into my salon? Poor fellow! he lies dead and cold now, and they said in the village he had put an end to himself, but those of the household knew better. Oh! I need not be afraid; Jacques was gone, no one knew where; but with such people it was not safe to upbraid or insist. Monsieur would be at home the next day, and it would not be long to wait.

But I felt as if I could not exist till the next day, without the letter. It might be to say that my father was ill, dying—he might cry for his daughter from his death-bed! In short, there was no end to the thoughts and fancies that haunted me. It was of no use for Amante to say that, after all, she might be mistaken— that she did not read writing well—that she had but a glimpse of the address; I let my coffee cool, my food all became distasteful, and I wrung my hands with impatience to get at the letter, and have some news of my dear ones at home. All the time, Amante kept her imperturbable good temper, first reasoning, then scolding. At last she said, as if wearied out, that if I would consent to make a good supper, she would see what could be done as to our going to monsieur's room in search of the letter, after the servants were all gone to bed. We agreed to go together when all was still, and look over the letters; there could be no harm in that; and yet, somehow, we were such cowards we dared not do it openly and in the face of the household.

Presently my supper came up—partridges, bread, fruits, and cream. How well I remember that supper! We put the untouched cake away in a sort of buffet, and poured the cold coffee out of the window, in order that the servants might not take offence at the apparent fancifulness of sending down for food I could not eat. I was so anxious for all to be in bed, that I told the footman who served that he need not wait to take away the plates and dishes, but might go to bed. Long after I thought the house was quiet, Amante, in her caution, made me wait. It was past eleven before we set out, with cat-like steps and veiled light, along the passages, to go to my husband's room and steal my own letter, if it was indeed there; a fact about which Amante had become very uncertain in the progress of our discussion.

To make you understand my story, I must now try to explain to you the plan of the château. It had been at one time a fortified place of some strength, perched on the summit of a rock, which projected from the side of the mountain. But additions had been made to the old building (which must have borne a strong resemblance to the castles overhanging the Rhine), and these new buildings were placed so as to command a magnificent view, being on the steepest side of the rock, from which the mountain fell away, as it were, leaving the great plain of France in full survey. The ground-plan was something of the shape of three sides of an oblong; my apartments in the modern edifice occupied the narrow end, and had this grand prospect. The front of the castle was old, and ran parallel to the road far below. In this were contained the offices and public rooms of various descriptions, into which I never penetrated. The back wing (considering the new building, in which my apartments were, as the centre) consisted of many rooms, of a dark and gloomy character, as the mountain-side shut out much of the sun, and heavy pine woods came down within a few yards of the windows. Yet on this side—on a projecting plateau of the rock—my husband had formed the flower-garden of which I have spoken; for he was a great cultivator of flowers in his leisure moments.

Now my bedroom was the corner room of the new buildings on the part next to the mountain. Hence I could have let myself down into the flower-garden by my hands on the window-sill on one side, without danger of hurting myself; while the windows at right angles with these looked sheer down a descent of a hundred feet at least. Going still farther along this wing, you came to the old building; in fact, these two fragments of the ancient castle had formerly been attached by some such connecting apartments as my husband had rebuilt. These rooms belonged to M. de la Tourelle. His bedroom opened into mine, his dressing-room lay beyond; and that was pretty nearly all I knew, for the servants, as well as he himself, had a knack of turning me back, under some pretence, if ever they found me walking about alone, as I was inclined to do, when first I came, from a sort of curiosity to see the whole of the place of which I found myself mistress. M. de la Tourelle never encouraged me to go out alone, either in a carriage or for a walk, saying always that the roads were unsafe in those disturbed times; indeed, I have sometimes fancied since that the flower-garden, to which the only access from the castle was through his rooms, was designed in order to give me exercise and employment under his own eye.

But to return to that night. I knew, as I have said, that M. de la Tourelle's private room opened out of his dressing-room, and this out of his bedroom, which again opened into mine, the corner-room. But there were other doors into all these rooms, and these doors led into a long gallery, lighted by windows, looking into the inner court. I do not remember our consulting much about it; we went through my room into my husband's apartment through the dressing-room, but the door of communication into his study was locked, so there was nothing for it but to turn back and go by the gallery to the other door. I recollect noticing one or two things in these rooms, then seen by me for the first time. I remember the sweet perfume that hung in the air, the scent bottles of silver that decked his toilet-table, and the whole apparatus for bathing and dressing, more luxurious even than those which he had provided for me. But the room itself was less splendid in its proportions than mine. In truth, the new buildings ended at the entrance to my husband's dressing-room. There were deep window recesses in walls eight or nine feet thick, and even the partitions between the chambers were three feet deep; but over all these doors or windows there fell thick, heavy draperies, so that I should think no one could have heard in one room what passed in another. We went back into my room, and out into the gallery. We had to shade our candle, from a fear that possessed us, I don't know why, lest some of the servants in the opposite wing might trace our progress towards the part of the castle unused by any one except my husband. Somehow, I had always the feeling that all the domestics, except Amante, were spies upon me, and that I was trammelled in a web of observation and unspoken limitation extending over all my actions.

There was a light in the upper room; we paused, and Amante would have again retreated, but I was chafing under the delays. What was the harm of my seeking my father's unopened letter to me in my husband's study? I, generally the coward, now blamed Amante for her unusual timidity. But the truth was, she had far more reason for suspicion as to the proceedings of that terrible household than I had ever known of. I urged her on, I pressed on myself; we came to the door, locked, but with the key in it; we turned it, we entered; the letters lay on the table, their white oblongs catching the light in an instant, and revealing themselves to my eager eyes, hungering after the words of love from my peaceful, distant home. But just as I pressed forward to examine the letters, the candle which Amante held, caught in some draught, went out, and we were in darkness. Amante proposed that we should carry the letters back to my salon, collecting them as well as we could in the dark, and returning all but the expected one for me; but I begged her to return to my room, where I kept tinder and flint, and to strike a fresh light; and so she went, and I remained alone in the room, of which I could only just distinguish the size, and the principal articles of furniture: a large table, with a deep, overhanging cloth, in the middle, escritoires and other heavy articles against the walls; all this I could see as I stood there, my hand on the table close by the letters, my face towards the window, which, both from the darkness of the wood growing high up the mountain-side and the faint light of the declining moon, seemed only like an oblong of paler purpler black than the shadowy room. How much I remembered from my one instantaneous glance before the candle went out, how much I saw as my eyes became accustomed to the darkness, I do not know, but even now, in my dreams, comes up that room of horror, distinct in its profound shadow. Amante could hardly have been gone a minute before I felt an additional gloom before the window, and heard soft movements outside—soft, but resolute, and continued until the end was accomplished, and the window raised.

In mortal terror of people forcing an entrance at such an hour, and in such a manner as to leave no doubt of their purpose, I would have turned to fly when first I heard the noise, only that I feared by any quick motion to catch their attention, as I also ran the danger of doing by opening the door, which was all but closed, and to whose handlings I was unaccustomed. Again, quick as lightning, I bethought me of the hiding-place between the locked door to my husband's dressing-room and the portière which covered it; but I gave that up, I felt as if I could not reach it without screaming or fainting. So I sank down softly, and crept under the table, hidden, as I hoped, by the great, deep table-cover, with its heavy fringe. I had not recovered my swooning senses fully, and was trying to reassure myself as to my being in a place of comparative safety, for, above all things, I dreaded the betrayal of fainting, and struggled hard for such courage as I might attain by deadening myself to the danger I was in by inflicting intense pain on myself. You have often asked me the reason of that mark on my hand; it was where, in my agony, I bit out a piece of flesh with my relentless teeth, thankful for the pain, which helped to numb my terror. I say, I was but just concealed when I heard the window lifted, and one after another stepped over the sill, and stood by me so close that I could have touched their feet. Then they laughed and whispered; my brain swam so that I could not tell the meaning of their words, but I heard my husband's laughter among the rest—low, hissing, scornful—as he kicked something heavy that they had dragged in over the floor, and which lay near me; so near, that my husband's kick, in touching it, touched me too. I don't know why—I can't tell how—but some feeling, and not curiosity, prompted me to put out my hand, ever so softly, ever so little, and feel in the darkness for what lay spurned beside me. I stole my groping palm upon the clenched and chilly hand of a corpse!

Strange to say, this roused me to instant vividness of thought. Till this moment I had almost forgotten Amante; now I planned with feverish rapidity how I could give her a warning not to return; or rather, I should say, I tried to plan, for all my projects were utterly futile, as I might have seen from the first. I could only hope she would hear the voices of those who were now busy in trying to kindle a light, swearing awful oaths at the mislaid articles which would have enabled them to strike fire. I heard her step outside coming nearer and nearer; I saw from my hiding-place the line of light beneath the door more and more distinctly; close to it her footstep paused; the men inside—at the time I thought they had been only two, but I found out afterwards there were three—paused in their endeavours, and were quite still, as breathless as myself, I suppose. Then she slowly pushed the door open with gentle motion, to save her flickering candle from being again extinguished. For a moment all was still. Then I heard my husband say, as he advanced towards her (he wore riding-boots, the shape of which I knew well, as I could see them in the light),—

"Amante, may I ask what brings you here into my private room?"

He stood between her and the dead body of a man, from which ghastly heap I shrank away as it almost touched me, so close were we all together. I could not tell whether she saw it or not; I could give her no warning, nor make any dumb utterance of signs to bid her what to say—if, indeed, I knew myself what would be best for her to say.

Her voice was quite changed when she spoke; quite hoarse, and very low; yet it was steady enough as she said, what was the truth, that she had come to look for a letter which she believed had arrived for me from Germany. Good, brave Amante! Not a word about me. M. de la Tourelle answered with a grim blasphemy and a fearful threat. He would have no one prying into his premises; madame should have her letters, if there were any, when he chose to give them to her, if, indeed, he thought it well to give them to her at all. As for Amante, this was her first warning, but it was also her last; and, taking the candle out of her hand, he turned her out of the room, his companions discreetly making a screen, so as to throw the corpse into deep shadow. I heard the key turn in the door after her—if I had ever had any thought of escape it was gone now. I only hoped that whatever was to befal me might soon be over, for the tension of nerve was growing more than I could bear. The instant she could be supposed to be out of hearing, two voices began speaking in the most angry terms to my husband, upbraiding him for not having detained her, gagged her—nay, one was for killing her, saying he had seen her eye fall on the face of the dead man, whom he now kicked in his passion. Though the form of their speech was as if they were speaking to equals, yet in their tone there was something of fear. I am sure my husband was their superior, or captain, or somewhat. He replied to them almost as if he were scoffing at them, saying it was such an expenditure of labour having to do with fools; that, ten to one, the woman was only telling the simple truth, and that she was frightened enough by discovering her master in his room to be thankful to escape and return to her mistress, to whom he could easily explain on the morrow how he happened to return in the dead of night. But his companions fell to cursing me, and saying that since M. de la Tourelle had been married he was fit for nothing but to dress himself fine and scent himself with perfume; that, as for me, they could have got him twenty girls prettier, and with far more spirit in them. He quietly answered that I suited him, and that was enough. All this time they were doing something—I could not see what—to the corpse; sometimes they were too busy rifling the dead body, I believe, to talk; again they let it fall with a heavy, resistless thud, and took to quarrelling. They taunted my husband with angry vehemence, enraged at his scoffing and scornful replies, his mocking laughter. Yes, holding up his poor dead victim, the better to strip him of whatever he wore that was valuable, I heard my husband laugh just as he had done when exchanging repartees in the little salon of the Rupprechts at Carlsruhe. I hated and dreaded him from that moment. At length, as if to make an end of the subject, he said, with cool determination in his voice,—

"Now, my good friends, what is the use of all this talking, when you know in your hearts that, if I suspected my wife of knowing more than I chose of my affairs, she would not outlive the day? Remember Victorine. Because she merely joked about my affairs in an imprudent manner, and rejected my advice to keep a prudent tongue—to see what she liked, but ask nothing and say nothing—she has gone a long journey—longer than to Paris."

"But this one is different to her; we knew all that Madame Victorine knew, she was such a chatterbox; but this one may find out a vast deal, and never breathe a word about it, she is so sly. Some fine day we may have the country raised, and the gendarmes down upon us from Strasburg, and all owing to your pretty doll, with her cunning ways of coming over you."

I think this roused M. de la Tourelle a little from his contemptuous indifference, for he ground an oath through his teeth, and said, "Feel! this dagger is sharp, Henri. If my wife breathes a word, and I am such a fool as not to have stopped her mouth effectually before she can bring down gendarmes upon us, just let that good steel find its way to my heart. Let her guess but one tittle, let her have but one slight suspicion that I am not a 'grand propriétaire,' much less imagine that I am a chief of Chauffeurs, and she follows Victorine on the long journey beyond Paris that very day."

"She'll outwit you yet; or I never judged women well. Those still silent ones are the devil. She'll be off during some of your absences, having picked out some secret that will break us all on the wheel."

"Bah!" said his voice; and then in a minute he added, "Let her go if she will. But, where she goes, I will follow; so don't cry before you're hurt."

By this time, they had nearly stripped the body; and the conversation turned on what they should do with it. I learnt that the dead man was the Sieur de Poissy, a neighbouring gentleman, whom I had often heard of as hunting with my husband. I had never seen him, but they spoke as if he had come upon them while they were robbing some Cologne merchant, torturing him after the cruel practice of the Chauffeurs, by roasting the feet of their victims in order to compel them to reveal any hidden circumstances connected with their wealth, of which the Chauffeurs afterwards made use; and this Sieur de Poissy coming down upon them, and recognising M. de la Tourelle, they had killed him, and brought him thither after nightfall. I heard him whom I called my husband, laugh his little light laugh as he spoke of the way in which the dead body had been strapped before one of the riders, in such a way that it appeared to any passer-by as if, in truth, the murderer were tenderly supporting some sick person. He repeated some mocking reply of double meaning, which he himself had given to some one who made inquiry. He enjoyed the play upon words, softly applauding his own wit. And all the time the poor helpless outstretched arms of the dead lay close to his dainty boot! Then another stooped (my heart stopped beating), and picked up a letter lying on the ground—a letter that had dropped out of M. de Poissy's pocket—a letter from his wife, full of tender words of endearment and pretty babblings of love. This was read aloud, with coarse ribald comments on every sentence, each trying to outdo the previous speaker. When they came to some pretty words about a sweet Maurice, their little child away with its mother on some visit, they laughed at M. de la Tourelle, and told him that he would be hearing such woman's drivelling some day. Up to that moment, I think, I had only feared him, but his unnatural, half-ferocious reply made me hate even more than I dreaded him. But now they grew weary of their savage merriment; the jewels and watch had been apprised, the money and papers examined; and apparently there was some necessity for the body being interred quietly and before daybreak. They had not dared to leave him where he was slain for fear lest people should come and recognise him, and raise the hue and cry upon them. For they all along spoke as if it was their constant endeavour to keep the immediate neighbourhood of Les Rochers in the most orderly and tranquil condition, so as never to give cause for visits from the gendarmes. They disputed a little as to whether they should make their way into the castle larder through the gallery, and satisfy their hunger before the hasty interment, or afterwards. I listened with eager feverish interest as soon as this meaning of their speeches reached my hot and troubled brain, for at the time the words they uttered seemed only to stamp themselves with terrible force on my memory, so that I could hardly keep from repeating them aloud like a dull, miserable, unconscious echo; but my brain was numb to the sense of what they said, unless I myself were named, and then, I suppose, some instinct of self-preservation stirred within me, and quickened my sense. And how I strained my ears, and nerved my hands and limbs, beginning to twitch with convulsive movements, which I feared might betray me! I gathered every word they spoke, not knowing which proposal to wish for, but feeling that whatever was finally decided upon, my only chance of escape was drawing near. I once feared lest my husband should go to his bedroom before I had had that one chance, in which case he would most likely have perceived my absence. He said that his hands were soiled (I shuddered, for it might be with life-blood), and he would go and cleanse them; but some bitter jest turned his purpose, and he left the room with the other two—left it by the gallery door. Left me alone in the dark with the stiffening corpse!

Now, now was my time, if ever; and yet I could not move. It was not my cramped and stiffened joints that crippled me, it was the sensation of that dead man's close presence. I almost fancied—I almost fancy still—I heard the arm nearest to me move; lift itself up, as if once more imploring, and fall in dead despair. At that fancy—if fancy it were—I screamed aloud in mad terror, and the sound of my own strange voice broke the spell. I drew myself to the side of the table farthest from the corpse, with as much slow caution as if I really could have feared the clutch of that poor dead arm, powerless for evermore. I softly raised myself up, and stood sick and trembling, holding by the table, too dizzy to know what to do next. I nearly fainted, when a low voice spoke—when Amante, from the outside of the door, whispered, "Madame!" The faithful creature had been on the watch, had heard my scream, and having seen the three ruffians troop along the gallery down the stairs, and across the court to the offices in the other wing of the castle, she had stolen to the door of the room in which I was. The sound of her voice gave me strength; I walked straight towards it, as one benighted on a dreary moor, suddenly perceiving the small steady light which tells of human dwellings, takes heart, and steers straight onward. Where I was, where that voice was, I knew not; but go to it I must, or die. The door once opened—I know not by which of us—I fell upon her neck, grasping her tight, till my hands ached with the tension of their hold. Yet she never uttered a word. Only she took me up in her vigorous arms, and bore me to my room, and laid me on my bed. I do not know more; as soon as I was placed there I lost sense; I came to myself with a horrible dread lest my husband was by me, with a belief that he was in the room, in hiding, waiting to hear my first words, watching for the least sign of the terrible knowledge I possessed to murder me. I dared not breathe quicker, I measured and timed each heavy inspiration; I did not speak, nor move, nor even open my eyes, for long after I was in my full, my miserable senses. I heard some one treading softly about the room, as if with a purpose, not as if for curiosity, or merely to beguile the time; some one passed in and out of the salon; and I still lay quiet, feeling as if death were inevitable, but wishing that the agony of death were past. Again faintness stole over me; but just as I was sinking into the horrible feeling of nothingness, I heard Amante's voice close to me, saying,—

"Drink this, madame, and let us begone. All is ready."

I let her put her arm under my head and raise me, and pour something down my throat. All the time she kept talking in a quiet, measured voice, unlike her own, so dry and authoritative; she told me that a suit of her clothes lay ready for me, that she herself was as much disguised as the circumstances permitted her to be, that what provisions I had left from my supper were stowed away in her pockets, and so she went on, dwelling on little details of the most commonplace description, but never alluding for an instant to the fearful cause why flight was necessary. I made no inquiry as to how she knew, or what she knew. I never asked her either then or afterwards, I could not bear it—we kept our dreadful secret close. But I suppose she must have been in the dressing-room adjoining, and heard all.

In fact, I dared not speak even to her, as if there were anything beyond the most common event in life in our preparing thus to leave the house of blood by stealth in the dead of night. She gave me directions— short condensed directions, without reasons—just as you do to a child; and like a child I obeyed her. She went often to the door and listened; and often, too, she went to the window, and looked anxiously out. For me, I saw nothing but her, and I dared not let my eyes wander from her for a minute; and I heard nothing in the deep midnight silence but her soft movements, and the heavy beating of my own heart. At last she took my hand, and led me in the dark, through the salon, once more into the terrible gallery, where across the black darkness the windows admitted pale sheeted ghosts of light upon the floor. Clinging to her I went; unquestioning—for she was human sympathy to me after the isolation of my unspeakable terror. On we went, turning to the left instead of to the right, past my suite of sitting-rooms where the gilding was red with blood, into that unknown wing of the castle that fronted the main road lying parallel far below. She guided me along the basement passages to which we had now descended, until we came to a little open door, through which the air blew chill and cold, bringing for the first time a sensation of life to me. The door led into a kind of cellar, through which we groped our way to an opening like a window, but which, instead of being glazed, was only fenced with iron bars, two of which were loose, as Amante evidently knew, for she took them out with the ease of one who had performed the action often before, and then helped me to follow her out into the free, open air.

We stole round the end of the building, and on turning the corner—she first—I felt her hold on me tighten for an instant, and the next step I, too, heard distant voices, and the blows of a spade upon the heavy soil, for the night was very warm and still.

We had not spoken a word; we did not speak now. Touch was safer and as expressive. She turned down towards the high road; I followed. I did not know the path; we stumbled again and again, and I was much bruised; so doubtless was she; but bodily pain did me good. At last, we were on the plainer path of the high road.

I had such faith in her that I did not venture to speak, even when she paused, as wondering to which hand she should turn. But now, for the first time, she spoke:—

"Which way did you come when he brought you here first?"

I pointed, I could not speak.

We turned in the opposite direction; still going along the high road. In about an hour, we struck up to the mountain-side, scrambling far up before we even dared to rest; far up and away again before day had fully dawned. Then we looked about for some place of rest and concealment: and now we dared to speak in whispers. Amante told me that she had locked the door of communication between his bedroom and mine, and, as in a dream, I was aware that she had also locked and brought away the key of the door between the latter and the salon.

"He will have been too busy this night to think much about you—he will suppose you are asleep—I shall be the first to be missed; but they will only just now be discovering our loss."

I remember those last words of hers made me pray to go on; I felt as if we were losing precious time in thinking either of rest or concealment; but she hardly replied to me, so busy was she in seeking out some hiding-place. At length, giving it up in despair, we proceeded onwards a little way; the mountain-side sloped downwards rapidly, and in the full morning light we saw ourselves in a narrow valley, made by a stream which forced its way along it. About a mile lower down there rose the pale blue smoke of a village, a mill-wheel was lashing up the water close at hand, though out of sight. Keeping under the cover of every sheltering tree or bush, we worked our way down past the mill, down to a one-arched bridge, which doubtless formed part of the road between the village and the mill.

"This will do," said she; and we crept under the space, and climbing a little way up the rough stone-work, we seated ourselves on a projecting ledge, and crouched in the deep damp shadow. Amante sat a little above me, and made me lay my head on her lap. Then she fed me, and took some food herself; and opening out her great dark cloak, she covered up every light-coloured speck about us; and thus we sat, shivering and shuddering, yet feeling a kind of rest through it all, simply from the fact that motion was no longer imperative, and that during the daylight our only chance of safety was to be still. But the damp shadow in which we were sitting was blighting, from the circumstance of the sunlight never penetrating there; and I dreaded lest, before night and the time for exertion again came on, I should feel illness creeping all over me. To add to our discomfort, it had rained the whole day long, and the stream, fed by a thousand little mountain brooklets, began to swell into a torrent, rushing over the stones with a perpetual and dizzying noise.

Every now and then I was wakened from the painful doze into which I continually fell, by a sound of horses' feet over our head: sometimes lumbering heavily as if dragging a burden, sometimes rattling and galloping, and with the sharper cry of men's voices coming cutting through the roar of the waters. At length, day fell. We had to drop into the stream, which came above our knees as we waded to the bank. There we stood, stiff and shivering. Even Amante's courage seemed to fail.

"We must pass this night in shelter, somehow," said she. For indeed the rain was coming down pitilessly. I said nothing. I thought that surely the end must be death in some shape; and I only hoped that to death might not be added the terror of the cruelty of men. In a minute or so she had resolved on her course of action. We went up the stream to the mill. The familiar sounds, the scent of the wheat, the flour whitening the walls—all reminded me of home, and it seemed to me as if I must struggle out of this nightmare and waken, and find myself once more a happy girl by the Neckar-side. They were long in unbarring the door at which Amante had knocked: at length, an old feeble voice inquired who was there, and what was sought? Amante answered shelter from the storm for two women; but the old woman replied, with suspicious hesitation, that she was sure it was a man who was asking for shelter, and that she could not let us in. But at length she satisfied herself, and unbarred the heavy door, and admitted us. She was not an unkindly woman; but her thoughts all travelled in one circle, and that was, that her master, the miller, had told her on no account to let any man into the place during his absence, and that she did not know if he would not think two women as bad; and yet that as we were not men, no one could say she had disobeyed him, for it was a shame to let a dog be out such a night as this. Amante, with ready wit, told her to let no one know that we had taken shelter there that night, and that then her master could not blame her; and while she was thus enjoining secrecy as the wisest course, with a view to far other people than the miller, she was hastily helping me to take off my wet clothes, and spreading them, as well as the brown mantle that had covered us both, before the great stove which warmed the room with the effectual heat that the old woman's failing vitality required. All this time the poor creature was discussing with herself as to whether she had disobeyed orders, in a kind of garrulous way that made me fear much for her capability of retaining anything secret if she was questioned. By-and-by, she wandered away to an unnecessary revelation of her master's whereabouts: gone to help in the search for his landlord, the Sieur de Poissy, who lived at the château just above, and who had not returned from his chase the day before; so the intendant imagined he might have met with some accident, and had summoned the neighbours to beat the forest and the hill-side. She told us much besides, giving us to understand that she would fain meet with a place as housekeeper where there were more servants and less to do, as her life here was very lonely and dull, especially since her master's son had gone away—gone to the wars. She then took her supper, which was evidently apportioned out to her with a sparing hand, as, even if the idea had come into her head, she had not enough to offer us any. Fortunately, warmth was all that we required, and that, thanks to Amante's cares, was returning to our chilled bodies. After supper, the old woman grew drowsy; but she seemed uncomfortable at the idea of going to sleep and leaving us still in the house. Indeed, she gave us pretty broad hints as to the propriety of our going once more out into the bleak and stormy night; but we begged to be allowed to stay under shelter of some kind; and, at last, a bright idea came over her, and she bade us mount by a ladder to a kind of loft, which went half over the lofty mill-kitchen in which we were sitting. We obeyed her—what else could we do?—and found ourselves in a spacious floor, without any safeguard or wall, boarding, or railing, to keep us from falling over into the kitchen in case we went too near the edge. It was, in fact, the store-room or garret for the household. There was bedding piled up, boxes and chests, mill sacks, the winter store of apples and nuts, bundles of old clothes, broken furniture, and many other things. No sooner were we up there, than the old woman dragged the ladder, by which we had ascended, away with a chuckle, as if she was now secure that we could do no mischief, and sat herself down again once more, to doze and await her master's return. We pulled out some bedding, and gladly laid ourselves down in our dried clothes and in some warmth, hoping to have the sleep we so much needed to refresh us and prepare us for the next day. But I could not sleep, and I was aware, from her breathing, that Amante was equally wakeful. We could both see through the crevices between the boards that formed the flooring into the kitchen below, very partially lighted by the common lamp that hung against the wall near the stove on the opposite side to that on which we were.

PORTION III

Far on in the night there were voices outside reached us in our hiding-place; an angry knocking at the door, and we saw through the chinks the old woman rouse herself up to go and open it for her master, who came in, evidently half drunk. To my sick horror, he was followed by Lefebvre, apparently as sober and wily as ever. They were talking together as they came in, disputing about something; but the miller stopped the conversation to swear at the old woman for having fallen asleep, and, with tipsy anger, and even with blows, drove the poor old creature out of the kitchen to bed. Then he and Lefebvre went on talking—about the Sieur de Poissy's disappearance. It seemed that Lefebvre had been out all day, along with other of my husband's men, ostensibly assisting in the search; in all probability trying to blind the Sieur de Poissy's followers by putting them on a wrong scent, and also, I fancied, from one or two of Lefebvre's sly questions, combining the hidden purpose of discovering us.

Although the miller was tenant and vassal to the Sieur de Poissy, he seemed to me to be much more in league with the people of M. de la Tourelle. He was evidently aware, in part, of the life which Lefebvre and the others led; although, again, I do not suppose he knew or imagined one-half of their crimes; and also, I think, he was seriously interested in discovering the fate of his master, little suspecting Lefebvre of murder or violence. He kept talking himself, and letting out all sorts of thoughts and opinions; watched by the keen eyes of Lefebvre gleaming out below his shaggy eyebrows. It was evidently not the cue of the latter to let out that his master's wife had escaped from that vile and terrible den; but though he never breathed a word relating to us, not the less was I certain he was thirsting for our blood, and lying in wait for us at every turn of events. Presently he got up and took his leave; and the miller bolted him out, and stumbled off to bed. Then we fell asleep, and slept sound and long.

The next morning, when I awoke, I saw Amante, half raised, resting on one hand, and eagerly gazing, with straining eyes, into the kitchen below. I looked too, and both heard and saw the miller and two of his men eagerly and loudly talking about the old woman, who had not appeared as usual to make the fire in the stove, and prepare her master's breakfast, and who now, late on in the morning, had been found dead in her bed; whether from the effect of her master's blows the night before, or from natural causes, who can tell? The miller's conscience upbraided him a little, I should say, for he was eagerly declaring his value for his housekeeper, and repeating how often she had spoken of the happy life she led with him. The men might have their doubts, but they did not wish to offend the miller, and all agreed that the necessary steps should be taken for a speedy funeral. And so they went out, leaving us in our loft, but so much alone, that, for the first time almost, we ventured to speak freely, though still in a hushed voice, pausing to listen continually. Amante took a more cheerful view of the whole occurrence than I did. She said that, had the old woman lived, we should have had to depart that morning, and that this quiet departure would have been the best thing we could have had to hope for, as, in all probability, the housekeeper would have told her master of us and of our resting-place, and this fact would, sooner or later, have been brought to the knowledge of those from whom we most desired to keep it concealed; but that now we had time to rest, and a shelter to rest in, during the first hot pursuit, which we knew to a fatal certainty was being carried on. The remnants of our food, and the stored-up fruit, would supply us with provision; the only thing to be feared was, that something might be required from the loft, and the miller or some one else mount up in search of it. But even then, with a little arrangement of boxes and chests, one part might be so kept in shadow that we might yet escape observation. All this comforted me a little; but, I asked, how were we ever to escape? The ladder was taken away, which was our only means of descent. But Amante replied that she could make a sufficient ladder of the rope lying coiled among other things, to drop us down the ten feet or so—with the advantage of its being portable, so that we might carry it away, and thus avoid all betrayal of the fact that any one had ever been hidden in the loft.

During the two days that intervened before we did escape, Amante made good use of her time. She looked into every box and chest during the man's absence at his mill; and finding in one box an old suit of man's clothes, which had probably belonged to the miller's absent son, she put them on to see if they would fit her; and, when she found that they did, she cut her own hair to the shortness of a man's, made me clip her black eyebrows as close as though they had been shaved, and by cutting up old corks into pieces such as would go into her cheeks, she altered both the shape of her face and her voice to a degree which I should not have believed possible.

All this time I lay like one stunned; my body resting, and renewing its strength, but I myself in an almost idiotic state—else surely I could not have taken the stupid interest which I remember I did in all Amante's energetic preparations for disguise. I absolutely recollect once the feeling of a smile coming over my stiff face as some new exercise of her cleverness proved a success.

But towards the second day, she required me, too, to exert myself; and then all my heavy despair returned. I let her dye my fair hair and complexion with the decaying shells of the stored-up walnuts, I let her blacken my teeth, and even voluntarily broke a front tooth the better to effect my disguise. But through it all I had no hope of evading my terrible husband. The third night the funeral was over, the drinking ended, the guests gone; the miller put to bed by his men, being too drunk to help himself. They stopped a little while in the kitchen, talking and laughing about the new housekeeper likely to come; and they, too, went off, shutting, but not locking the door. Everything favoured us. Amante had tried her ladder on one of the two previous nights, and could, by a dexterous throw from beneath, unfasten it from the hook to which it was fixed, when it had served its office; she made up a bundle of worthless old clothes in order that we might the better preserve our characters of a travelling pedlar and his wife; she stuffed a hump on her back, she thickened my figure, she left her own clothes deep down beneath a heap of others in the chest from which she had taken the man's dress which she wore; and with a few francs in her pocket—the sole money we had either of us had about us when we escaped—we let ourselves down the ladder, unhooked it, and passed into the cold darkness of night again.

We had discussed the route which it would be well for us to take while we lay perdues in our loft. Amante had told me then that her reason for inquiring, when we first left Les Rochers, by which way I had first been brought to it, was to avoid the pursuit which she was sure would first be made in the direction of Germany; but that now she thought we might return to that district of country where my German fashion of speaking French would excite least observation. I thought that Amante herself had something peculiar in her accent, which I had heard M. de la Tourelle sneer at as Norman patois; but I said not a word beyond agreeing to her proposal that we should bend our steps towards Germany. Once there, we should, I thought, be safe. Alas! I forgot the unruly time that was overspreading all Europe, overturning all law, and all the protection which law gives.

How we wandered—not daring to ask our way—how we lived, how we struggled through many a danger and still more terrors of danger, I shall not tell you now. I will only relate two of our adventures before we reached Frankfort. The first, although fatal to an innocent lady, was yet, I believe, the cause of my safety; the second I shall tell you, that you may understand why I did not return to my former home, as I had hoped to do when we lay in the miller's loft, and I first became capable of groping after an idea of what my future life might be. I cannot tell you how much in these doubtings and wanderings I became attached to Amante. I have sometimes feared since, lest I cared for her only because she was so necessary to my own safety; but, no! it was not so; or not so only, or principally. She said once that she was flying for her own life as well as for mine; but we dared not speak much on our danger, or on the horrors that had gone before. We planned a little what was to be our future course; but even for that we did not look forward long; how could we, when every day we scarcely knew if we should see the sun go down? For Amante knew or conjectured far more than I did of the atrocity of the gang to which M. de la Tourelle belonged; and every now and then, just as we seemed to be sinking into the calm of security, we fell upon traces of a pursuit after us in all directions. Once I remember—we must have been nearly three weeks wearily walking through unfrequented ways, day after day, not daring to make inquiry as to our whereabouts, nor yet to seem purposeless in our wanderings—we came to a kind of lonely roadside farrier's and blacksmith's. I was so tired, that Amante declared that, come what might, we would stay there all night; and accordingly she entered the house, and boldly announced herself as a travelling tailor, ready to do any odd jobs of work that might be required, for a night's lodging and food for herself and wife. She had adopted this plan once or twice before, and with good success; for her father had been a tailor in Rouen, and as a girl she had often helped him with his work, and knew the tailors' slang and habits, down to the particular whistle and cry which in France tells so much to those of a trade. At this blacksmith's, as at most other solitary houses far away from a town, there was not only a store of men's clothes laid by as wanting mending when the housewife could afford time, but there was a natural craving after news from a distance, such news as a wandering tailor is bound to furnish. The early November afternoon was closing into evening, as we sat down, she cross-legged on the great table in the blacksmith's kitchen, drawn close to the window, I close behind her, sewing at another part of the same garment, and from time to time well scolded by my seeming husband. All at once she turned round to speak to me. It was only one word, "Courage!" I had seen nothing; I sat out of the light; but I turned sick for an instant, and then I braced myself up into a strange strength of endurance to go through I knew not what.

The blacksmith's forge was in a shed beside the house, and fronting the road. I heard the hammers stop plying their continual rhythmical beat. She had seen why they ceased. A rider had come up to the forge and dismounted, leading his horse in to be re-shod. The broad red light of the forge-fire had revealed the face of the rider to Amante, and she apprehended the consequence that really ensued.

The rider, after some words with the blacksmith, was ushered in by him into the house-place where we sat.

"Here, good wife, a cup of wine and some galette for this gentleman."

"Anything, anything, madame, that I can eat and drink in my hand while my horse is being shod. I am in haste, and must get on to Forbach to-night."

The blacksmith's wife lighted her lamp; Amante had asked her for it five minutes before. How thankful we were that she had not more speedily complied with our request! As it was, we sat in dusk shadow, pretending to stitch away, but scarcely able to see. The lamp was placed on the stove, near which my husband, for it was he, stood and warmed himself. By-and-by he turned round, and looked all over the room, taking us in with about the same degree of interest as the inanimate furniture. Amante, cross-legged, fronting him, stooped over her work, whistling softly all the while. He turned again to the stove, impatiently rubbing his hands. He had finished his wine and galette, and wanted to be off.

"I am in haste, my good woman. Ask thy husband to get on more quickly. I will pay him double if he makes haste."

The woman went out to do his bidding; and he once more turned round to face us. Amante went on to the second part of the tune. He took it up, whistled a second for an instant or so, and then the blacksmith's wife re-entering, he moved towards her, as if to receive her answer the more speedily.

"One moment, monsieur—only one moment. There was a nail out of the off-foreshoe which my husband is replacing; it would delay monsieur again if that shoe also came off."

"Madame is right," said he, "but my haste is urgent. If madame knew my reasons, she would pardon my impatience. Once a happy husband, now a deserted and betrayed man, I pursue a wife on whom I lavished all my love, but who has abused my confidence, and fled from my house, doubtless to some paramour; carrying off with her all the jewels and money on which she could lay her hands. It is possible madame may have heard or seen something of her; she was accompanied in her flight by a base, profligate woman from Paris, whom I, unhappy man, had myself engaged for my wife's waiting-maid, little dreaming what corruption I was bringing into my house!"

"Is it possible?" said the good woman, throwing up her hands.

Amante went on whistling a little lower, out of respect to the conversation.

"However, I am tracing the wicked fugitives; I am on their track" (and the handsome, effeminate face looked as ferocious as any demon's). "They will not escape me; but every minute is a minute of misery to me, till I meet my wife. Madame has sympathy, has she not?"

He drew his face into a hard, unnatural smile, and then both went out to the forge, as if once more to hasten the blacksmith over his work.

Amante stopped her whistling for one instant.

"Go on as you are, without change of an eyelid even; in a few minutes he will be gone, and it will be over!"

It was a necessary caution, for I was on the point of giving way, and throwing myself weakly upon her neck. We went on; she whistling and stitching, I making semblance to sew. And it was well we did so; for almost directly he came back for his whip, which he had laid down and forgotten; and again I felt one of those sharp, quick-scanning glances, sent all round the room, and taking in all.

Then we heard him ride away; and then, it had been long too dark to see well, I dropped my work, and gave way to my trembling and shuddering. The blacksmith's wife returned. She was a good creature. Amante told her I was cold and weary, and she insisted on my stopping my work, and going to sit near the stove; hastening, at the same time, her preparations for supper, which, in honour of us, and of monsieur's liberal payment, was to be a little less frugal than ordinary. It was well for me that she made me taste a little of the cider-soup she was preparing, or I could not have held up, in spite of Amante's warning look, and the remembrance of her frequent exhortations to act resolutely up to the characters we had assumed, whatever befel. To cover my agitation, Amante stopped her whistling, and began to talk; and, by the time the blacksmith came in, she and the good woman of the house were in full flow. He began at once upon the handsome gentleman, who had paid him so well; all his sympathy was with him, and both he and his wife only wished he might overtake his wicked wife, and punish her as she deserved. And then the conversation took a turn, not uncommon to those whose lives are quiet and monotonous; every one seemed to vie with each other in telling about some horror; and the savage and mysterious band of robbers called the Chauffeurs, who infested all the roads leading to the Rhine, with Schinderhannes at their head, furnished many a tale which made the very marrow of my bones run cold, and quenched even Amante's power of talking. Her eyes grew large and wild, her cheeks blanched, and for once she sought by her looks help from me. The new call upon me roused me. I rose and said, with their permission my husband and I would seek our bed, for that we had travelled far and were early risers. I added that we would get up betimes, and finish our piece of work. The blacksmith said we should be early birds if we rose before him; and the good wife seconded my proposal with kindly bustle. One other such story as those they had been relating, and I do believe Amante would have fainted.

As it was, a night's rest set her up; we arose and finished our work betimes, and shared the plentiful breakfast of the family. Then we had to set forth again; only knowing that to Forbach we must not go, yet believing, as was indeed the case, that Forbach lay between us and that Germany to which we were directing our course. Two days more we wandered on, making a round, I suspect, and returning upon the road to Forbach, a league or two nearer to that town than the blacksmith's house. But as we never made inquiries I hardly knew where we were, when we came one night to a small town, with a good large rambling inn in the very centre of the principal street. We had begun to feel as if there were more safety in towns than in the loneliness of the country. As we had parted with a ring of mine not many days before to a travelling jeweller, who was too glad to purchase it far below its real value to make many inquiries as to how it came into the possession of a poor working tailor, such as Amante seemed to be, we resolved to stay at this inn all night, and gather such particulars and information as we could by which to direct our onward course.

We took our supper in the darkest corner of the salle-à-manger, having previously bargained for a small bedroom across the court, and over the stables. We needed food sorely; but we hurried on our meal from dread of any one entering that public room who might recognize us. Just in the middle of our meal, the public diligence drove lumbering up under the porte-cochère, and disgorged its passengers. Most of them turned into the room where we sat, cowering and fearful, for the door was opposite to the porter's lodge, and both opened on to the wide-covered entrance from the street. Among the passengers came in a young, fair-haired lady, attended by an elderly French maid. The poor young creature tossed her head, and shrank away from the common room, full of evil smells and promiscuous company, and demanded, in German French, to be taken to some private apartment. We heard that she and her maid had come in the coupé, and, probably from pride, poor young lady! she had avoided all association with her fellow-passengers, thereby exciting their dislike and ridicule. All these little pieces of hearsay had a significance to us afterwards, though, at the time, the only remark made that bore upon the future was Amante's whisper to me that the young lady's hair was exactly the colour of mine, which she had cut off and burnt in the stove in the miller's kitchen in one of her descents from our hiding-place in the loft.

As soon as we could, we struck round in the shadow, leaving the boisterous and merry fellow-passengers to their supper. We crossed the court, borrowed a lantern from the ostler, and scrambled up the rude steps to our chamber above the stable. There was no door into it; the entrance was the hole into which the ladder fitted. The window looked into the court. We were tired and soon fell asleep. I was wakened by a noise in the stable below. One instant of listening, and I wakened Amante, placing my hand on her mouth, to prevent any exclamation in her half-roused state. We heard my husband speaking about his horse to the ostler. It was his voice. I am sure of it. Amante said so too. We durst not move to rise and satisfy ourselves. For five minutes or so he went on giving directions. Then he left the stable, and, softly stealing to our window, we saw him cross the court and re-enter the inn. We consulted as to what we should do. We feared to excite remark or suspicion by descending and leaving our chamber, or else immediate escape was our strongest idea. Then the ostler left the stable, locking the door on the outside.

"We must try and drop through the window—if, indeed, it is well to go at all," said Amante.

With reflection came wisdom. We should excite suspicion by leaving without paying our bill. We were on foot, and might easily be pursued. So we sat on our bed's edge, talking and shivering, while from across the court the laughter rang merrily, and the company slowly dispersed one by one, their lights flitting past the windows as they went upstairs and settled each one to his rest.

We crept into our bed, holding each other tight, and listening to every sound, as if we thought we were tracked, and might meet our death at any moment. In the dead of night, just at the profound stillness preceding the turn into another day, we heard a soft, cautious step crossing the yard. The key into the stable was turned—some one came into the stable—we felt rather than heard him there. A horse started a little, and made a restless movement with his feet, then whinnied recognition. He who had entered made two or three low sounds to the animal, and then led him into the court. Amante sprang to the window with the noiseless activity of a cat. She looked out, but dared not speak a word. We heard the great door into the street open—a pause for mounting, and the horse's footsteps were lost in distance.

Then Amante came back to me. "It was he! he is gone!" said she, and once more we lay down, trembling and shaking.

This time we fell sound asleep. We slept long and late. We were wakened by many hurrying feet, and many confused voices; all the world seemed awake and astir. We rose and dressed ourselves, and coming down we looked around among the crowd collected in the court-yard, in order to assure ourselves he was not there before we left the shelter of the stable.

The instant we were seen, two or three people rushed to us.

"Have you heard?—Do you know?—That poor young lady—oh, come and see!" and so we were hurried, almost in spite of ourselves, across the court, and up the great open stairs of the main building of the inn, into a bed-chamber, where lay the beautiful young German lady, so full of graceful pride the night before, now white and still in death. By her stood the French maid, crying and gesticulating.

"Oh, madame! if you had but suffered me to stay with you! Oh! the baron, what will he say?" and so she went on. Her state had but just been discovered; it had been supposed that she was fatigued, and was sleeping late, until a few minutes before. The surgeon of the town had been sent for, and the landlord of the inn was trying vainly to enforce order until he came, and, from time to time, drinking little cups of brandy, and offering them to the guests, who were all assembled there, pretty much as the servants were doing in the court-yard.

At last the surgeon came. All fell back, and hung on the words that were to fall from his lips.

"See!" said the landlord. "This lady came last night by the diligence with her maid. Doubtless a great lady, for she must have a private sitting-room—"

"She was Madame the Baroness de Roeder," said the French maid.

—"And was difficult to please in the matter of supper, and a sleeping-room. She went to bed well, though fatigued. Her maid left her—"

"I begged to be allowed to sleep in her room, as we were in a strange inn, of the character of which we knew nothing; but she would not let me, my mistress was such a great lady."

—"And slept with my servants," continued the landlord. "This morning we thought madame was still slumbering; but when eight, nine, ten, and near eleven o'clock came, I bade her maid use my pass-key, and enter her room—"

"The door was not locked, only closed. And here she was found—dead is she not, monsieur?—with her face down on her pillow, and her beautiful hair all scattered wild; she never would let me tie it up, saying it made her head ache. Such hair!" said the waiting-maid, lifting up a long golden tress, and letting it fall again.

I remembered Amante's words the night before, and crept close up to her.

Meanwhile, the doctor was examining the body underneath the bed-clothes, which the landlord, until now, had not allowed to be disarranged. The surgeon drew out his hand, all bathed and stained with blood; and holding up a short, sharp knife, with a piece of paper fastened round it.

"Here has been foul play," he said. "The deceased lady has been murdered. This dagger was aimed straight at her heart." Then, putting on his spectacles, he read the writing on the bloody paper, dimmed and horribly obscured as it was:—

NUMÉRO UN.   Ainsi les Chauffeurs se vengent.

"Let us go!" said I to Amante. "Oh, let us leave this horrible place!"

"Wait a little," said she. "Only a few minutes more. It will be better."

Immediately the voices of all proclaimed their suspicions of the cavalier who had arrived last the night before. He had, they said, made so many inquiries about the young lady, whose supercilious conduct all in the salle-à-manger had been discussing on his entrance. They were talking about her as we left the room; he must have come in directly afterwards, and not until he had learnt all about her, had he spoken of the business which necessitated his departure at dawn of day, and made his arrangements with both landlord and ostler for the possession of the keys of the stable and porte-cochère. In short, there was no doubt as to the murderer, even before the arrival of the legal functionary who had been sent for by the surgeon; but the word on the paper chilled every one with terror. Les Chauffeurs, who were they? No one knew, some of the gang might even then be in the room overhearing, and noting down fresh objects for vengeance. In Germany, I had heard little of this terrible gang, and I had paid no greater heed to the stories related once or twice about them in Carlsruhe than one does to tales about ogres. But here in their very haunts, I learnt the full amount of the terror they inspired. No one would be legally responsible for any evidence criminating the murderer. The public prosecutor shrank from the duties of his office. What do I say? Neither Amante nor I, knowing far more of the actual guilt of the man who had killed that poor sleeping young lady, durst breathe a word. We appeared to be wholly ignorant of everything: we, who might have told so much. But how could we? we were broken down with terrific anxiety and fatigue, with the knowledge that we, above all, were doomed victims; and that the blood, heavily dripping from the bed-clothes on to the floor, was dripping thus out of the poor dead body, because, when living, she had been mistaken for me.

At length Amante went up to the landlord, and asked permission to leave his inn, doing all openly and humbly, so as to excite neither ill-will nor suspicion. Indeed, suspicion was otherwise directed, and he willingly gave us leave to depart. A few days afterwards we were across the Rhine, in Germany, making our way towards Frankfort, but still keeping our disguises, and Amante still working at her trade.

On the way, we met a young man, a wandering journeyman from Heidelberg. I knew him, although I did not choose that he should know me. I asked him, as carelessly as I could, how the old miller was now? He told me he was dead. This realization of the worst apprehensions caused by his long silence shocked me inexpressibly. It seemed as though every prop gave way from under me. I had been talking to Amante only that very day of the safety and comfort of the home that awaited her in my father's house; of the gratitude which the old man would feel towards her; and how there, in that peaceful dwelling, far away from the terrible land of France, she should find ease and security for all the rest of her life. All this I thought I had to promise, and even yet more had I looked for, for myself. I looked to the unburdening of my heart and conscience by telling all I knew to my best and wisest friend. I looked to his love as a sure guidance as well as a comforting stay, and, behold, he was gone away from me for ever!

I had left the room hastily on hearing of this sad news from the Heidelberger. Presently, Amante followed:

"Poor madame," said she, consoling me to the best of her ability. And then she told me by degrees what more she had learned respecting my home, about which she knew almost as much as I did, from my frequent talks on the subject both at Les Rochers and on the dreary, doleful road we had come along. She had continued the conversation after I left, by asking about my brother and his wife. Of course, they lived on at the mill, but the man said (with what truth I know not, but I believed it firmly at the time) that Babette had completely got the upper hand of my brother, who only saw through her eyes and heard with her ears. That there had been much Heidelberg gossip of late days about her sudden intimacy with a grand French gentleman who had appeared at the mill—a relation, by marriage—married, in fact, to the miller's sister, who, by all accounts, had behaved abominably and ungratefully. But that was no reason for Babette's extreme and sudden intimacy with him, going about everywhere with the French gentleman; and since he left (as the Heidelberger said he knew for a fact) corresponding with him constantly. Yet her husband saw no harm in it all, seemingly; though, to be sure, he was so out of spirits, what with his father's death and the news of his sister's infamy, that he hardly knew how to hold up his head.

"Now," said Amante, "all this proves that M. de la Tourelle has suspected that you would go back to the nest in which you were reared, and that he has been there, and found that you have not yet returned; but probably he still imagines that you will do so, and has accordingly engaged your sister-in-law as a kind of informant. Madame has said that her sister-in-law bore her no extreme good-will; and the defamatory story he has got the start of us in spreading, will not tend to increase the favour in which your sister-in-law holds you. No doubt the assassin was retracing his steps when we met him near Forbach, and having heard of the poor German lady, with her French maid, and her pretty blonde complexion, he followed her. If madame will still be guided by me—and, my child, I beg of you still to trust me," said Amante, breaking out of her respectful formality into the way of talking more natural to those who had shared and escaped from common dangers—more natural, too, where the speaker was conscious of a power of protection which the other did not possess—"we will go on to Frankfort, and lose ourselves, for a time, at least, in the numbers of people who throng a great town; and you have told me that Frankfort is a great town. We will still be husband and wife; we will take a small lodging, and you shall housekeep and live in-doors. I, as the rougher and the more alert, will continue my father's trade, and seek work at the tailors' shops."

I could think of no better plan, so we followed this out. In a back street at Frankfort we found two furnished rooms to let on a sixth story. The one we entered had no light from day; a dingy lamp swung perpetually from the ceiling, and from that, or from the open door leading into the bedroom beyond, came our only light. The bedroom was more cheerful, but very small. Such as it was, it almost exceeded our possible means. The money from the sale of my ring was almost exhausted, and Amante was a stranger in the place, speaking only French, moreover, and the good Germans were hating the French people right heartily. However, we succeeded better than our hopes, and even laid by a little against the time of my confinement. I never stirred abroad, and saw no one, and Amante's want of knowledge of German kept her in a state of comparative isolation.

At length my child was born—my poor worse than fatherless child. It was a girl, as I had prayed for. I had feared lest a boy might have something of the tiger nature of its father, but a girl seemed all my own. And yet not all my own, for the faithful Amante's delight and glory in the babe almost exceeded mine; in outward show it certainly did.

We had not been able to afford any attendance beyond what a neighbouring sage-femme could give, and she came frequently, bringing in with her a little store of gossip, and wonderful tales culled out of her own experience, every time. One day she began to tell me about a great lady in whose service her daughter had lived as scullion, or some such thing. Such a beautiful lady! with such a handsome husband. But grief comes to the palace as well as to the garret, and why or wherefore no one knew, but somehow the Baron de Roeder must have incurred the vengeance of the terrible Chauffeurs; for not many months ago, as madame was going to see her relations in Alsace, she was stabbed dead as she lay in bed at some hotel on the road. Had I not seen it in the Gazette? Had I not heard? Why, she had been told that as far off as Lyons there were placards offering a heavy reward on the part of the Baron de Roeder for information respecting the murderer of his wife. But no one could help him, for all who could bear evidence were in such terror of the Chauffeurs; there were hundreds of them she had been told, rich and poor, great gentlemen and peasants, all leagued together by most frightful oaths to hunt to the death any one who bore witness against them; so that even they who survived the tortures to which the Chauffeurs subjected many of the people whom they plundered, dared not to recognise them again, would not dare, even did they see them at the bar of a court of justice; for, if one were condemned, were there not hundreds sworn to avenge his death?

I told all this to Amante, and we began to fear that if M. de la Tourelle, or Lefebvre, or any of the gang at Les Rochers, had seen these placards, they would know that the poor lady stabbed by the former was the Baroness de Roeder, and that they would set forth again in search of me.

This fresh apprehension told on my health and impeded my recovery. We had so little money we could not call in a physician, at least, not one in established practice. But Amante found out a young doctor for whom, indeed, she had sometimes worked; and offering to pay him in kind, she brought him to see me, her sick wife. He was very gentle and thoughtful, though, like ourselves, very poor. But he gave much time and consideration to the case, saying once to Amante that he saw my constitution had experienced some severe shock from which it was probable that my nerves would never entirely recover. By-and-by I shall name this doctor, and then you will know, better than I can describe, his character.

I grew strong in time—stronger, at least. I was able to work a little at home, and to sun myself and my baby at the garret-window in the roof. It was all the air I dared to take. I constantly wore the disguise I had first set out with; as constantly had I renewed the disfiguring dye which changed my hair and complexion. But the perpetual state of terror in which I had been during the whole months succeeding my escape from Les Rochers made me loathe the idea of ever again walking in the open daylight, exposed to the sight and recognition of every passer-by. In vain Amante reasoned—in vain the doctor urged. Docile in every other thing, in this I was obstinate. I would not stir out. One day Amante returned from her work, full of news—some of it good, some such as to cause us apprehension. The good news was this; the master for whom she worked as journeyman was going to send her with some others to a great house at the other side of Frankfort, where there were to be private theatricals, and where many new dresses and much alteration of old ones would be required. The tailors employed were all to stay at this house until the day of representation was over, as it was at some distance from the town, and no one could tell when their work would be ended. But the pay was to be proportionately good.

The other thing she had to say was this: she had that day met the travelling jeweller to whom she and I had sold my ring. It was rather a peculiar one, given to me by my husband; we had felt at the time that it might be the means of tracing us, but we were penniless and starving, and what else could we do? She had seen that this Frenchman had recognised her at the same instant that she did him, and she thought at the same time that there was a gleam of more than common intelligence on his face as he did so. This idea had been confirmed by his following her for some way on the other side of the street; but she had evaded him with her better knowledge of the town, and the increasing darkness of the night. Still it was well that she was going to such a distance from our dwelling on the next day; and she had brought me in a stock of provisions, begging me to keep within doors, with a strange kind of fearful oblivion of the fact that I had never set foot beyond the threshold of the house since I had first entered it—scarce ever ventured down the stairs. But, although my poor, my dear, very faithful Amante was like one possessed that last night, she spoke continually of the dead, which is a bad sign for the living. She kissed you—yes! it was you, my daughter, my darling, whom I bore beneath my bosom away from the fearful castle of your father—I call him so for the first time, I must call him so once again before I have done—Amante kissed you, sweet baby, blessed little comforter, as if she never could leave off. And then she went away, alive.

Two days, three days passed away. That third evening I was sitting within my bolted doors—you asleep on your pillow by my side—when a step came up the stair, and I knew it must be for me; for ours were the topmost rooms. Some one knocked; I held my very breath. But some one spoke, and I knew it was the good Doctor Voss. Then I crept to the door, and answered.

"Are you alone?" asked I.

"Yes," said he, in a still lower voice. "Let me in." I let him in, and he was as alert as I in bolting and barring the door. Then he came and whispered to me his doleful tale. He had come from the hospital in the opposite quarter of the town, the hospital which he visited; he should have been with me sooner, but he had feared lest he should be watched. He had come from Amante's death-bed. Her fears of the jeweller were too well founded. She had left the house where she was employed that morning, to transact some errand connected with her work in the town; she must have been followed, and dogged on her way back through solitary wood-paths, for some of the wood-rangers belonging to the great house had found her lying there, stabbed to death, but not dead; with the poniard again plunged through the fatal writing, once more; but this time with the word "un" underlined, so as to show that the assassin was aware of his previous mistake.

Numéro Un.   Ainsi les Chauffeurs se vengent.

They had carried her to the house, and given her restoratives till she had recovered the feeble use of her speech. But, oh, faithful, dear friend and sister! even then she remembered me, and refused to tell (what no one else among her fellow workmen knew), where she lived or with whom. Life was ebbing away fast, and they had no resource but to carry her to the nearest hospital, where, of course, the fact of her sex was made known. Fortunately both for her and for me, the doctor in attendance was the very Doctor Voss whom we already knew. To him, while awaiting her confessor, she told enough to enable him to understand the position in which I was left; before the priest had heard half her tale Amante was dead.

Doctor Voss told me he had made all sorts of détours, and waited thus, late at night, for fear of being watched and followed. But I do not think he was. At any rate, as I afterwards learnt from him, the Baron Roeder, on hearing of the similitude of this murder with that of his wife in every particular, made such a search after the assassins, that, although they were not discovered, they were compelled to take to flight for the time.

I can hardly tell you now by what arguments Dr. Voss, at first merely my benefactor, sparing me a portion of his small modicum, at length persuaded me to become his wife. His wife he called it, I called it; for we went through the religious ceremony too much slighted at the time, and as we were both Lutherans, and M. de la Tourelle had pretended to be of the reformed religion, a divorce from the latter would have been easily procurable by German law both ecclesiastical and legal, could we have summoned so fearful a man into any court.

The good doctor took me and my child by stealth to his modest dwelling; and there I lived in the same deep retirement, never seeing the full light of day, although when the dye had once passed away from my face my husband did not wish me to renew it. There was no need; my yellow hair was grey, my complexion was ashen-coloured, no creature could have recognized the fresh-coloured, bright-haired young woman of eighteen months before. The few people whom I saw knew me only as Madame Voss; a widow much older than himself, whom Dr. Voss had secretly married. They called me the Grey Woman.

He made me give you his surname. Till now you have known no other father—while he lived you needed no father's love. Once only, only once more, did the old terror come upon me. For some reason which I forget, I broke through my usual custom, and went to the window of my room for some purpose, either to shut or to open it. Looking out into the street for an instant, I was fascinated by the sight of M. de la Tourelle, gay, young, elegant as ever, walking along on the opposite side of the street. The noise I had made with the window caused him to look up; he saw me, an old grey woman, and he did not recognize me! Yet it was not three years since we had parted, and his eyes were keen and dreadful like those of the lynx.

I told M. Voss, on his return home, and he tried to cheer me, but the shock of seeing M. de la Tourelle had been too terrible for me. I was ill for long months afterwards.

Once again I saw him. Dead. He and Lefebvre were at last caught; hunted down by the Baron de Roeder in some of their crimes. Dr. Voss had heard of their arrest; their condemnation, their death; but he never said a word to me, until one day he bade me show him that I loved him by my obedience and my trust. He took me a long carriage journey, where to I know not, for we never spoke of that day again; I was led through a prison, into a closed court-yard, where, decently draped in the last robes of death, concealing the marks of decapitation, lay M. de la Tourelle, and two or three others, whom I had known at Les Rochers.

After that conviction Dr. Voss tried to persuade me to return to a more natural mode of life, and to go out more. But although I sometimes complied with his wish, yet the old terror was ever strong upon me, and he, seeing what an effort it was, gave up urging me at last.

You know all the rest. How we both mourned bitterly the loss of that dear husband and father—for such I will call him ever—and as such you must consider him, my child, after this one revelation is over.

Why has it been made, you ask. For this reason, my child. The lover, whom you have only known as M. Lebrun, a French artist, told me but yesterday his real name, dropped because the blood-thirsty republicans might consider it as too aristocratic. It is Maurice de Poissy.

CURIOUS IF TRUE

(EXTRACT FROM A LETTER FROM RICHARD WHITTINGHAM, ESQ.)

You were formerly so much amused at my pride in my descent from that sister of Calvin's, who married a Whittingham, Dean of Durham, that I doubt if you will be able to enter into the regard for my distinguished relation that has led me to France, in order to examine registers and archives, which, I thought, might enable me to discover collateral descendants of the great reformer, with whom I might call cousins. I shall not tell you of my troubles and adventures in this research; you are not worthy to hear of them; but something so curious befel me one evening last August, that if I had not been perfectly certain I was wide awake, I might have taken it for a dream.

For the purpose I have named, it was necessary that I should make Tours my head-quarters for a time. I had traced descendants of the Calvin family out of Normandy into the centre of France; but I found it was necessary to have a kind of permission from the bishop of the diocese before I could see certain family papers, which had fallen into the possession of the Church; and, as I had several English friends at Tours, I awaited the answer to my request to Monseigneur de —, at that town. I was ready to accept any invitation; but I received very few; and was sometimes a little at a loss what to do with my evenings. The table d'hôte was at five o'clock; I did not wish to go to the expense of a private sitting-room, disliked the dinnery atmosphere of the salle à manger, could not play either at pool or billiards, and the aspect of my fellow guests was unprepossessing enough to make me unwilling to enter into any tête-à-tête gamblings with them. So I usually rose from table early, and tried to make the most of the remaining light of the August evenings in walking briskly off to explore the surrounding country; the middle of the day was too hot for this purpose, and better employed in lounging on a bench in the Boulevards, lazily listening to the distant band, and noticing with equal laziness the faces and figures of the women who passed by.

One Thursday evening, the 18th of August it was, I think, I had gone further than usual in my walk, and I found that it was later than I had imagined when I paused to turn back. I fancied I could make a round; I had enough notion of the direction in which I was, to see that by turning up a narrow straight lane to my left I should shorten my way back to Tours. And so I believe I should have done, could I have found an outlet at the right place, but field-paths are almost unknown in that part of France, and my lane, stiff and straight as any street, and marked into terribly vanishing perspective by the regular row of poplars on each side, seemed interminable. Of course night came on, and I was in darkness. In England I might have had a chance of seeing a light in some cottage only a field or two off, and asking my way from the inhabitants; but here I could see no such welcome sight; indeed, I believe French peasants go to bed with the summer daylight, so if there were any habitations in the neighbourhood I never saw them. At last—I believe I must have walked two hours in the darkness,—I saw the dusky outline of a wood on one side of the weariful lane, and, impatiently careless of all forest laws and penalties for trespassers, I made my way to it, thinking that if the worst came to the worst, I could find some covert—some shelter where I could lie down and rest, until the morning light gave me a chance of finding my way back to Tours. But the plantation, on the outskirts of what appeared to me a dense wood, was of young trees, too closely planted to be more than slender stems growing up to a good height, with scanty foliage on their summits. On I went towards the thicker forest, and once there I slackened my pace, and began to look about me for a good lair. I was as dainty as Lochiel's grandchild, who made his grandsire indignant at the luxury of his pillow of snow: this brake was too full of brambles, that felt damp with dew; there was no hurry, since I had given up all hope of passing the night between four walls; and I went leisurely groping about, and trusting that there were no wolves to be poked up out of their summer drowsiness by my stick, when all at once I saw a château before me, not a quarter of a mile off, at the end of what seemed to be an ancient avenue (now overgrown and irregular), which I happened to be crossing, when I looked to my right, and saw the welcome sight. Large, stately, and dark was its outline against the dusky night-sky; there were pepper-boxes and tourelles and what-not fantastically going up into the dim starlight. And more to the purpose still, though I could not see the details of the building that I was now facing, it was plain enough that there were lights in many windows, as if some great entertainment was going on.

"They are hospitable people, at any rate," thought I. "Perhaps they will give me a bed. I don't suppose French propriétaires have traps and horses quite as plentiful as English gentlemen; but they are evidently having a large party, and some of their guests may be from Tours, and will give me a cast back to the Lion d'Or. I am not proud, and I am dog-tired. I am not above hanging on behind, if need be."

So, putting a little briskness and spirit into my walk, I went up to the door, which was standing open, most hospitably, and showing a large lighted hall, all hung round with spoils of the chase, armour, &c, the details of which I had not time to notice, for the instant I stood on the threshold a huge porter appeared, in a strange, old-fashioned dress, a kind of livery which well befitted the general appearance of the house. He asked me, in French (so curiously pronounced that I thought I had hit upon a new kind of patois), my name, and whence I came. I thought he would not be much the wiser, still it was but civil to give it before I made my request for assistance; so, in reply, I said—

"My name is Whittingham—Richard Whittingham, an English gentleman, staying at —." To my infinite surprise, a light of pleased intelligence came over the giant's face; he made me a low bow, and said (still in the same curious dialect) that I was welcome, that I was long expected.

"Long expected!" What could the fellow mean? Had I stumbled on a nest of relations by John Calvin's side, who had heard of my genealogical inquiries, and were gratified and interested by them? But I was too much pleased to be under shelter for the night to think it necessary to account for my agreeable reception before I enjoyed it. Just as he was opening the great heavy battants of the door that led from the hall to the interior, he turned round and said,—

"Apparently Monsieur le Géanquilleur is not come with you."

"No! I am all alone; I have lost my way,"—and I was going on with my explanation, when he, as if quite indifferent to it, led the way up a great stone staircase, as wide as many rooms, and having on each landing-place massive iron wickets, in a heavy framework; these the porter unlocked with the solemn slowness of age. Indeed, a strange, mysterious awe of the centuries that had passed away since this château was built, came over me as I waited for the turning of the ponderous keys in the ancient locks. I could almost have fancied that I heard a mighty rushing murmur (like the ceaseless sound of a distant sea, ebbing and flowing for ever and for ever), coming forth from the great vacant galleries that opened out on each side of the broad staircase, and were to be dimly perceived in the darkness above us. It was as if the voices of generations of men yet echoed and eddied in the silent air. It was strange, too, that my friend the porter going before me, ponderously infirm, with his feeble old hands striving in vain to keep the tall flambeau he held steadily before him,—strange, I say, that he was the only domestic I saw in the vast halls and passages, or met with on the grand staircase. At length we stood before the gilded doors that led into the saloon where the family—or it might be the company, so great was the buzz of voices—was assembled. I would have remonstrated when I found he was going to introduce me, dusty and travel-smeared, in a morning costume that was not even my best, into this grand salon, with nobody knew how many ladies and gentlemen assembled; but the obstinate old man was evidently bent upon taking me straight to his master, and paid no heed to my words.

The doors flew open, and I was ushered into a saloon curiously full of pale light, which did not culminate on any spot, nor proceed from any centre, nor flicker with any motion of the air, but filled every nook and corner, making all things deliciously distinct; different from our light of gas or candle, as is the difference between a clear southern atmosphere and that of our misty England.

At the first moment, my arrival excited no attention, the apartment was so full of people, all intent on their own conversation. But my friend the porter went up to a handsome lady of middle age, richly attired in that antique manner which fashion has brought round again of late years, and, waiting first in an attitude of deep respect till her attention fell upon him, told her my name and something about me, as far as I could guess from the gestures of the one and the sudden glance of the eye of the other.

She immediately came towards me with the most friendly actions of greeting, even before she had advanced near enough to speak. Then,—and was it not strange?—her words and accent were that of the commonest peasant of the country. Yet she herself looked high-bred, and would have been dignified had she been a shade less restless, had her countenance worn a little less lively and inquisitive expression. I had been poking a good deal about the old parts of Tours, and had had to understand the dialect of the people who dwelt in the Marché au Vendredi and similar places, or I really should not have understood my handsome hostess, as she offered to present me to her husband, a henpecked, gentlemanly man, who was more quaintly attired than she in the very extreme of that style of dress. I thought to myself that in France, as in England, it is the provincials who carry fashion to such an excess as to become ridiculous.

However, he spoke (still in the patois) of his pleasure in making my acquaintance, and led me to a strange uneasy easy-chair, much of a piece with the rest of the furniture, which might have taken its place without any anachronism by the side of that in the Hôtel Cluny. Then again began the clatter of French voices, which my arrival had for an instant interrupted, and I had leisure to look about me. Opposite to me sat a very sweet-looking lady, who must have been a great beauty in her youth, I should think, and would be charming in old age, from the sweetness of her countenance. She was, however, extremely fat, and on seeing her feet laid up before her on a cushion, I at once perceived that they were so swollen as to render her incapable of walking, which probably brought on her excessive embonpoint. Her hands were plump and small, but rather coarse-grained in texture, not quite so clean as they might have been, and altogether not so aristocratic-looking as the charming face. Her dress was of superb black velvet, ermine-trimmed, with diamonds thrown all abroad over it.

Not far from her stood the least little man I had ever seen; of such admirable proportions no one could call him a dwarf, because with that word we usually associate something of deformity; but yet with an elfin look of shrewd, hard, worldly wisdom in his face that marred the impression which his delicate regular little features would otherwise have conveyed. Indeed, I do not think he was quite of equal rank with the rest of the company, for his dress was inappropriate to the occasion (and he apparently was an invited, while I was an involuntary guest); and one or two of his gestures and actions were more like the tricks of an uneducated rustic than anything else. To explain what I mean: his boots had evidently seen much service, and had been re-topped, re-heeled, re-soled to the extent of cobbler's powers. Why should he have come in them if they were not his best—his only pair? And what can be more ungenteel than poverty? Then again he had an uneasy trick of putting his hand up to his throat, as if he expected to find something the matter with it; and he had the awkward habit—which I do not think he could have copied from Dr. Johnson, because most probably he had never heard of him—of trying always to retrace his steps on the exact boards on which he had trodden to arrive at any particular part of the room. Besides, to settle the question, I once heard him addressed as Monsieur Poucet, without any aristocratic "de" for a prefix; and nearly every one else in the room was a marquis, at any rate.

I say, "nearly every one;" for some strange people had the entrée; unless, indeed, they were, like me, benighted. One of the guests I should have taken for a servant, but for the extraordinary influence he seemed to have over the man I took for his master, and who never did anything without, apparently, being urged thereto by this follower. The master, magnificently dressed, but ill at ease in his clothes, as if they had been made for some one else, was a weak-looking, handsome man, continually sauntering about, and I almost guessed an object of suspicion to some of the gentlemen present, which, perhaps, drove him on the companionship of his follower, who was dressed something in the style of an ambassador's chasseur; yet it was not a chasseur's dress after all; it was something more thoroughly old-world; boots half way up his ridiculously small legs, which clattered as he walked along, as if they were too large for his little feet; and a great quantity of grey fur, as trimming to coat, court-mantle, boots, cap—everything. You know the way in which certain countenances remind you perpetually of some animal, be it bird or beast! Well, this chasseur (as I will call him for want of a better name) was exceedingly like the great Tom-cat that you have seen so often in my chambers, and laughed at almost as often for his uncanny gravity of demeanour. Grey whiskers has my Tom—grey whiskers had the chasseur: grey hair overshadows the upper lip of my Tom—grey mustachios hid that of the chasseur. The pupils of Tom's eyes dilate and contract as I had thought cats' pupils only could do, until I saw those of the chasseur. To be sure, canny as Tom is, the chasseur had the advantage in the more intelligent expression. He seemed to have obtained most complete sway over his master or patron, whose looks he watched, and whose steps he followed, with a kind of distrustful interest that puzzled me greatly.

There were several other groups in the more distant part of the saloon, all of the stately old school, all grand and noble, I conjectured from their bearing. They seemed perfectly well acquainted with each other, as if they were in the habit of meeting. But I was interrupted in my observations by the tiny little gentleman on the opposite side of the room coming across to take a place beside me. It is no difficult matter to a Frenchman to slide into conversation, and so gracefully did my pigmy friend keep up the character of the nation, that we were almost confidential before ten minutes had elapsed.

Now I was quite aware that the welcome which all had extended to me, from the porter up to the vivacious lady and meek lord of the castle, was intended for some other person. But it required either a degree of moral courage, of which I cannot boast, or the self-reliance and conversational powers of a bolder and cleverer man than I, to undeceive people who had fallen into so fortunate a mistake for me. Yet the little man by my side insinuated himself so much into my confidence, that I had half a mind to tell him of my exact situation, and to turn him into a friend and an ally.

"Madame is perceptibly growing older," said he, in the midst of my perplexity, glancing at our hostess.

"Madame is still a very fine woman," replied I.

"Now, is it not strange," continued he, lowering his voice, "how women almost invariably praise the absent, or departed, as if they were angels of light, while as for the present, or the living"—here he shrugged up his little shoulders, and made an expressive pause. "Would you believe it! Madame is always praising her late husband to monsieur's face; till, in fact, we guests are quite perplexed how to look: for, you know, the late M. de Retz's character was quite notorious,—everybody has heard of him." All the world of Touraine, thought I, but I made an assenting noise.

At this instant, monsieur our host came up to me, and with a civil look of tender interest (such as some people put on when they inquire after your mother, about whom they do not care one straw), asked if I had heard lately how my cat was? "How my cat was!" What could the man mean? My cat! Could he mean the tailless Tom, born in the Isle of Man, and now supposed to be keeping guard against the incursions of rats and mice into my chambers in London? Tom is, as you know, on pretty good terms with some of my friends, using their legs for rubbing-posts without scruple, and highly esteemed by them for his gravity of demeanour, and wise manner of winking his eyes. But could his fame have reached across the Channel? However, an answer must be returned to the inquiry, as monsieur's face was bent down to mine with a look of polite anxiety; so I, in my turn, assumed an expression of gratitude, and assured him that, to the best of my belief, my cat was in remarkably good health.

"And the climate agrees with her?"

"Perfectly," said I, in a maze of wonder at this deep solicitude in a tailless cat who had lost one foot and half an ear in some cruel trap. My host smiled a sweet smile, and, addressing a few words to my little neighbour, passed on.

"How wearisome those aristocrats are!" quoth my neighbour, with a slight sneer. "Monsieur's conversation rarely extends to more than two sentences to any one. By that time his faculties are exhausted, and he needs the refreshment of silence. You and I, monsieur, are, at any rate, indebted to our own wits for our rise in the world!"

Here again I was bewildered! As you know, I am rather proud of my descent from families which, if not noble themselves, are allied to nobility,—and as to my "rise in the world"—if I had risen, it would have been rather for balloon-like qualities than for mother-wit, to being unencumbered with heavy ballast either in my head or my pockets. However, it was my cue to agree: so I smiled again.

"For my part," said he, "if a man does not stick at trifles, if he knows how to judiciously add to, or withhold facts, and is not sentimental in his parade of humanity, he is sure to do well; sure to affix a de or von to his name, and end his days in comfort. There is an example of what I am saying"—and he glanced furtively at the weak-looking master of the sharp, intelligent servant, whom I have called the chasseur.

"Monsieur le Marquis would never have been anything but a miller's son, if it had not been for the talents of his servant. Of course you know his antecedents?"

I was going to make some remarks on the changes in the order of the peerage since the days of Louis XVI.—going, in fact, to be very sensible and historical—when there was a slight commotion among the people at the other end of the room. Lacqueys in quaint liveries must have come in from behind the tapestry, I suppose (for I never saw them enter, though I sate right opposite to the doors), and were handing about the slight beverages and slighter viands which are considered sufficient refreshments, but which looked rather meagre to my hungry appetite. These footmen were standing solemnly opposite to a lady,—beautiful, splendid as the dawn, but—sound asleep in a magnificent settee. A gentleman who showed so much irritation at her ill-timed slumbers, that I think he must have been her husband, was trying to awaken her with actions not far removed from shakings. All in vain; she was quite unconscious of his annoyance, or the smiles of the company, or the automatic solemnity of the waiting footman, or the perplexed anxiety of monsieur and madame.

My little friend sat down with a sneer, as if his curiosity was quenched in contempt.

"Moralists would make an infinity of wise remarks on that scene," said he. "In the first place, note the ridiculous position into which their superstitious reverence for rank and title puts all these people. Because monsieur is a reigning prince over some minute principality, the exact situation of which no one has as yet discovered, no one must venture to take their glass of eau sucré till Madame la Princesse awakens; and, judging from past experience, those poor lacqueys may have to stand for a century before that happens. Next—always speaking as a moralist, you will observe—note how difficult it is to break off bad habits acquired in youth!"

Just then the prince succeeded, by what means I did not see, in awaking the beautiful sleeper. But at first she did not remember where she was, and looking up at her husband with loving eyes, she smiled and said:

"Is it you, my prince?"

But he was too conscious of the suppressed amusement of the spectators and his own consequent annoyance, to be reciprocally tender, and turned away with some little French expression, best rendered into English by "Pooh, pooh, my dear!"

After I had had a glass of delicious wine of some unknown quality, my courage was in rather better plight than before, and I told my cynical little neighbour—whom I must say I was beginning to dislike— that I had lost my way in the wood, and had arrived at the château quite by mistake.

He seemed mightily amused at my story; said that the same thing had happened to himself more than once; and told me that I had better luck than he had on one of these occasions, when, from his account, he must have been in considerable danger of his life. He ended his story by making me admire his boots, which he said he still wore, patched though they were, and all their excellent quality lost by patching, because they were of such a first-rate make for long pedestrian excursions. "Though, indeed," he wound up by saying, "the new fashion of railroads would seem to supersede the necessity for this description of boots."

When I consulted him as to whether I ought to make myself known to my host and hostess as a benighted traveller, instead of the guest whom they had taken me for, he exclaimed, "By no means! I hate such squeamish morality." And he seemed much offended by my innocent question, as if it seemed by implication to condemn something in himself. He was offended and silent; and just at this moment I caught the sweet, attractive eyes of the lady opposite—that lady whom I named at first as being no longer in the bloom of youth, but as being somewhat infirm about the feet, which were supported on a raised cushion before her. Her looks seemed to say, "Come here, and let us have some conversation together;" and, with a bow of silent excuse to my little companion, I went across to the lame old lady. She acknowledged my coming with the prettiest gesture of thanks possible; and, half apologetically, said, "It is a little dull to be unable to move about on such evenings as this; but it is a just punishment to me for my early vanities. My poor feet, that were by nature so small, are now taking their revenge for my cruelty in forcing them into such little slippers.... Besides, monsieur," with a pleasant smile, "I thought it was possible you might be weary of the malicious sayings of your little neighbour. He has not borne the best character in his youth, and such men are sure to be cynical in their old age."

"Who is he?" asked I, with English abruptness.

"His name is Poucet, and his father was, I believe, a wood-cutter, or charcoal burner, or something of the sort. They do tell sad stories of connivance at murder, ingratitude, and obtaining money on false pretences—but you will think me as bad as he if I go on with my slanders. Rather let us admire the lovely lady coming up towards us, with the roses in her hand—I never see her without roses, they are so closely connected with her past history, as you are doubtless aware. Ah, beauty!" said my companion to the lady drawing near to us, "it is like you to come to me, now that I can no longer go to you." Then turning to me, and gracefully drawing me into the conversation, she said, "You must know that, although we never met until we were both married, we have been almost like sisters ever since. There have been so many points of resemblance in our circumstances, and I think I may say in our characters. We had each two elder sisters—mine were but half-sisters, though—who were not so kind to us as they might have been."

"But have been sorry for it since," put in the other lady.

"Since we have married princes," continued the same lady, with an arch smile that had nothing of unkindness in it, "for we both have married far above our original stations in life; we are both unpunctual in our habits, and, in consequence of this failing of ours, we have both had to suffer mortification and pain."

"And both are charming," said a whisper close behind me. "My lord the marquis, say it—say, 'And both are charming.'"

"And both are charming," was spoken aloud by another voice. I turned, and saw the wily cat-like chasseur, prompting his master to make civil speeches.

The ladies bowed with that kind of haughty acknowledgment which shows that compliments from such a source are distasteful. But our trio of conversation was broken up, and I was sorry for it. The marquis looked as if he had been stirred up to make that one speech, and hoped that he would not be expected to say more; while behind him stood the chasseur, half impertinent and half servile in his ways and attitudes. The ladies, who were real ladies, seemed to be sorry for the awkwardness of the marquis, and addressed some trifling questions to him, adapting themselves to the subjects on which he could have no trouble in answering. The chasseur, meanwhile, was talking to himself in a growling tone of voice. I had fallen a little into the background at this interruption in a conversation which promised to be so pleasant, and I could not help hearing his words.

"Really, De Carabas grows more stupid every day. I have a great mind to throw off his boots, and leave him to his fate. I was intended for a court, and to a court I will go, and make my own fortune as I have made his. The emperor will appreciate my talents."

And such are the habits of the French, or such his forgetfulness of good manners in his anger, that he spat right and left on the parquetted floor.

Just then a very ugly, very pleasant-looking man, came towards the two ladies to whom I had lately been speaking, leading up to them a delicate, fair woman, dressed all in the softest white, as if she were vouée au blanc. I do not think there was a bit of colour about her. I thought I heard her making, as she came along, a little noise of pleasure, not exactly like the singing of a tea-kettle, nor yet like the cooing of a dove, but reminding me of each sound.

"Madame de Mioumiou was anxious to see you," said he, addressing the lady with the roses, "so I have brought her across to give you a pleasure!" What an honest, good face! but oh! how ugly! And yet I liked his ugliness better than most persons' beauty. There was a look of pathetic acknowledgment of his ugliness, and a deprecation of your too hasty judgment, in his countenance that was positively winning. The soft, white lady kept glancing at my neighbour the chasseur, as if they had had some former acquaintance, which puzzled me very much, as they were of such different rank. However, their nerves were evidently strung to the same tune, for at a sound behind the tapestry, which was more like the scuttering of rats and mice than anything else, both Madame de Mioumiou and the chasseur started with the most eager look of anxiety on their countenances, and by their restless movements— madame's panting, and the fiery dilation of his eyes—one might see that commonplace sounds affected them both in a manner very different to the rest of the company. The ugly husband of the lovely lady with the roses now addressed himself to me.

"We are much disappointed," he said, "in finding that monsieur is not accompanied by his countryman— le grand Jean d'Angleterre; I cannot pronounce his name rightly"—and he looked at me to help him out.

"Le grand Jean d'Angleterre!" now who was le grand Jean d'Angleterre? John Bull? John Russell? John Bright?

"Jean—Jean"—continued the gentleman, seeing my embarrassment. "Ah, these terrible English names—'Jean de Géanquilleur!'"

I was as wise as ever. And yet the name struck me as familiar, but slightly disguised. I repeated it to myself. It was mighty like John the Giant-killer, only his friends always call that worthy "Jack." I said the name aloud.

"Ah, that is it!" said he. "But why has he not accompanied you to our little reunion to-night?"

I had been rather puzzled once or twice before, but this serious question added considerably to my perplexity. Jack the Giant-killer had once, it is true, been rather an intimate friend of mine, as far as (printer's) ink and paper can keep up a friendship, but I had not heard his name mentioned for years; and for aught I knew he lay enchanted with King Arthur's knights, who lie entranced until the blast of the trumpets of four mighty kings shall call them to help at England's need. But the question had been asked in serious earnest by that gentleman, whom I more wished to think well of me than I did any other person in the room. So I answered respectfully that it was long since I had heard anything of my countryman; but that I was sure it would have given him as much pleasure as it was doing myself to have been present at such an agreeable gathering of friends. He bowed, and then the lame lady took up the word.

"To-night is the night when, of all the year, this great old forest surrounding the castle is said to be haunted by the phantom of a little peasant girl who once lived hereabouts; the tradition is that she was devoured by a wolf. In former days I have seen her on this night out of yonder window at the end of the gallery. Will you, ma belle, take monsieur to see the view outside by the moonlight (you may possibly see the phantom-child); and leave me to a little tête-à-tête with your husband?"

With a gentle movement the lady with the roses complied with the other's request, and we went to a great window, looking down on the forest, in which I had lost my way. The tops of the far-spreading and leafy trees lay motionless beneath us in that pale, wan light, which shows objects almost as distinct in form, though not in colour, as by day. We looked down on the countless avenues, which seemed to converge from all quarters to the great old castle; and suddenly across one, quite near to us, there passed the figure of a little girl, with the "capuchon" on, that takes the place of a peasant girl's bonnet in France. She had a basket on one arm, and by her, on the side to which her head was turned, there went a wolf. I could almost have said it was licking her hand, as if in penitent love, if either penitence or love had ever been a quality of wolves,—but though not of living, perhaps it may be of phantom wolves.

"There, we have seen her!" exclaimed my beautiful companion. "Though so long dead, her simple story of household goodness and trustful simplicity still lingers in the hearts of all who have ever heard of her; and the country-people about here say that seeing that phantom-child on this anniversary brings good luck for the year. Let us hope that we shall share in the traditionary good fortune. Ah! here is Madame de Retz—she retains the name of her first husband, you know, as he was of higher rank than the present." We were joined by our hostess.

"If monsieur is fond of the beauties of nature and art," said she, perceiving that I had been looking at the view from the great window, "he will perhaps take pleasure in seeing the picture." Here she sighed, with a little affectation of grief. "You know the picture I allude to," addressing my companion, who bowed assent, and smiled a little maliciously, as I followed the lead of madame.

I went after her to the other end of the saloon, noting by the way with what keen curiosity she caught up what was passing either in word or action on each side of her. When we stood opposite to the end wall, I perceived a full-length picture of a handsome, peculiar-looking man, with—in spite of his good looks—a very fierce and scowling expression. My hostess clasped her hands together as her arms hung down in front, and sighed once more. Then, half in soliloquy, she said—

"He was the love of my youth; his stern yet manly character first touched this heart of mine. When—when shall I cease to deplore his loss!"

Not being acquainted with her enough to answer this question (if, indeed, it were not sufficiently answered by the fact of her second marriage), I felt awkward; and, by way of saying something, I remarked,—

"The countenance strikes me as resembling something I have seen before—in an engraving from an historical picture, I think; only, it is there the principal figure in a group: he is holding a lady by her hair, and threatening her with his scimitar, while two cavaliers are rushing up the stairs, apparently only just in time to save her life."

"Alas, alas!" said she, "you too accurately describe a miserable passage in my life, which has often been represented in a false light. The best of husbands"—here she sobbed, and became slightly inarticulate with her grief—"will sometimes be displeased. I was young and curious, he was justly angry with my disobedience—my brothers were too hasty—the consequence is, I became a widow!"

After due respect for her tears, I ventured to suggest some commonplace consolation. She turned round sharply:—

"No, monsieur: my only comfort is that I have never forgiven the brothers who interfered so cruelly, in such an uncalled-for manner, between my dear husband and myself. To quote my friend Monsieur Sganarelle—'Ce sont petites choses qui sont de temps en temps necessaires dans l'amitié; et cinq ou six coups d'épée entre gens qui s'aiment ne font que ragaillardir l'affection.' You observe the colouring is not quite what it should be?"

"In this light the beard is of rather a peculiar tint," said I.

"Yes: the painter did not do it justice. It was most lovely, and gave him such a distinguished air, quite different from the common herd. Stay, I will show you the exact colour, if you will come near this flambeau!" And going near the light, she took off a bracelet of hair, with a magnificent clasp of pearls. It was peculiar, certainly. I did not know what to say. "His precious lovely beard!" said she. "And the pearls go so well with the delicate blue!"

Her husband, who had come up to us, and waited till her eye fell upon him before venturing to speak, now said, "It is strange Monsieur Ogre is not yet arrived!"

"Not at all strange," said she, tartly. "He was always very stupid, and constantly falls into mistakes, in which he comes worse off; and it is very well he does, for he is a credulous and cowardly fellow. Not at all strange! If you will"—turning to her husband, so that I hardly heard her words, until I caught—"Then everybody would have their rights, and we should have no more trouble. Is it not, monsieur?" addressing me.

"If I were in England, I should imagine madame was speaking of the reform bill, or the millennium,—but I am in ignorance."

And just as I spoke, the great folding-doors were thrown open wide, and every one started to their feet to greet a little old lady, leaning on a thin black wand—and—

"Madame la Féemarraine," was announced by a chorus of sweet shrill voices.

And in a moment I was lying in the grass close by a hollow oak-tree, with the slanting glory of the dawning day shining full in my face, and thousands of little birds and delicate insects piping and warbling out their welcome to the ruddy splendour.

SIX WEEKS AT HEPPENHEIM

After I left Oxford, I determined to spend some months in travel before settling down in life. My father had left me a few thousands, the income arising from which would be enough to provide for all the necessary requirements of a lawyer's education; such as lodgings in a quiet part of London, fees and payment to the distinguished barrister with whom I was to read; but there would be small surplus left over for luxuries or amusements; and as I was rather in debt on leaving college, since I had forestalled my income, and the expenses of my travelling would have to be defrayed out of my capital, I determined that they should not exceed fifty pounds. As long as that sum would last me I would remain abroad; when it was spent my holiday should be over, and I would return and settle down somewhere in the neighbourhood of Russell Square, in order to be near Mr. —'s chambers in Lincoln's-inn. I had to wait in London for one day while my passport was being made out, and I went to examine the streets in which I purposed to live; I had picked them out, from studying a map, as desirable; and so they were, if judged entirely by my reason; but their aspect was very depressing to one country-bred, and just fresh from the beautiful street-architecture of Oxford. The thought of living in such a monotonous gray district for years made me all the more anxious to prolong my holiday by all the economy which could eke out my fifty pounds. I thought I could make it last for one hundred days at least. I was a good walker, and had no very luxurious tastes in the matter of accommodation or food; I had as fair a knowledge of German and French as any untravelled Englishman can have; and I resolved to avoid expensive hotels such as my own countrymen frequented.

I have stated this much about myself to explain how I fell in with the little story that I am going to record, but with which I had not much to do,—my part in it being little more than that of a sympathizing spectator. I had been through France into Switzerland, where I had gone beyond my strength in the way of walking, and I was on my way home, when one evening I came to the village of Heppenheim, on the Berg-Strasse. I had strolled about the dirty town of Worms all morning, and dined in a filthy hotel; and after that I had crossed the Rhine, and walked through Lorsch to Heppenheim. I was unnaturally tired and languid as I dragged myself up the rough-paved and irregular village street to the inn recommended to me. It was a large building, with a green court before it. A cross-looking but scrupulously clean hostess received me, and showed me into a large room with a dinner-table in it, which, though it might have accommodated thirty or forty guests, only stretched down half the length of the eating-room. There were windows at each end of the room; two looked to the front of the house, on which the evening shadows had already fallen; the opposite two were partly doors, opening into a large garden full of trained fruit-trees and beds of vegetables, amongst which rose-bushes and other flowers seemed to grow by permission, not by original intention. There was a stove at each end of the room, which, I suspect, had originally been divided into two. The door by which I had entered was exactly in the middle, and opposite to it was another, leading to a great bed-chamber, which my hostess showed me as my sleeping quarters for the night.

If the place had been much less clean and inviting, I should have remained there; I was almost surprised myself at my vis inertiæ; once seated in the last warm rays of the slanting sun by the garden window, I was disinclined to move, or even to speak. My hostess had taken my orders as to my evening meal, and had left me. The sun went down, and I grew shivery. The vast room looked cold and bare; the darkness brought out shadows that perplexed me, because I could not fully make out the objects that produced them after dazzling my eyes by gazing out into the crimson light.

Some one came in; it was the maiden to prepare for my supper. She began to lay the cloth at one end of the large table. There was a smaller one close by me. I mustered up my voice, which seemed a little as if it was getting beyond my control, and called to her,—

"Will you let me have my supper here on this table?"

She came near; the light fell on her while I was in shadow. She was a tall young woman, with a fine strong figure, a pleasant face, expressive of goodness and sense, and with a good deal of comeliness about it, too, although the fair complexion was bronzed and reddened by weather, so as to have lost much of its delicacy, and the features, as I had afterwards opportunity enough of observing, were anything but regular. She had white teeth, however, and well-opened blue eyes—grave-looking eyes which had shed tears for past sorrow—plenty of light-brown hair, rather elaborately plaited, and fastened up by two great silver pins. That was all—perhaps more than all—I noticed that first night. She began to lay the cloth where I had directed. A shiver passed over me: she looked at me, and then said,—

"The gentleman is cold: shall I light the stove?"

Something vexed me—I am not usually so impatient: it was the coming-on of serious illness—I did not like to be noticed so closely; I believed that food would restore me, and I did not want to have my meal delayed, as I feared it might be by the lighting of the stove; and most of all I was feverishly annoyed by movement. I answered sharply and abruptly,—

"No; bring supper quickly; that is all I want."

Her quiet, sad eyes met mine for a moment; but I saw no change in their expression, as if I had vexed her by my rudeness: her countenance did not for an instant lose its look of patient sense, and that is pretty nearly all I can remember of Thekla that first evening at Heppenheim.

I suppose I ate my supper, or tried to do so, at any rate; and I must have gone to bed, for days after I became conscious of lying there, weak as a new-born babe, and with a sense of past pain in all my weary limbs. As is the case in recovering from fever, one does not care to connect facts, much less to reason upon them; so how I came to be lying in that strange bed, in that large, half-furnished room; in what house that room was; in what town, in what country, I did not take the trouble to recal. It was of much more consequence to me then to discover what was the well-known herb that gave the scent to the clean, coarse sheets in which I lay. Gradually I extended my observations, always confining myself to the present. I must have been well cared-for by some one, and that lately, too, for the window was shaded, so as to prevent the morning sun from coming in upon the bed; there was the crackling of fresh wood in the great white china stove, which must have been newly replenished within a short time.

By-and-by the door opened slowly. I cannot tell why, but my impulse was to shut my eyes as if I were still asleep. But I could see through my apparently closed eyelids. In came, walking on tip-toe, with a slow care that defeated its object, two men. The first was aged from thirty to forty, in the dress of a Black Forest peasant,—old-fashioned coat and knee-breeches of strong blue cloth, but of a thoroughly good quality; he was followed by an older man, whose dress, of more pretension as to cut and colour (it was all black), was, nevertheless, as I had often the opportunity of observing afterwards, worn threadbare.

Their first sentences, in whispered German, told me who they were: the landlord of the inn where I was lying a helpless log, and the village doctor who had been called in. The latter felt my pulse, and nodded his head repeatedly in approbation. I had instinctively known that I was getting better, and hardly cared for this confirmation; but it seemed to give the truest pleasure to the landlord, who shook the hand of the doctor, in a pantomime expressive of as much thankfulness as if I had been his brother. Some low-spoken remarks were made, and then some question was asked, to which, apparently, my host was unable to reply. He left the room, and in a minute or two returned, followed by Thekla, who was questioned by the doctor, and replied with a quiet clearness, showing how carefully the details of my illness had been observed by her. Then she left the room, and, as if every minute had served to restore to my brain its power of combining facts, I was suddenly prompted to open my eyes, and ask in the best German I could muster what day of the month it was; not that I clearly remembered the date of my arrival at Heppenheim, but I knew it was about the beginning of September.

Again the doctor conveyed his sense of extreme satisfaction in a series of rapid pantomimic nods, and then replied in deliberate but tolerable English, to my great surprise,—

"It is the 29th of September, my dear sir. You must thank the dear God. Your fever has made its course of twenty-one days. Now patience and care must be practised. The good host and his household will have the care; you must have the patience. If you have relations in England, I will do my endeavours to tell them the state of your health."

"I have no near relations," said I, beginning in my weakness to cry, as I remembered, as if it had been a dream, the days when I had father, mother, sister.

"Chut, chut!" said he; then, turning to the landlord, he told him in German to make Thekla bring me one of her good bouillons; after which I was to have certain medicines, and to sleep as undisturbedly as possible. For days, he went on, I should require constant watching and careful feeding; every twenty minutes I was to have something, either wine or soup, in small quantities.

A dim notion came into my hazy mind that my previous husbandry of my fifty pounds, by taking long walks and scanty diet, would prove in the end very bad economy; but I sank into dozing unconsciousness before I could quite follow out my idea. I was roused by the touch of a spoon on my lips; it was Thekla feeding me. Her sweet, grave face had something approaching to a mother's look of tenderness upon it, as she gave me spoonful after spoonful with gentle patience and dainty care: and then I fell asleep once more. When next I wakened it was night; the stove was lighted, and the burning wood made a pleasant crackle, though I could only see the outlines and edges of red flame through the crevices of the small iron door. The uncurtained window on my left looked into the purple, solemn night. Turning a little, I saw Thekla sitting near a table, sewing diligently at some great white piece of household work. Every now and then she stopped to snuff the candle; sometimes she began to ply her needle again immediately; but once or twice she let her busy hands lie idly in her lap, and looked into the darkness, and thought deeply for a moment or two; these pauses always ended in a kind of sobbing sigh, the sound of which seemed to restore her to self-consciousness, and she took to her sewing even more diligently than before. Watching her had a sort of dreamy interest for me; this diligence of hers was a pleasant contrast to my repose; it seemed to enhance the flavour of my rest. I was too much of an animal just then to have my sympathy, or even my curiosity, strongly excited by her look of sad remembrance, or by her sighs.

After a while she gave a little start, looked at a watch lying by her on the table, and came, shading the candle by her hand, softly to my bedside. When she saw my open eyes she went to a porringer placed at the top of the stove, and fed me with soup. She did not speak while doing this. I was half aware that she had done it many times since the doctor's visit, although this seemed to be the first time that I was fully awake. She passed her arm under the pillow on which my head rested, and raised me a very little; her support was as firm as a man's could have been. Again back to her work, and I to my slumbers, without a word being exchanged.

It was broad daylight when I wakened again; I could see the sunny atmosphere of the garden outside stealing in through the nicks at the side of the shawl hung up to darken the room—a shawl which I was sure had not been there when I had observed the window in the night. How gently my nurse must have moved about while doing her thoughtful act!

My breakfast was brought me by the hostess; she who had received me on my first arrival at this hospitable inn. She meant to do everything kindly, I am sure; but a sick room was not her place; by a thousand little mal-adroitnesses she fidgeted me past bearing; her shoes creaked, her dress rustled; she asked me questions about myself which it irritated me to answer; she congratulated me on being so much better, while I was faint for want of the food which she delayed giving me in order to talk. My host had more sense in him when he came in, although his shoes creaked as well as hers. By this time I was somewhat revived, and could talk a little; besides, it seemed churlish to be longer without acknowledging so much kindness received.

"I am afraid I have been a great trouble," said I. "I can only say that I am truly grateful."

His good broad face reddened, and he moved a little uneasily.

"I don't see how I could have done otherwise than I—than we, did," replied he, in the soft German of the district. "We were all glad enough to do what we could; I don't say it was a pleasure, because it is our busiest time of year,—but then," said he, laughing a little awkwardly, as if he feared his expression might have been misunderstood, "I don't suppose it has been a pleasure to you either, sir, to be laid up so far from home."

"No, indeed."

"I may as well tell you now, sir, that we had to look over your papers and clothes. In the first place, when you were so ill I would fain have let your kinsfolk know, if I could have found a clue; and besides, you needed linen."

"I am wearing a shirt of yours though," said I, touching my sleeve.

"Yes, sir!" said he again, reddening a little. "I told Thekla to take the finest out of the chest; but I am afraid you find it coarser than your own."

For all answer I could only lay my weak hand on the great brown paw resting on the bed-side. He gave me a sudden squeeze in return that I thought would have crushed my bones.

"I beg your pardon, sir," said he, misinterpreting the sudden look of pain which I could not repress; "but watching a man come out of the shadow of death into life makes one feel very friendly towards him."

"No old or true friend that I have had could have done more for me than you, and your wife, and Thekla, and the good doctor."

"I am a widower," said he, turning round the great wedding-ring that decked his third finger. "My sister keeps house for me, and takes care of the children,—that is to say, she does it with the help of Thekla, the house-maiden. But I have other servants," he continued. "I am well to do, the good God be thanked! I have land, and cattle, and vineyards. It will soon be our vintage-time, and then you must go and see my grapes as they come into the village. I have a 'chasse,' too, in the Odenwald; perhaps one day you will be strong enough to go and shoot the 'chevreuil' with me."

His good, true heart was trying to make me feel like a welcome guest. Some time afterwards I learnt from the doctor that—my poor fifty pounds being nearly all expended—my host and he had been brought to believe in my poverty, as the necessary examination of my clothes and papers showed so little evidence of wealth. But I myself have but little to do with my story; I only name these things, and repeat these conversations, to show what a true, kind, honest man my host was. By the way, I may as well call him by his name henceforward, Fritz Müller. The doctor's name, Wiedermann.

I was tired enough with this interview with Fritz Müller; but when Dr. Wiedermann came he pronounced me to be much better; and through the day much the same course was pursued as on the previous one: being fed, lying still, and sleeping, were my passive and active occupations. It was a hot, sunshiny day, and I craved for air. Fresh air does not enter into the pharmacopoeia of a German doctor; but somehow I obtained my wish. During the morning hours the window through which the sun streamed—the window looking on to the front court—was opened a little; and through it I heard the sounds of active life, which gave me pleasure and interest enough. The hen's cackle, the cock's exultant call when he had found the treasure of a grain of corn,—the movements of a tethered donkey, and the cooing and whirring of the pigeons which lighted on the window-sill, gave me just subjects enough for interest. Now and then a cart or carriage drove up,—I could hear them ascending the rough village street long before they stopped at the "Halbmond," the village inn. Then there came a sound of running and haste in the house; and Thekla was always called for in sharp, imperative tones. I heard little children's footsteps, too, from time to time; and once there must have been some childish accident or hurt, for a shrill, plaintive little voice kept calling out, "Thekla, Thekla, liebe Thekla." Yet, after the first early morning hours, when my hostess attended on my wants, it was always Thekla who came to give me my food or my medicine; who redded up my room; who arranged the degree of light, shifting the temporary curtain with the shifting sun; and always as quietly and deliberately as though her attendance upon me were her sole work. Once or twice my hostess came into the large eating-room (out of which my room opened), and called Thekla away from whatever was her occupation in my room at the time, in a sharp, injured, imperative whisper. Once I remember it was to say that sheets were wanted for some stranger's bed, and to ask where she, the speaker, could have put the keys, in a tone of irritation, as though Thekla were responsible for Fräulein Müller's own forgetfulness.

Night came on; the sounds of daily life died away into silence; the children's voices were no more heard; the poultry were all gone to roost; the beasts of burden to their stables; and travellers were housed. Then Thekla came in softly and quietly, and took up her appointed place, after she had done all in her power for my comfort. I felt that I was in no state to be left all those weary hours which intervened between sunset and sunrise; but I did feel ashamed that this young woman, who had watched by me all the previous night, and for aught I knew, for many before, and had worked hard, been run off her legs, as English servants would say, all day long, should come and take up her care of me again; and it was with a feeling of relief that I saw her head bend forwards, and finally rest on her arms, which had fallen on the white piece of sewing spread before her on the table. She slept; and I slept. When I wakened dawn was stealing into the room, and making pale the lamplight. Thekla was standing by the stove, where she had been preparing the bouillon I should require on wakening. But she did not notice my half-open eyes, although her face was turned towards the bed. She was reading a letter slowly, as if its words were familiar to her, yet as though she were trying afresh to extract some fuller or some different meaning from their construction. She folded it up softly and slowly, and replaced it in her pocket with the quiet movement habitual to her. Then she looked before her, not at me, but at vacancy filled up by memories; and as the enchanter brought up the scenes and people which she saw, but I could not, her eyes filled with tears—tears that gathered almost imperceptibly to herself as it would seem—for when one large drop fell on her hands (held slightly together before her as she stood) she started a little, and brushed her eyes with the back of her hand, and then came towards the bed to see if I was awake. If I had not witnessed her previous emotion, I could never have guessed that she had any hidden sorrow or pain from her manner; tranquil, self-restrained as usual. The thought of this letter haunted me, especially as more than once I, wakeful or watchful during the ensuing nights, either saw it in her hands, or suspected that she had been recurring to it from noticing the same sorrowful, dreamy look upon her face when she thought herself unobserved. Most likely every one has noticed how inconsistently out of proportion some ideas become when one is shut up in any place without change of scene or thought. I really grew quite irritated about this letter. If I did not see it, I suspected it lay perdu in her pocket. What was in it? Of course it was a love-letter; but if so, what was going wrong in the course of her love? I became like a spoilt child in my recovery; every one whom I saw for the time being was thinking only of me, so it was perhaps no wonder that I became my sole object of thought; and at last the gratification of my curiosity about this letter seemed to me a duty that I owed to myself. As long as my fidgety inquisitiveness remained ungratified, I felt as if I could not get well. But to do myself justice, it was more than inquisitiveness. Thekla had tended me with the gentle, thoughtful care of a sister, in the midst of her busy life. I could often hear the Fräulein's sharp voice outside blaming her for something that had gone wrong; but I never heard much from Thekla in reply. Her name was called in various tones by different people, more frequently than I could count, as if her services were in perpetual requisition, yet I was never neglected, or even long uncared-for. The doctor was kind and attentive; my host friendly and really generous; his sister subdued her acerbity of manner when in my room, but Thekla was the one of all to whom I owed my comforts, if not my life. If I could do anything to smooth her path (and a little money goes a great way in these primitive parts of Germany), how willingly would I give it? So one night I began—she was no longer needed to watch by my bedside, but she was arranging my room before leaving me for the night—

"Thekla," said I, "you don't belong to Heppenheim, do you?"

She looked at me, and reddened a little.

"No. Why do you ask?"

"You have been so good to me that I cannot help wanting to know more about you. I must needs feel interested in one who has been by my side through my illness as you have. Where do your friends live? Are your parents alive?"

All this time I was driving at the letter.

"I was born at Altenahr. My father is an innkeeper there. He owns the 'Golden Stag.' My mother is dead, and he has married again, and has many children."

"And your stepmother is unkind to you," said I, jumping to a conclusion.

"Who said so?" asked she, with a shade of indignation in her tone. "She is a right good woman, and makes my father a good wife."

"Then why are you here living so far from home?"

Now the look came back to her face which I had seen upon it during the night hours when I had watched her by stealth; a dimming of the grave frankness of her eyes, a light quiver at the corners of her mouth. But all she said was, "It was better."

Somehow, I persisted with the wilfulness of an invalid. I am half ashamed of it now.

"But why better, Thekla? Was there—" How should I put it? I stopped a little, and then rushed blindfold at my object: "Has not that letter which you read so often something to do with your being here?"

She fixed me with her serious eyes till I believe I reddened far more than she; and I hastened to pour out, incoherently enough, my conviction that she had some secret care, and my desire to help her if she was in any trouble.

"You cannot help me," said she, a little softened by my explanation, though some shade of resentment at having been thus surreptitiously watched yet lingered in her manner. "It is an old story; a sorrow gone by, past, at least it ought to be, only sometimes I am foolish"—her tones were softening now—"and it is punishment enough that you have seen my folly."

"If you had a brother here, Thekla, you would let him give you his sympathy if he could not give you his help, and you would not blame yourself if you had shown him your sorrow, should you? I tell you again, let me be as a brother to you."

"In the first place, sir"—this "sir" was to mark the distinction between me and the imaginary brother—"I should have been ashamed to have shown even a brother my sorrow, which is also my reproach and my disgrace." These were strong words; and I suppose my face showed that I attributed to them a still stronger meaning than they warranted; but honi soit qui mal y pense—for she went on dropping her eyes and speaking hurriedly.

"My shame and my reproach is this: I have loved a man who has not loved me"—she grasped her hands together till the fingers made deep white dents in the rosy flesh—"and I can't make out whether he ever did, or whether he did once and is changed now; if only he did once love me, I could forgive myself."

With hasty, trembling hands she began to rearrange the tisane and medicines for the night on the little table at my bed-side. But, having got thus far, I was determined to persevere.

"Thekla," said I, "tell me all about it, as you would to your mother, if she were alive. There are often misunderstandings which, never set to rights, make the misery and desolation of a life-time."

She did not speak at first. Then she pulled out the letter, and said, in a quiet, hopeless tone of voice:—

"You can read German writing? Read that, and see if I have any reason for misunderstanding."

The letter was signed "Franz Weber," and dated from some small town in Switzerland—I forget what—about a month previous to the time when I read it. It began with acknowledging the receipt of some money which had evidently been requested by the writer, and for which the thanks were almost fulsome; and then, by the quietest transition in the world, he went on to consult her as to the desirability of his marrying some girl in the place from which he wrote, saying that this Anna Somebody was only eighteen and very pretty, and her father a well-to-do shopkeeper, and adding, with coarse coxcombry, his belief that he was not indifferent to the maiden herself. He wound up by saying that, if this marriage did take place, he should certainly repay the various sums of money which Thekla had lent him at different times.

I was some time in making out all this. Thekla held the candle for me to read it; held it patiently and steadily, not speaking a word till I had folded up the letter again, and given it back to her. Then our eyes met.

"There is no misunderstanding possible, is there, sir?" asked she, with a faint smile.

"No," I replied; "but you are well rid of such a fellow."

She shook her head a little. "It shows his bad side, sir. We have all our bad sides. You must not judge him harshly; at least, I cannot. But then we were brought up together."

"At Altenahr?"

"Yes; his father kept the other inn, and our parents, instead of being rivals, were great friends. Franz is a little younger than I, and was a delicate child. I had to take him to school, and I used to be so proud of it and of my charge. Then he grew strong, and was the handsomest lad in the village. Our fathers used to sit and smoke together, and talk of our marriage, and Franz must have heard as much as I. Whenever he was in trouble, he would come to me for what advice I could give him; and he danced twice as often with me as with any other girl at all the dances, and always brought his nosegay to me. Then his father wished him to travel, and learn the ways at the great hotels on the Rhine before he settled down in Altenahr. You know that is the custom in Germany, sir. They go from town to town as journeymen, learning something fresh everywhere, they say."

"I knew that was done in trades," I replied.

"Oh, yes; and among inn-keepers, too," she said. "Most of the waiters at the great hotels in Frankfort, and Heidelberg, and Mayence, and, I daresay, at all the other places, are the sons of innkeepers in small towns, who go out into the world to learn new ways, and perhaps to pick up a little English and French; otherwise, they say, they should never get on. Franz went off from Altenahr on his journeyings four years ago next May-day; and before he went, he brought me back a ring from Bonn, where he bought his new clothes. I don't wear it now; but I have got it upstairs, and it comforts me to see something that shows me it was not all my silly fancy. I suppose he fell among bad people, for he soon began to play for money,—and then he lost more than he could always pay—and sometimes I could help him a little, for we wrote to each other from time to time, as we knew each other's addresses; for the little ones grew around my father's hearth, and I thought that I, too, would go forth into the world and earn my own living, so that—well, I will tell the truth—I thought that by going into service, I could lay by enough for buying a handsome stock of household linen, and plenty of pans and kettles against—against what will never come to pass now."

"Do the German women buy the pots and kettles, as you call them, when they are married?" asked I, awkwardly, laying hold of a trivial question to conceal the indignant sympathy with her wrongs which I did not like to express.

"Oh, yes; the bride furnishes all that is wanted in the kitchen, and all the store of house-linen. If my mother had lived, it would have been laid by for me, as she could have afforded to buy it, but my stepmother will have hard enough work to provide for her own four little girls. However," she continued, brightening up, "I can help her, for now I shall never marry; and my master here is just and liberal, and pays me sixty florins a year, which is high wages." (Sixty florins are about five pounds sterling.) "And now, good-night, sir. This cup to the left holds the tisane, that to the right the acorn-tea." She shaded the candle, and was leaving the room. I raised myself on my elbow, and called her back.

"Don't go on thinking about this man," said I. "He was not good enough for you. You are much better unmarried."

"Perhaps so," she answered gravely. "But you cannot do him justice; you do not know him."

A few minutes after, I heard her soft and cautious return; she had taken her shoes off, and came in her stockinged feet up to my bedside, shading the light with her hand. When she saw that my eyes were open, she laid down two letters on the table, close by my night-lamp.

"Perhaps, some time, sir, you would take the trouble to read these letters; you would then see how noble and clever Franz really is. It is I who ought to be blamed, not he."

No more was said that night.

Some time the next morning I read the letters. They were filled with vague, inflated, sentimental descriptions of his inner life and feelings; entirely egotistical, and intermixed with quotations from second-rate philosophers and poets. There was, it must be said, nothing in them offensive to good principle or good feeling, however much they might be opposed to good taste. I was to go into the next room that afternoon for the first time of leaving my sick chamber. All morning I lay and ruminated. From time to time I thought of Thekla and Franz Weber. She was the strong, good, helpful character, he the weak and vain; how strange it seemed that she should have cared for one so dissimilar; and then I remembered the various happy marriages when to an outsider it seemed as if one was so inferior to the other that their union would have appeared a subject for despair if it had been looked at prospectively. My host came in, in the midst of these meditations, bringing a great flowered dressing-gown, lined with flannel, and the embroidered smoking-cap which he evidently considered as belonging to this Indian-looking robe. They had been his father's, he told me; and as he helped me to dress, he went on with his communications on small family matters. His inn was flourishing; the numbers increased every year of those who came to see the church at Heppenheim: the church which was the pride of the place, but which I had never yet seen. It was built by the great Kaiser Karl. And there was the Castle of Starkenburg, too, which the Abbots of Lorsch had often defended, stalwart churchmen as they were, against the temporal power of the emperors. And Melibocus was not beyond a walk either. In fact, it was the work of one person to superintend the inn alone; but he had his farm and his vineyards beyond, which of themselves gave him enough to do. And his sister was oppressed with the perpetual calls made upon her patience and her nerves in an inn; and would rather go back and live at Worms. And his children wanted so much looking after. By the time he had placed himself in a condition for requiring my full sympathy, I had finished my slow toilette; and I had to interrupt his confidences, and accept the help of his good strong arm to lead me into the great eating-room, out of which my chamber opened. I had a dreamy recollection of the vast apartment. But how pleasantly it was changed! There was the bare half of the room, it is true, looking as it had done on that first afternoon, sunless and cheerless, with the long, unoccupied table, and the necessary chairs for the possible visitors; but round the windows that opened on the garden a part of the room was enclosed by the household clothes'-horses hung with great pieces of the blue homespun cloth of which the dress of the Black Forest peasant is made. This shut-in space was warmed by the lighted stove, as well as by the lowering rays of the October sun. There was a little round walnut table with some flowers upon it, and a great cushioned armchair placed so as to look out upon the garden and the hills beyond. I felt sure that this was all Thekla's arrangement; I had rather wondered that I had seen so little of her this day. She had come once or twice on necessary errands into my room in the morning, but had appeared to be in great haste, and had avoided meeting my eye. Even when I had returned the letters, which she had entrusted to me with so evident a purpose of placing the writer in my good opinion, she had never inquired as to how far they had answered her design; she had merely taken them with some low word of thanks, and put them hurriedly into her pocket. I suppose she shrank from remembering how fully she had given me her confidence the night before, now that daylight and actual life pressed close around her. Besides, there surely never was anyone in such constant request as Thekla. I did not like this estrangement, though it was the natural consequence of my improved health, which would daily make me less and less require services which seemed so urgently claimed by others. And, moreover, after my host left me—I fear I had cut him a little short in the recapitulation of his domestic difficulties, but he was too thorough and good-hearted a man to bear malice—I wanted to be amused or interested. So I rang my little hand-bell, hoping that Thekla would answer it, when I could have fallen into conversation with her, without specifying any decided want. Instead of Thekla the Fräulein came, and I had to invent a wish; for I could not act as a baby, and say that I wanted my nurse. However, the Fräulein is better than no one, so I asked her if I could have some grapes, which had been provided for me on every day but this, and which were especially grateful to my feverish palate. She was a good, kind woman, although, perhaps, her temper was not the best in the world; and she expressed the sincerest regret as she told me that there were no more in the house. Like an invalid I fretted at my wish not being granted, and spoke out.

"But Thekla told me the vintage was not till the fourteenth; and you have a vineyard close beyond the garden on the slope of the hill out there, have you not?"

"Yes; and grapes for the gathering. But perhaps the gentleman does not know our laws. Until the vintage—(the day of beginning the vintage is fixed by the Grand Duke, and advertised in the public papers)—until the vintage, all owners of vineyards may only go on two appointed days in every week to gather their grapes; on those two days (Tuesdays and Fridays this year) they must gather enough for the wants of their families; and if they do not reckon rightly, and gather short measure, why they have to go without. And these two last days the Half-Moon has been besieged with visitors, all of whom have asked for grapes. But to-morrow the gentleman can have as many as he will; it is the day for gathering them."

"What a strange kind of paternal law," I grumbled out. "Why is it so ordained? Is it to secure the owners against pilfering from their unfenced vineyards?"

"I am sure I cannot tell," she replied. "Country people in these villages have strange customs in many ways, as I daresay the English gentleman has perceived. If he would come to Worms he would see a different kind of life."

"But not a view like this," I replied, caught by a sudden change of light—some cloud passing away from the sun, or something. Right outside of the windows was, as I have so often said, the garden. Trained plum-trees with golden leaves, great bushes of purple, Michaelmas daisy, late flowering roses, apple-trees partly stripped of their rosy fruit, but still with enough left on their boughs to require the props set to support the luxuriant burden; to the left an arbour covered over with honeysuckle and other sweet-smelling creepers—all bounded by a low gray stone wall which opened out upon the steep vineyard, that stretched up the hill beyond, one hill of a series rising higher and higher into the purple distance. "Why is there a rope with a bunch of straw tied in it stretched across the opening of the garden into the vineyard?" I inquired, as my eye suddenly caught upon the object.

"It is the country way of showing that no one must pass along that path. To-morrow the gentleman will see it removed; and then he shall have the grapes. Now I will go and prepare his coffee." With a curtsey, after the fashion of Worms gentility, she withdrew. But an under-servant brought me my coffee; and with her I could not exchange a word: she spoke in such an execrable patois. I went to bed early, weary, and depressed. I must have fallen asleep immediately, for I never heard any one come to arrange my bed-side table; yet in the morning I found that every usual want or wish of mine had been attended to.

I was wakened by a tap at my door, and a pretty piping child's voice asking, in broken German, to come in. On giving the usual permission, Thekla entered, carrying a great lovely boy of two years old, or thereabouts, who had only his little night-shirt on, and was all flushed with sleep. He held tight in his hands a great cluster of muscatel and noble grapes. He seemed like a little Bacchus, as she carried him towards me with an expression of pretty loving pride upon her face as she looked at him. But when he came close to me—the grim, wasted, unshorn—he turned quick away, and hid his face in her neck, still grasping tight his bunch of grapes. She spoke to him rapidly and softly, coaxing him as I could tell full well, although I could not follow her words; and in a minute or two the little fellow obeyed her, and turned and stretched himself almost to overbalancing out of her arms, and half-dropped the fruit on the bed by me. Then he clutched at her again, burying his face in her kerchief, and fastening his little fists in her luxuriant hair.

"It is my master's only boy," said she, disentangling his fingers with quiet patience, only to have them grasp her braids afresh. "He is my little Max, my heart's delight, only he must not pull so hard. Say his 'to-meet-again,' and kiss his hand lovingly, and we will go." The promise of a speedy departure from my dusky room proved irresistible; he babbled out his Aufwiedersehen, and kissing his chubby hand, he was borne away joyful and chattering fast in his infantile half-language. I did not see Thekla again until late afternoon, when she brought me in my coffee. She was not like the same creature as the blooming, cheerful maiden whom I had seen in the morning; she looked wan and careworn, older by several years.

"What is the matter, Thekla?" said I, with true anxiety as to what might have befallen my good, faithful nurse.

She looked round before answering. "I have seen him," she said. "He has been here, and the Fräulein has been so angry! She says she will tell my master. Oh, it has been such a day!" The poor young woman, who was usually so composed and self-restrained, was on the point of bursting into tears; but by a strong effort she checked herself, and tried to busy herself with rearranging the white china cup, so as to place it more conveniently to my hand.

"Come, Thekla," said I, "tell me all about it. I have heard loud voices talking, and I fancied something had put the Fräulein out; and Lottchen looked flurried when she brought me my dinner. Is Franz here? How has he found you out?"

"He is here. Yes, I am sure it is he; but four years makes such a difference in a man; his whole look and manner seemed so strange to me; but he knew me at once, and called me all the old names which we used to call each other when we were children; and he must needs tell me how it had come to pass that he had not married that Swiss Anna. He said he had never loved her; and that now he was going home to settle, and he hoped that I would come too, and—" There she stopped short.

"And marry him, and live at the inn at Altenahr," said I, smiling, to reassure her, though I felt rather disappointed about the whole affair.

"No," she replied. "Old Weber, his father, is dead; he died in debt, and Franz will have no money. And he was always one that needed money. Some are, you know; and while I was thinking, and he was standing near me, the Fräulein came in; and—and—I don't wonder—for poor Franz is not a pleasant-looking man now-a-days—she was very angry, and called me a bold, bad girl, and said she could have no such goings on at the 'Halbmond,' but would tell my master when he came home from the forest."

"But you could have told her that you were old friends." I hesitated, before saying the word lovers, but, after a pause, out it came.

"Franz might have said so," she replied, a little stiffly. "I could not; but he went off as soon as she bade him. He went to the 'Adler' over the way, only saying he would come for my answer to-morrow morning. I think it was he that should have told her what we were—neighbours' children and early friends—not have left it all to me. Oh," said she, clasping her hands tight together, "she will make such a story of it to my master."

"Never mind," said I, "tell the master I want to see him, as soon as he comes in from the forest, and trust me to set him right before the Fräulein has the chance to set him wrong."

She looked up at me gratefully, and went away without any more words. Presently the fine burly figure of my host stood at the opening to my enclosed sitting-room. He was there, three-cornered hat in hand, looking tired and heated as a man does after a hard day's work, but as kindly and genial as ever, which is not what every man is who is called to business after such a day, before he has had the necessary food and rest.

I had been reflecting a good deal on Thekla's story; I could not quite interpret her manner to-day to my full satisfaction; but yet the love which had grown with her growth, must assuredly have been called forth by her lover's sudden reappearance; and I was inclined to give him some credit for having broken off an engagement to Swiss Anna, which had promised so many worldly advantages; and, again, I had considered that if he was a little weak and sentimental, it was Thekla, who would marry him by her own free will, and perhaps she had sense and quiet resolution enough for both. So I gave the heads of the little history I have told you to my good friend and host, adding that I should like to have a man's opinion of this man; but that if he were not an absolute good-for-nothing, and if Thekla still loved him, as I believed, I would try and advance them the requisite money towards establishing themselves in the hereditary inn at Altenahr.

Such was the romantic ending to Thekla's sorrows, I had been planning and brooding over for the last hour. As I narrated my tale, and hinted at the possible happy conclusion that might be in store, my host's face changed. The ruddy colour faded, and his look became almost stern—certainly very grave in expression. It was so unsympathetic, that I instinctively cut my words short. When I had done, he paused a little, and then said: "You would wish me to learn all I can respecting this stranger now at the 'Adler,' and give you the impression I receive of the fellow."

"Exactly so," said I; "I want to learn all I can about him for Thekla's sake."

"For Thekla's sake I will do it," he gravely repeated.

"And come to me to-night, even if I am gone to bed?"

"Not so," he replied. "You must give me all the time you can in a matter like this."

"But he will come for Thekla's answer in the morning."

"Before he comes you shall know all I can learn."

I was resting during the fatigues of dressing the next day, when my host tapped at my door. He looked graver and sterner than I had ever seen him do before; he sat down almost before I had begged him to do so.

"He is not worthy of her," he said. "He drinks brandy right hard; he boasts of his success at play, and"—here he set his teeth hard—"he boasts of the women who have loved him. In a village like this, sir, there are always those who spend their evenings in the gardens of the inns; and this man, after he had drank his fill, made no secrets; it needed no spying to find out what he was, else I should not have been the one to do it."

"Thekla must be told of this," said I. "She is not the woman to love any one whom she cannot respect."

Herr Müller laughed a low bitter laugh, quite unlike himself. Then he replied,—

"As for that matter, sir, you are young; you have had no great experience of women. From what my sister tells me there can be little doubt of Thekla's feeling towards him. She found them standing together by the window; his arm round Thekla's waist, and whispering in her ear—and to do the maiden justice she is not the one to suffer such familiarities from every one. No"—continued he, still in the same contemptuous tone—"you'll find she will make excuses for his faults and vices; or else, which is perhaps more likely, she will not believe your story, though I who tell it you can vouch for the truth of every word I say." He turned short away and left the room. Presently I saw his stalwart figure in the hill-side vineyard, before my windows, scaling the steep ascent with long regular steps, going to the forest beyond. I was otherwise occupied than in watching his progress during the next hour; at the end of that time he re-entered my room, looking heated and slightly tired, as if he had been walking fast, or labouring hard; but with the cloud off his brows, and the kindly light shining once again out of his honest eyes.

"I ask your pardon, sir," he began, "for troubling you afresh. I believe I was possessed by the devil this morning. I have been thinking it over. One has perhaps no right to rule for another person's happiness. To have such a"—here the honest fellow choked a little—"such a woman as Thekla to love him ought to raise any man. Besides, I am no judge for him or for her. I have found out this morning that I love her myself, and so the end of it is, that if you, sir, who are so kind as to interest yourself in the matter, and if you think it is really her heart's desire to marry this man—which ought to be his salvation both for earth and heaven—I shall be very glad to go halves with you in any place for setting them up in the inn at Altenahr; only allow me to see that whatever money we advance is well and legally tied up, so that it is secured to her. And be so kind as to take no notice of what I have said about my having found out that I have loved her; I named it as a kind of apology for my hard words this morning, and as a reason why I was not a fit judge of what was best." He had hurried on, so that I could not have stopped his eager speaking even had I wished to do so; but I was too much interested in the revelation of what was passing in his brave tender heart to desire to stop him. Now, however, his rapid words tripped each other up, and his speech ended in an unconscious sigh.

"But," I said, "since you were here Thekla has come to me, and we have had a long talk. She speaks now as openly to me as she would if I were her brother; with sensible frankness, where frankness is wise, with modest reticence, where confidence would be unbecoming. She came to ask me, if I thought it her duty to marry this fellow, whose very appearance, changed for the worse, as she says it is, since she last saw him four years ago, seemed to have repelled her."

"She could let him put his arm round her waist yesterday," said Herr Müller, with a return of his morning's surliness.

"And she would marry him now if she could believe it to be her duty. For some reason of his own, this Franz Weber has tried to work upon this feeling of hers. He says it would be the saving of him."

"As if a man had not strength enough in him—a man who is good for aught—to save himself, but needed a woman to pull him through life!"

"Nay," I replied, hardly able to keep from smiling. "You yourself said, not five minutes ago, that her marrying him might be his salvation both for earth and heaven."

"That was when I thought she loved the fellow," he answered quick. "Now—but what did you say to her, sir?"

"I told her, what I believe to be as true as gospel, that as she owned she did not love him any longer now his real self had come to displace his remembrance, that she would be sinning in marrying him; doing evil that possible good might come. I was clear myself on this point, though I should have been perplexed how to advise, if her love had still continued."

"And what answer did she make?"

"She went over the history of their lives; she was pleading against her wishes to satisfy her conscience. She said that all along through their childhood she had been his strength; that while under her personal influence he had been negatively good; away from her, he had fallen into mischief—"

"Not to say vice," put in Herr Müller.

"And now he came to her penitent, in sorrow, desirous of amendment, asking her for the love she seems to have considered as tacitly plighted to him in years gone by—"

"And which he has slighted and insulted. I hope you told her of his words and conduct last night in the 'Adler' gardens?"

"No. I kept myself to the general principle, which, I am sure, is a true one. I repeated it in different forms; for the idea of the duty of self-sacrifice had taken strong possession of her fancy. Perhaps, if I had failed in setting her notion of her duty in the right aspect, I might have had recourse to the statement of facts, which would have pained her severely, but would have proved to her how little his words of penitence and promises of amendment were to be trusted to."

"And it ended?"

"Ended by her being quite convinced that she would be doing wrong instead of right if she married a man whom she had entirely ceased to love, and that no real good could come from a course of action based on wrong-doing."

"That is right and true," he replied, his face broadening into happiness again.

"But she says she must leave your service, and go elsewhere."

"Leave my service she shall; go elsewhere she shall not."

"I cannot tell what you may have the power of inducing her to do; but she seems to me very resolute."

"Why?" said he, firing round at me, as if I had made her resolute.

"She says your sister spoke to her before the maids of the household, and before some of the townspeople, in a way that she could not stand; and that you yourself by your manner to her last night showed how she had lost your respect. She added, with her face of pure maidenly truth, that he had come into such close contact with her only the instant before your sister had entered the room."

"With your leave, sir," said Herr Müller, turning towards the door, "I will go and set all that right at once."

It was easier said than done. When I next saw Thekla, her eyes were swollen up with crying, but she was silent, almost defiant towards me. A look of resolute determination had settled down upon her face. I learnt afterwards that parts of my conversation with Herr Müller had been injudiciously quoted by him in the talk he had had with her. I thought I would leave her to herself, and wait till she unburdened herself of the feeling of unjust resentment towards me. But it was days before she spoke to me with anything like her former frankness. I had heard all about it from my host long before.

He had gone to her straight on leaving me; and like a foolish, impetuous lover, had spoken out his mind and his wishes to her in the presence of his sister, who, it must be remembered, had heard no explanation of the conduct which had given her propriety so great a shock the day before. Herr Müller thought to re-instate Thekla in his sister's good opinion by giving her in the Fräulein's very presence the highest possible mark of his own love and esteem. And there in the kitchen, where the Fräulein was deeply engaged in the hot work of making some delicate preserve on the stove, and ordering Thekla about with short, sharp displeasure in her tones, the master had come in, and possessing himself of the maiden's hand, had, to her infinite surprise—to his sister's infinite indignation—made her the offer of his heart, his wealth, his life; had begged of her to marry him. I could gather from his account that she had been in a state of trembling discomfiture at first; she had not spoken, but had twisted her hand out of his, and had covered her face with her apron. And then the Fräulein had burst forth—"accursed words" he called her speech. Thekla uncovered her face to listen; to listen to the end; to listen to the passionate recrimination between the brother and the sister. And then she went up, close up to the angry Fräulein, and had said quite quietly, but with a manner of final determination which had evidently sunk deep into her suitor's heart, and depressed him into hopelessness, that the Fräulein had no need to disturb herself; that on this very day she had been thinking of marrying another man, and that her heart was not like a room to let, into which as one tenant went out another might enter. Nevertheless, she felt the master's goodness. He had always treated her well from the time when she had entered the house as his servant. And she should be sorry to leave him; sorry to leave the children; very sorry to leave little Max: yes, she should even be sorry to leave the Fräulein, who was a good woman, only a little too apt to be hard on other women. But she had already been that very day and deposited her warning at the police office; the busy time would be soon over, and she should be glad to leave their service on All Saints' Day. Then (he thought) she had felt inclined to cry, for she suddenly braced herself up, and said, yes, she should be very glad; for somehow, though they had been kind to her, she had been very unhappy at Heppenheim; and she would go back to her home for a time, and see her old father and kind stepmother, and her nursling half-sister Ida, and be among her own people again.

I could see it was this last part that most of all rankled in Herr Müller's mind. In all probability Franz Weber was making his way back to Heppenheim too; and the bad suspicion would keep welling up that some lingering feeling for her old lover and disgraced playmate was making her so resolute to leave and return to Altenahr.

For some days after this I was the confidant of the whole household, excepting Thekla. She, poor creature, looked miserable enough; but the hardy, defiant expression was always on her face. Lottchen spoke out freely enough; the place would not be worth having if Thekla left it; it was she who had the head for everything, the patience for everything; who stood between all the under-servants and the Fräulein's tempers. As for the children, poor motherless children! Lottchen was sure that the master did not know what he was doing when he allowed his sister to turn Thekla away—and all for what? for having a lover, as every girl had who could get one. Why, the little boy Max slept in the room which Lottchen shared with Thekla; and she heard him in the night as quickly as if she was his mother; when she had been sitting up with me, when I was so ill, Lottchen had had to attend to him; and it was weary work after a hard day to have to get up and soothe a teething child; she knew she had been cross enough sometimes; but Thekla was always good and gentle with him, however tired he was. And as Lottchen left the room I could hear her repeating that she thought she should leave when Thekla went, for that her place would not be worth having.

Even the Fräulein had her word of regret—regret mingled with self-justification. She thought she had been quite right in speaking to Thekla for allowing such familiarities; how was she to know that the man was an old friend and playmate? He looked like a right profligate good-for-nothing. And to have a servant take up her scolding as an unpardonable offence, and persist in quitting her place, just when she had learnt all her work, and was so useful in the household—so useful that the Fräulein could never put up with any fresh, stupid house-maiden, but, sooner than take the trouble of teaching the new servant where everything was, and how to give out the stores if she was busy, she would go back to Worms. For, after all, housekeeping for a brother was thankless work; there was no satisfying men; and Heppenheim was but a poor ignorant village compared to Worms.

She must have spoken to her brother about her intention of leaving him, and returning to her former home; indeed a feeling of coolness had evidently grown up between the brother and sister during these latter days. When one evening Herr Müller brought in his pipe, and, as his custom had sometimes been, sat down by my stove to smoke, he looked gloomy and annoyed. I let him puff away, and take his own time. At length he began,—

"I have rid the village of him at last. I could not bear to have him here disgracing Thekla with speaking to her whenever she went to the vineyard or the fountain. I don't believe she likes him a bit."

"No more do I," I said. He turned on me.

"Then why did she speak to him at all? Why cannot she like an honest man who likes her? Why is she so bent on going home to Altenahr?"

"She speaks to him because she has known him from a child, and has a faithful pity for one whom she has known so innocent, and who is now so lost in all good men's regard. As for not liking an honest man—(though I may have my own opinion about that)—liking goes by fancy, as we say in English; and Altenahr is her home; her father's house is at Altenahr, as you know."

"I wonder if he will go there," quoth Herr Müller, after two or three more puffs. "He was fast at the 'Adler;' he could not pay his score, so he kept on staying here, saying that he should receive a letter from a friend with money in a day or two; lying in wait, too, for Thekla, who is well-known and respected all through Heppenheim: so his being an old friend of hers made him have a kind of standing. I went in this morning and paid his score, on condition that he left the place this day; and he left the village as merrily as a cricket, caring no more for Thekla than for the Kaiser who built our church: for he never looked back at the 'Halbmond,' but went whistling down the road."

"That is a good riddance," said I.

"Yes. But my sister says she must return to Worms. And Lottchen has given notice; she says the place will not be worth having when Thekla leaves. I wish I could give notice too."

"Try Thekla again."

"Not I," said he, reddening. "It would seem now as if I only wanted her for a housekeeper. Besides, she avoids me at every turn, and will not even look at me. I am sure she bears me some ill-will about that ne'er-do-well."

There was silence between us for some time, which he at length broke.

"The pastor has a good and comely daughter. Her mother is a famous housewife. They often have asked me to come to the parsonage and smoke a pipe. When the vintage is over, and I am less busy, I think I will go there, and look about me."

"When is the vintage?" asked I. "I hope it will take place soon, for I am growing so well and strong I fear I must leave you shortly; but I should like to see the vintage first."

"Oh, never fear! you must not travel yet awhile; and Government has fixed the grape-gathering to begin on the fourteenth."

"What a paternal Government! How does it know when the grapes will be ripe? Why cannot every man fix his own time for gathering his own grapes?"

"That has never been our way in Germany. There are people employed by the Government to examine the vines, and report when the grapes are ripe. It is necessary to make laws about it; for, as you must have seen, there is nothing but the fear of the law to protect our vineyards and fruit-trees; there are no enclosures along the Berg-Strasse, as you tell me you have in England; but, as people are only allowed to go into the vineyards on stated days, no one, under pretence of gathering his own produce, can stray into his neighbour's grounds and help himself, without some of the duke's foresters seeing him."

"Well," said I, "to each country its own laws."

I think it was on that very evening that Thekla came in for something. She stopped arranging the tablecloth and the flowers, as if she had something to say, yet did not know how to begin. At length I found that her sore, hot heart, wanted some sympathy; her hand was against every one's, and she fancied every one had turned against her. She looked up at me, and said, a little abruptly,—

"Does the gentleman know that I go on the fifteenth?"

"So soon?" said I, with surprise. "I thought you were to remain here till All Saints' Day."

"So I should have done—so I must have done—if the Fräulein had not kindly given me leave to accept of a place—a very good place too—of housekeeper to a widow lady at Frankfort. It is just the sort of situation I have always wished for. I expect I shall be so happy and comfortable there."

"Methinks the lady doth profess too much," came into my mind. I saw she expected me to doubt the probability of her happiness, and was in a defiant mood.

"Of course," said I, "you would hardly have wished to leave Heppenheim if you had been happy here; and every new place always promises fair, whatever its performance may be. But wherever you go, remember you have always a friend in me."

"Yes," she replied, "I think you are to be trusted. Though, from my experience, I should say that of very few men."

"You have been unfortunate," I answered; "many men would say the same of women."

She thought a moment, and then said, in a changed tone of voice, "The Fräulein here has been much more friendly and helpful of these late days than her brother; yet I have served him faithfully, and have cared for his little Max as though he were my own brother. But this morning he spoke to me for the first time for many days,—he met me in the passage, and, suddenly stopping, he said he was glad I had met with so comfortable a place, and that I was at full liberty to go whenever I liked: and then he went quickly on, never waiting for my answer."

"And what was wrong in that? It seems to me he was trying to make you feel entirely at your ease, to do as you thought best, without regard to his own interests."

"Perhaps so. It is silly, I know," she continued, turning full on me her grave, innocent eyes; "but one's vanity suffers a little when every one is so willing to part with one."

"Thekla! I owe you a great debt—let me speak to you openly. I know that your master wanted to marry you, and that you refused him. Do not deceive yourself. You are sorry for that refusal now?"

She kept her serious look fixed upon me; but her face and throat reddened all over.

"No," said she, at length; "I am not sorry. What can you think I am made of; having loved one man ever since I was a little child until a fortnight ago, and now just as ready to love another? I know you do not rightly consider what you say, or I should take it as an insult."

"You loved an ideal man; he disappointed you, and you clung to your remembrance of him. He came, and the reality dispelled all illusions."

"I do not understand philosophy," said she. "I only know that I think that Herr Müller had lost all respect for me from what his sister had told him; and I know that I am going away; and I trust I shall be happier in Frankfort than I have been here of late days." So saying, she left the room.

I was wakened up on the morning of the fourteenth by the merry ringing of church bells, and the perpetual firing and popping off of guns and pistols. But all this was over by the time I was up and dressed, and seated at breakfast in my partitioned room. It was a perfect October day; the dew not yet off the blades of grass, glistening on the delicate gossamer webs, which stretched from flower to flower in the garden, lying in the morning shadow of the house. But beyond the garden, on the sunny hill-side, men, women, and children were clambering up the vineyards like ants,—busy, irregular in movement, clustering together, spreading wide apart,—I could hear the shrill merry voices as I sat,—and all along the valley, as far as I could see, it was much the same; for every one filled his house for the day of the vintage, that great annual festival. Lottchen, who had brought in my breakfast, was all in her Sunday best, having risen early to get her work done and go abroad to gather grapes. Bright colours seemed to abound; I could see dots of scarlet, and crimson, and orange through the fading leaves; it was not a day to languish in the house; and I was on the point of going out by myself, when Herr Müller came in to offer me his sturdy arm, and help me in walking to the vineyard. We crept through the garden scented with late flowers and sunny fruit,—we passed through the gate I had so often gazed at from the easy-chair, and were in the busy vineyard; great baskets lay on the grass already piled nearly full of purple and yellow grapes. The wine made from these was far from pleasant to my taste; for the best Rhine wine is made from a smaller grape, growing in closer, harder clusters; but the larger and less profitable grape is by far the most picturesque in its mode of growth, and far the best to eat into the bargain.

Wherever we trod, it was on fragrant, crushed vine-leaves; every one we saw had his hands and face stained with the purple juice. Presently I sat down on a sunny bit of grass, and my host left me to go farther afield, to look after the more distant vineyards. I watched his progress. After he left me, he took off coat and waistcoat, displaying his snowy shirt and gaily-worked braces; and presently he was as busy as any one. I looked down on the village; the gray and orange and crimson roofs lay glowing in the noonday sun. I could see down into the streets; but they were all empty—even the old people came toiling up the hill-side to share in the general festivity. Lottchen had brought up cold dinners for a regiment of men; every one came and helped himself. Thekla was there, leading the little Karoline, and helping the toddling steps of Max; but she kept aloof from me; for I knew, or suspected, or had probed too much. She alone looked sad and grave, and spoke so little, even to her friends, that it was evident to see that she was trying to wean herself finally from the place. But I could see that she had lost her short, defiant manner. What she did say was kindly and gently spoken. The Fräulein came out late in the morning, dressed, I suppose, in the latest Worms fashion—quite different to anything I had ever seen before. She came up to me, and talked very graciously to me for some time.

"Here comes the proprietor (squire) and his lady, and their dear children. See, the vintagers have tied bunches of the finest grapes on to a stick, heavier than the children or even the lady can carry. Look! look! how he bows!—one can tell he has been an attaché at Vienna. That is the court way of bowing there—holding the hat right down before them, and bending the back at right angles. How graceful! And here is the doctor! I thought he would spare time to come up here. Well, doctor, you will go all the more cheerfully to your next patient for having been up into the vineyards. Nonsense, about grapes making other patients for you. Ah, here is the pastor and his wife, and the Fräulein Anna. Now, where is my brother, I wonder? Up in the far vineyard, I make no doubt. Mr. Pastor, the view up above is far finer than what it is here, and the best grapes grow there; shall I accompany you and madame, and the dear Fräulein? The gentleman will excuse me."

I was left alone. Presently I thought I would walk a little farther, or at any rate change my position. I rounded a corner in the pathway, and there I found Thekla, watching by little sleeping Max. He lay on her shawl; and over his head she had made an arching canopy of broken vine-branches, so that the great leaves threw their cool, flickering shadows on his face. He was smeared all over with grape-juice, his sturdy fingers grasped a half-eaten bunch even in his sleep. Thekla was keeping Lina quiet by teaching her how to weave a garland for her head out of field-flowers and autumn-tinted leaves. The maiden sat on the ground, with her back to the valley beyond, the child kneeling by her, watching the busy fingers with eager intentness. Both looked up as I drew near, and we exchanged a few words.

"Where is the master?" I asked. "I promised to await his return; he wished to give me his arm down the wooden steps; but I do not see him."

"He is in the higher vineyard," said Thekla, quietly, but not looking round in that direction. "He will be some time there, I should think. He went with the pastor and his wife; he will have to speak to his labourers and his friends. My arm is strong, and I can leave Max in Lina's care for five minutes. If you are tired, and want to go back, let me help you down the steps; they are steep and slippery."

I had turned to look up the valley. Three or four hundred yards off, in the higher vineyard, walked the dignified pastor, and his homely, decorous wife. Behind came the Fräulein Anna, in her short-sleeved Sunday gown, daintily holding a parasol over her luxuriant brown hair. Close behind her came Herr Müller, stopping now to speak to his men,—again, to cull out a bunch of grapes to tie on to the

Fräulein's stick; and by my feet sate the proud serving-maid in her country dress, waiting for my answer, with serious, up-turned eyes, and sad, composed face.

"No, I am much obliged to you, Thekla; and if I did not feel so strong I would have thankfully taken your arm. But I only wanted to leave a message for the master, just to say that I have gone home."

"Lina will give it to the father when he comes down," said Thekla.

I went slowly down into the garden. The great labour of the day was over, and the younger part of the population had returned to the village, and were preparing the fireworks and pistol-shootings for the evening. Already one or two of those well-known German carts (in the shape of a V) were standing near the vineyard gates, the patient oxen meekly waiting while basketful after basketful of grapes were being emptied into the leaf-lined receptacle.

As I sat down in my easy-chair close to the open window through which I had entered, I could see the men and women on the hill-side drawing to a centre, and all stand round the pastor, bareheaded, for a minute or so. I guessed that some words of holy thanksgiving were being said, and I wished that I had stayed to hear them, and mark my especial gratitude for having been spared to see that day. Then I heard the distant voices, the deep tones of the men, the shriller pipes of women and children, join in the German harvest-hymn, which is generally sung on such occasions;[1] then silence, while I concluded that a blessing was spoken by the pastor, with outstretched arms; and then they once more dispersed, some to the village, some to finish their labours for the day among the vines. I saw Thekla coming through the garden with Max in her arms, and Lina clinging to her woollen skirts. Thekla made for my open window; it was rather a shorter passage into the house than round by the door. "I may come through, may I not?" she asked, softly. "I fear Max is not well; I cannot understand his look, and he wakened up so strange!" She paused to let me see the child's face; it was flushed almost to a crimson look of heat, and his breathing was laboured and uneasy, his eyes half-open and filmy.

"Something is wrong, I am sure," said I. "I don't know anything about children, but he is not in the least like himself."

She bent down and kissed the cheek so tenderly that she would not have bruised the petal of a rose. "Heart's darling," she murmured. He quivered all over at her touch, working his fingers in an unnatural kind of way, and ending with a convulsive twitching all over his body. Lina began to cry at the grave, anxious look on our faces.

"You had better call the Fräulein to look at him," said I. "I feel sure he ought to have a doctor; I should say he was going to have a fit."

"The Fräulein and the master are gone to the pastor's for coffee, and Lottchen is in the higher vineyard, taking the men their bread and beer. Could you find the kitchen girl, or old Karl? he will be in the stables, I think. I must lose no time." Almost without waiting for my reply, she had passed through the room, and in the empty house I could hear her firm, careful footsteps going up the stair; Lina's pattering beside her; and the one voice wailing, the other speaking low comfort.

I was tired enough, but this good family had treated me too much like one of their own for me not to do what I could in such a case as this. I made my way out into the street, for the first time since I had come to the house on that memorable evening six weeks ago. I bribed the first person I met to guide me to the doctor's, and send him straight down to the "Halbmond," not staying to listen to the thorough scolding he fell to giving me; then on to the parsonage, to tell the master and the Fräulein of the state of things at home.

I was sorry to be the bearer of bad news into such a festive chamber as the pastor's. There they sat, resting after heat and fatigue, each in their best gala dress, the table spread with "Dicker-milch," potato-salad, cakes of various shapes and kinds—all the dainty cates dear to the German palate. The pastor was talking to Herr Müller, who stood near the pretty young Fräulein Anna, in her fresh white chemisette, with her round white arms, and her youthful coquettish airs, as she prepared to pour out the coffee; our Fräulein was talking busily to the Frau Mama; the younger boys and girls of the family filling up the room. A ghost would have startled the assembled party less than I did, and would probably have been more welcome, considering the news I brought. As he listened, the master caught up his hat and went forth, without apology or farewell. Our Fräulein made up for both, and questioned me fully; but now she, I could see, was in haste to go, although restrained by her manners, and the kind-hearted Frau Pastorin soon set her at liberty to follow her inclination. As for me I was dead-beat, and only too glad to avail myself of the hospitable couple's pressing request that I would stop and share their meal. Other magnates of the village came in presently, and relieved me of the strain of keeping up a German conversation about nothing at all with entire strangers. The pretty Fräulein's face had clouded over a little at Herr Müller's sudden departure; but she was soon as bright as could be, giving private chase and sudden little scoldings to her brothers, as they made raids upon the dainties under her charge. After I was duly rested and refreshed, I took my leave; for I, too, had my quieter anxieties about the sorrow in the Müller family.

The only person I could see at the "Halbmond" was Lottchen; every one else was busy about the poor little Max, who was passing from one fit into another. I told Lottchen to ask the doctor to come in and see me before he took his leave for the night, and tired as I was, I kept up till after his visit, though it was very late before he came; I could see from his face how anxious he was. He would give me no opinion as to the child's chances of recovery, from which I guessed that he had not much hope. But when I expressed my fear he cut me very short.

"The truth is, you know nothing about it; no more do I, for that matter. It is enough to try any man, much less a father, to hear his perpetual moans—not that he is conscious of pain, poor little worm; but if she stops for a moment in her perpetual carrying him backwards and forwards, he plains so piteously it is enough to—enough to make a man bless the Lord who never led him into the pit of matrimony. To see the father up there, following her as she walks up and down the room, the child's head over her shoulder, and Müller trying to make the heavy eyes recognize the old familiar ways of play, and the chirruping sounds which he can scarce make for crying—I shall be here to-morrow early, though before that either life or death will have come without the old doctor's help."

All night long I dreamt my feverish dream—of the vineyard—the carts, which held little coffins instead of baskets of grapes—of the pastor's daughter, who would pull the dying child out of Thekla's arms; it was a bad, weary night! I slept long into the morning; the broad daylight filled my room, and yet no one had been near to waken me! Did that mean life or death? I got up and dressed as fast as I could; for I was aching all over with the fatigue of the day before. Out into the sitting-room; the table was laid for breakfast, but no one was there. I passed into the house beyond, up the stairs, blindly seeking for the room where I might know whether it was life or death. At the door of a room I found Lottchen crying; at the sight of me in that unwonted place she started, and began some kind of apology, broken both by tears and smiles, as she told me that the doctor said the danger was over—past, and that Max was sleeping a gentle peaceful slumber in Thekla's arms—arms that had held him all through the livelong night.

"Look at him, sir; only go in softly; it is a pleasure to see the child to-day; tread softly, sir."

She opened the chamber-door. I could see Thekla sitting, propped up by cushions and stools, holding her heavy burden, and bending over him with a look of tenderest love. Not far off stood the Fräulein, all disordered and tearful, stirring or seasoning some hot soup, while the master stood by her impatient. As soon as it was cooled or seasoned enough he took the basin and went to Thekla, and said something very low; she lifted up her head, and I could see her face; pale, weary with watching, but with a soft peaceful look upon it, which it had not worn for weeks. Fritz Müller began to feed her, for her hands were occupied in holding his child; I could not help remembering Mrs. Inchbald's pretty description of Dorriforth's anxiety in feeding Miss Milner; she compares it, if I remember rightly, to that of a tender-hearted boy, caring for his darling bird, the loss of which would embitter all the joys of his holidays. We closed the door without noise, so as not to waken the sleeping child. Lottchen brought me my coffee and bread; she was ready either to laugh or to weep on the slightest occasion. I could not tell if it was in innocence or mischief. She asked me the following question,—

"Do you think Thekla will leave to-day, sir?"

In the afternoon I heard Thekla's step behind my extemporary screen. I knew it quite well. She stopped for a moment before emerging into my view.

She was trying to look as composed as usual, but, perhaps because her steady nerves had been shaken by her night's watching, she could not help faint touches of dimples at the corners of her mouth, and her eyes were veiled from any inquisitive look by their drooping lids.

"I thought you would like to know that the doctor says Max is quite out of danger now. He will only require care."

"Thank you, Thekla; Doctor — has been in already this afternoon to tell me so, and I am truly glad."

She went to the window, and looked out for a moment. Many people were in the vineyards again to-day; although we, in our household anxiety, had paid them but little heed. Suddenly she turned round into the room, and I saw that her face was crimson with blushes. In another instant Herr Müller entered by the window.

"Has she told you, sir?" said he, possessing himself of her hand, and looking all a-glow with happiness. "Hast thou told our good friend?" addressing her.

"No. I was going to tell him, but I did not know how to begin."

"Then I will prompt thee. Say after me—'I have been a wilful, foolish woman—'"

She wrenched her hand out of his, half-laughing—"I am a foolish woman, for I have promised to marry him. But he is a still more foolish man, for he wishes to marry me. That is what I say."

"And I have sent Babette to Frankfort with the pastor. He is going there, and will explain all to Frau v. Schmidt; and Babette will serve her for a time. When Max is well enough to have the change of air the doctor prescribes for him, thou shalt take him to Altenahr, and thither will I also go; and become known to thy people and thy father. And before Christmas the gentleman here shall dance at our wedding."

"I must go home to England, dear friends, before many days are over. Perhaps we may travel together as far as Remagen. Another year I will come back to Heppenheim and see you."

As I planned it, so it was. We left Heppenheim all together on a lovely All-Saints' Day. The day before—the day of All-Souls—I had watched Fritz and Thekla lead little Lina up to the Acre of God, the Field of Rest, to hang the wreath of immortelles on her mother's grave. Peace be with the dead and the living.

LIBBIE MARSH'S THREE ERAS

ERA I

VALENTINE'S DAY

Last November but one, there was a flitting in our neighbourhood; hardly a flitting, after all, for it was only a single person changing her place of abode from one lodging to another; and instead of a cartload of drawers and baskets, dressers and beds, with old king clock at the top of all, it was only one large wooden chest to be carried after the girl, who moved slowly and heavily along the streets, listless and depressed, more from the state of her mind than of her body. It was Libbie Marsh, who had been obliged to quit her room in Dean Street, because the acquaintances whom she had been living with were leaving Manchester. She tried to think herself fortunate in having met with lodgings rather more out of the town, and with those who were known to be respectable; she did indeed try to be contented, but in spite of her reason, the old feeling of desolation came over her, as she was now about to be thrown again entirely among strangers.

No. 2, — Court, Albemarle Street, was reached at last, and the pace, slow as it was, slackened as she drew near the spot where she was to be left by the man who carried her box, for, trivial as her acquaintance with him was, he was not quite a stranger, as every one else was, peering out of their open doors, and satisfying themselves it was only "Dixon's new lodger."

Dixon's house was the last on the left-hand side of the court. A high dead brick wall connected it with its opposite neighbour. All the dwellings were of the same monotonous pattern, and one side of the court looked at its exact likeness opposite, as if it were seeing itself in a looking-glass.

Dixon's house was shut up, and the key left next door; but the woman in whose charge it was left knew that Libbie was expected, and came forward to say a few explanatory words, to unlock the door, and stir the dull grey ashes that were lazily burning in the grate: and then she returned to her own house, leaving poor Libbie standing alone with the great big chest in the middle of the house-place floor, with no one to say a word to (even a common-place remark would have been better than this dull silence), that could help her to repel the fast-coming tears.

Dixon and his wife, and their eldest girl, worked in factories, and were absent all day from the house: the youngest child, also a little girl, was boarded out on the week-days at the neighbour's where the door-key was deposited, but although busy making dirt-pies, at the entrance to the court, when Libbie came in, she was too young to care much about her parents' new lodger. Libbie knew that she was to sleep with the elder girl in the front bedroom, but, as you may fancy, it seemed a liberty even to go upstairs to take off her things, when no one was at home to marshal the way up the ladder-like steps. So she could only take off her bonnet, and sit down, and gaze at the now blazing fire, and think sadly on the past, and on the lonely creature she was in this wide world—father and mother gone, her little brother long since dead—he would been more than nineteen had he been alive, but she only thought of him as the darling baby; her only friends (to call friends) living far away at their new house; her employers, kind enough people in their way, but too rapidly twirling round on this bustling earth to have leisure to think of the little work-woman, excepting when they wanted gowns turned, carpets mended, or household linen darned; and hardly even the natural though hidden hope of a young girl's heart, to cheer her on with the bright visions of a home of her own at some future day, where, loving and beloved, she might fulfil a woman's dearest duties.

For Libbie was very plain, as she had known so long that the consciousness of it had ceased to mortify her. You can hardly live in Manchester without having some idea of your personal appearance: the factory lads and lasses take good care of that; and if you meet them at the hours when they are pouring out of the mills, you are sure to hear a good number of truths, some of them combined with such a spirit of impudent fun, that you can scarcely keep from laughing, even at the joke against yourself. Libbie had often and often been greeted by such questions as—"How long is it since you were a beauty?"—"What would you take a day to stand in the fields to scare away the birds?" &c., for her to linger under any impression as to her looks.

While she was thus musing, and quietly crying, under the pictures her fancy had conjured up, the Dixons came dropping in, and surprised her with her wet cheeks and quivering lips.

She almost wished to have the stillness again that had so oppressed her an hour ago, they talked and laughed so loudly and so much, and bustled about so noisily over everything they did. Dixon took hold of one iron handle of her box, and helped her to bump it upstairs, while his daughter Anne followed to see the unpacking, and what sort of clothes "little sewing body had gotten." Mrs. Dixon rattled out her tea-things, and put the kettle on, fetched home her youngest child, which added to the commotion. Then she called Anne downstairs, and sent her for this thing and that: eggs to put to the cream, it was so thin; ham, to give a relish to the bread and butter; some new bread, hot, if she could get it. Libbie heard all these orders, given at full pitch of Mrs. Dixon's voice, and wondered at their extravagance, so different from the habits of the place where she had last lodged. But they were fine spinners, in the receipt of good wages; and confined all day in an atmosphere ranging from seventy-five to eighty degrees. They had lost all natural, healthy appetite for simple food, and, having no higher tastes, found their greatest enjoyment in their luxurious meals.

When tea was ready, Libbie was called downstairs, with a rough but hearty invitation, to share their meal; she sat mutely at the corner of the tea-table, while they went on with their own conversation about people and things she knew nothing about, till at length she ventured to ask for a candle, to go and finish her unpacking before bedtime, as she had to go out sewing for several succeeding days. But once in the comparative peace of her bedroom, her energy failed her, and she contented herself with locking her Noah's ark of a chest, and put out her candle, and went to sit by the window, and gaze out at the bright heavens; for ever and ever "the blue sky, that bends over all," sheds down a feeling of sympathy with the sorrowful at the solemn hours when the ceaseless stars are seen to pace its depths.

By-and-by her eye fell down to gazing at the corresponding window to her own, on the opposite side of the court. It was lighted, but the blind was drawn down: upon the blind she saw, first unconsciously, the constant weary motion of a little spectral shadow, a child's hand and arm—no more; long, thin fingers hanging down from the wrist, while the arm moved up and down, as if keeping time to the heavy pulses of dull pain. She could not help hoping that sleep would soon come to still that incessant, feeble motion: and now and then it did cease, as if the little creature had dropped into a slumber from very weariness; but presently the arm jerked up with the fingers clenched, as if with a sudden start of agony. When Anne came up to bed, Libbie was still sitting, watching the shadow, and she directly asked to whom it belonged.

"It will be Margaret Hall's lad. Last summer, when it was so hot, there was no biding with the window shut at night, and theirs was open too: and many's the time he has waked me with his moans; they say he's been better sin' cold weather came."

"Is he always in bed? Whatten ails him?" asked Libbie.

"Summat's amiss wi' his backbone, folks say; he's better and worse, like. He's a nice little chap enough, and his mother's not that bad either; only my mother and her had words, so now we don't speak."

Libbie went on watching, and when she next spoke, to ask who and what his mother was, Anne Dixon was fast asleep.

Time passed away, and as usual unveiled the hidden things. Libbie found out that Margaret Hall was a widow, who earned her living as a washerwoman; that the little suffering lad was her only child, her dearly beloved. That while she scolded, pretty nearly, everybody else, "till her name was up" in the neighbourhood for a termagant, to him she was evidently most tender and gentle. He lay alone on his little bed, near the window, through the day, while she was away toiling for a livelihood. But when Libbie had plain sewing to do at her lodgings, instead of going out to sew, she used to watch from her bedroom window for the time when the shadows opposite, by their mute gestures, told that the mother had returned to bend over her child, to smooth his pillow, to alter his position, to get him his nightly cup of tea. And often in the night Libbie could not help rising gently from bed, to see if the little arm was waving up and down, as was his accustomed habit when sleepless from pain.

Libbie had a good deal of sewing to do at home that winter, and whenever it was not so cold as to benumb her fingers, she took it upstairs, in order to watch the little lad in her few odd moments of pause. On his better days he could sit up enough to peep out of his window, and she found he liked to look at her. Presently she ventured to nod to him across the court; and his faint smile, and ready nod back again, showed that this gave him pleasure. I think she would have been encouraged by this smile to have proceeded to a speaking acquaintance, if it had not been for his terrible mother, to whom it seemed to be irritation enough to know that Libbie was a lodger at the Dixons' for her to talk at her whenever they encountered each other, and to live evidently in wait for some good opportunity of abuse.

With her constant interest in him, Libbie soon discovered his great want of an object on which to occupy his thoughts, and which might distract his attention, when alone through the long day, from the pain he endured. He was very fond of flowers. It was November when she had first removed to her lodgings, but it had been very mild weather, and a few flowers yet lingered in the gardens, which the country people gathered into nosegays, and brought on market-days into Manchester. His mother had brought him a bunch of Michaelmas daisies the very day Libbie had become a neighbour, and she watched their history. He put them first in an old teapot, of which the spout was broken off and the lid lost; and he daily replenished the teapot from the jug of water his mother left near him to quench his feverish thirst. By-and-by, one or two of the constellation of lilac stars faded, and then the time he had hitherto spent in admiring, almost caressing them, was devoted to cutting off those flowers whose decay marred the beauty of the nosegay. It took him half the morning, with his feeble, languid motions, and his cumbrous old scissors, to trim up his diminished darlings. Then at last he seemed to think he had better preserve the few that remained by drying them; so they were carefully put between the leaves of the old Bible; and then, whenever a better day came, when he had strength enough to lift the ponderous book, he used to open the pages to look at his flower friends. In winter he could have no more living flowers to tend.

Libbie thought and thought, till at last an idea flashed upon her mind, that often made a happy smile steal over her face as she stitched away, and that cheered her through the solitary winter—for solitary it continued to be, though the Dixons were very good sort of people, never pressed her for payment, if she had had but little work to do that week; never grudged her a share of their extravagant meals, which were far more luxurious than she could have met with anywhere else, for her previously agreed payment in case of working at home; and they would fain have taught her to drink rum in her tea, assuring her that she should have it for nothing and welcome. But they were too touchy, too prosperous, too much absorbed in themselves, to take off Libbie's feeling of solitariness; not half as much as the little face by day, and the shadow by night, of him with whom she had never yet exchanged a word.

Her idea was this: her mother came from the east of England, where, as perhaps you know, they have the pretty custom of sending presents on St. Valentine's day, with the donor's name unknown, and, of course, the mystery constitutes half the enjoyment. The fourteenth of February was Libbie's birthday too, and many a year, in the happy days of old, had her mother delighted to surprise her with some little gift, of which she more than half-guessed the giver, although each Valentine's day the manner of its arrival was varied. Since then the fourteenth of February had been the dreariest of all the year, because the most haunted by memory of departed happiness. But now, this year, if she could not have the old gladness of heart herself, she would try and brighten the life of another. She would save, and she would screw, but she would buy a canary and a cage for that poor little laddie opposite, who wore out his monotonous life with so few pleasures, and so much pain.

I doubt I may not tell you here of the anxieties and the fears, of the hopes and the self-sacrifices—all, perhaps small in the tangible effect as the widow's mite, yet not the less marked by the viewless angels who go about continually among us—which varied Libbie's life before she accomplished her purpose. It is enough to say it was accomplished. The very day before the fourteenth she found time to go with her half-guinea to a barber's who lived near Albemarle Street, and who was famous for his stock of singing-birds. There are enthusiasts about all sorts of things, both good and bad, and many of the weavers in Manchester know and care more about birds than any one would easily credit. Stubborn, silent, reserved men on many things, you have only to touch on the subject of birds to light up their faces with brightness. They will tell you who won the prizes at the last canary show, where the prize birds may be seen, and give you all the details of those funny, but pretty and interesting mimicries of great people's cattle shows. Among these amateurs, Emanuel Morris the barber was an oracle.

He took Libbie into his little back room, used for private shaving of modest men, who did not care to be exhibited in the front shop decked out in the full glories of lather; and which was hung round with birds in rude wicker cages, with the exception of those who had won prizes, and were consequently honoured with gilt-wire prisons. The longer and thinner the body of the bird was, the more admiration it received, as far as external beauty went; and when, in addition to this, the colour was deep and clear, and its notes strong and varied, the more did Emanuel dwell upon its perfections. But these were all prize birds; and, on inquiry, Libbie heard, with some little sinking at heart, that their price ran from one to two guineas.

"I'm not over-particular as to shape and colour," said she, "I should like a good singer, that's all!"

She dropped a little in Emanuel's estimation. However, he showed her his good singers, but all were above Libbie's means.

"After all, I don't think I care so much about the singing very loud; it's but a noise after all, and sometimes noise fidgets folks."

"They must be nesh folks as is put out with the singing o' birds," replied Emanuel, rather affronted.

"It's for one who is poorly," said Libbie, deprecatingly.

"Well," said he, as if considering the matter, "folk that are cranky, often take more to them as shows 'em love, than to them as is clever and gifted. Happen yo'd rather have this'n," opening a cage-door, and calling to a dull-coloured bird, sitting moped up in a corner, "Here—Jupiter, Jupiter!"

The bird smoothed its feathers in an instant, and, uttering a little note of delight, flew to Emanuel, putting his beak to his lips, as if kissing him, and then, perching on his head, it began a gurgling warble of pleasure, not by any means so varied or so clear as the song of the others, but which pleased Libbie more; for she was always one to find out she liked the gooseberries that were accessible, better than the grapes that were beyond her reach. The price too was just right, so she gladly took possession of the cage, and hid it under her cloak, preparatory to carrying it home. Emanuel meanwhile was giving her directions as to its food, with all the minuteness of one loving his subject.

"Will it soon get to know any one?" asked she.

"Give him two days only, and you and he'll be as thick as him and me are now. You've only to open his door, and call him, and he'll follow you round the room; but he'll first kiss you, and then perch on your head. He only wants larning, which I've no time to give him, to do many another accomplishment."

"What's his name? I did not rightly catch it."

"Jupiter,—it's not common; but the town's o'errun with Bobbies and Dickies, and as my birds are thought a bit out o' the way, I like to have better names for 'em, so I just picked a few out o' my lad's school books. It's just as ready, when you're used to it, to say Jupiter as Dicky."

"I could bring my tongue round to Peter better; would he answer to Peter?" asked Libbie, now on the point of departing.

"Happen he might; but I think he'd come readier to the three syllables."

On Valentine's day, Jupiter's cage was decked round with ivy leaves, making quite a pretty wreath on the wicker work; and to one of them was pinned a slip of paper, with these words, written in Libbie's best round hand:—

"From your faithful Valentine. Please take notice his name is Peter, and he'll come if you call him, after a bit."

But little work did Libbie do that afternoon, she was so engaged in watching for the messenger who was to bear her present to her little valentine, and run away as soon as he had delivered up the canary, and explained to whom it was sent.

At last he came; then there was a pause before the woman of the house was at liberty to take it upstairs. Then Libbie saw the little face flush up into a bright colour, the feeble hands tremble with delighted eagerness, the head bent down to try and make out the writing (beyond his power, poor lad, to read), the rapturous turning round of the cage in order to see the canary in every point of view, head, tail, wings, and feet; an intention in which Jupiter, in his uneasiness at being again among strangers, did not second, for he hopped round so, as continually to present a full front to the boy. It was a source of never wearying delight to the little fellow, till daylight closed in; he evidently forgot to wonder who had sent it him, in his gladness at his possession of such a treasure; and when the shadow of his mother darkened on the blind, and the bird had been exhibited, Libbie saw her do what, with all her tenderness, seemed rarely to have entered into her thoughts—she bent down and kissed her boy, in a mother's sympathy with the joy of her child.

The canary was placed for the night between the little bed and window; and when Libbie rose once, to take her accustomed peep, she saw the little arm put fondly round the cage, as if embracing his new treasure even in his sleep. How Jupiter slept this first night is quite another thing.

So ended the first day in Libbie's three eras in last year.

ERA II

WHITSUNTIDE

The brightest, fullest daylight poured down into No. 2, — Court, Albemarle Street, and the heat, even at the early hour of five, as at the noontide on the June days of many years past.

The court seemed alive, and merry with voices and laughter. The bedroom windows were open wide, and had been so all night, on account of the heat; and every now and then you might see a head and a pair of shoulders, simply encased in shirt sleeves, popped out, and you might hear the inquiry passed from one to the other,—"Well, Jack, and where art thee bound for?"

"Dunham!"

"Why, what an old-fashioned chap thou be'st. Thy grandad afore thee went to Dunham: but thou wert always a slow coach. I'm off to Alderley,—me and my missis."

"Ay, that's because there's only thee and thy missis. Wait till thou hast gotten four childer, like me, and thou'lt be glad enough to take 'em to Dunham, oud-fashioned way, for fourpence apiece."

"I'd still go to Alderley; I'd not be bothered with my children; they should keep house at home."

A pair of hands, the person to whom they belonged invisible, boxed his ears on this last speech, in a very spirited, though playful, manner, and the neighbours all laughed at the surprised look of the speaker, at this assault from an unseen foe. The man who had been holding conversation with him cried out,—

"Served him right, Mrs. Slater: he knows nought about it yet; but when he gets them he'll be as loth to leave the babbies at home on a Whitsuntide as any on us. We shall live to see him in Dunham Park yet, wi' twins in his arms, and another pair on 'em clutching at daddy's coat-tails, let alone your share of youngsters, missis."

At this moment our friend Libbie appeared at her window, and Mrs. Slater, who had taken her discomfited husband's place, called out,—

"Elizabeth Marsh, where are Dixons and you bound to?"

"Dixons are not up yet; he said last night he'd take his holiday out in lying in bed. I'm going to the old-fashioned place, Dunham."

"Thou art never going by thyself, moping!"

"No. I'm going with Margaret Hall and her lad," replied Libbie, hastily withdrawing from the window, in order to avoid hearing any remarks on the associates she had chosen for her day of pleasure—the scold of the neighbourhood, and her sickly, ailing child!

But Jupiter might have been a dove, and his ivy leaves an olive branch, for the peace he had brought, the happiness he had caused, to three individuals at least. For of course it could not long be a mystery who had sent little Frank Hall his valentine; nor could his mother long entertain her hard manner towards one who had given her child a new pleasure. She was shy, and she was proud, and for some time she struggled against the natural desire of manifesting her gratitude; but one evening, when Libbie was returning home, with a bundle of work half as large as herself, as she dragged herself along through the heated streets, she was overtaken by Margaret Hall, her burden gently pulled from her, and her way home shortened, and her weary spirits soothed and cheered, by the outpourings of Margaret's heart; for the barrier of reserve once broken down, she had much to say, to thank her for days of amusement and happy employment for her lad, to speak of his gratitude, to tell of her hopes and fears,—the hopes and fears that made up the dates of her life. From that time, Libbie lost her awe of the termagant in interest for the mother, whose all was ventured in so frail a bark. From this time, Libbie was a fast friend with both mother and son, planning mitigations for the sorrowful days of the latter as eagerly as poor Margaret Hall, and with far more success. His life had flickered up under the charm and excitement of the last few months. He even seemed strong enough to undertake the journey to Dunham, which Libbie had arranged as a Whitsuntide treat, and for which she and his mother had been hoarding up for several weeks. The canal boat left Knott-mill at six, and it was now past five; so Libbie let herself out very gently, and went across to her friends. She knocked at the door of their lodging-room, and, without waiting for an answer, entered.

Franky's face was flushed, and he was trembling with excitement,—partly with pleasure, but partly with some eager wish not yet granted.

"He wants sore to take Peter with him," said his mother to Libbie, as if referring the matter to her. The boy looked imploringly at her.

"He would like it, I know; for one thing, he'd miss me sadly, and chirrup for me all day long, he'd be so lonely. I could not be half so happy a-thinking on him, left alone here by himself. Then, Libbie, he's just like a Christian, so fond of flowers and green leaves, and them sort of things. He chirrups to me so when mother brings me a pennyworth of wall-flowers to put round his cage. He would talk if he could, you know; but I can tell what he means quite as one as if he spoke. Do let Peter go, Libbie; I'll carry him in my own arms."

So Jupiter was allowed to be of the party. Now Libbie had overcome the great difficulty of conveying Franky to the boat, by offering to "slay" for a coach, and the shouts and exclamations of the neighbours told them that their conveyance awaited them at the bottom of the court. His mother carried Franky, light in weight, though heavy in helplessness, and he would hold the cage, believing that he was thus redeeming his pledge, that Peter should be a trouble to no one. Libbie proceeded to arrange the bundle containing their dinner, as a support in the corner of the coach. The neighbours came out with many blunt speeches, and more kindly wishes, and one or two of them would have relieved Margaret of her burden, if she would have allowed it. The presence of that little crippled fellow seemed to obliterate all the angry feelings which had existed between his mother and her neighbours, and which had formed the politics of that little court for many a day.

And now they were fairly off! Franky bit his lips in attempted endurance of the pain the motion caused him; he winced and shrank, until they were fairly on a Macadamized thoroughfare, when he closed his eyes, and seemed desirous of a few minutes' rest. Libbie felt very shy, and very much afraid of being seen by her employers, "set up in a coach!" and so she hid herself in a corner, and made herself as small as possible; while Mrs. Hall had exactly the opposite feeling, and was delighted to stand up, stretching out of the window, and nodding to pretty nearly every one they met or passed on the foot-paths; and they were not a few, for the streets were quite gay, even at that early hour, with parties going to this or that railway station, or to the boats which crowded the canals on this bright holiday week; and almost every one they met seemed to enter into Mrs. Hall's exhilaration of feeling, and had a smile or nod in return. At last she plumped down by Libbie, and exclaimed, "I never was in a coach but once afore, and that was when I was a-going to be married. It's like heaven; and all done over with such beautiful gimp, too!" continued she, admiring the lining of the vehicle. Jupiter did not enjoy it so much.

As if the holiday time, the lovely weather, and the "sweet hour of prime" had a genial influence, as no doubt they have, everybody's heart seemed softened towards poor Franky. The driver lifted him out with the tenderness of strength, and bore him carefully down to the boat; the people then made way, and gave him the best seat in their power,—or rather I should call it a couch, for they saw he was weary, and insisted on his lying down,—an attitude he would have been ashamed to assume without the protection of his mother and Libbie, who now appeared, bearing their baskets and carrying Peter.

Away the boat went, to make room for others, for every conveyance, both by land and water, is in requisition in Whitsun-week, to give the hard-worked crowds the opportunity of enjoying the charms of the country. Even every standing-place in the canal packets was occupied, and as they glided along, the banks were lined with people, who seemed to find it object enough to watch the boats go by, packed close and full with happy beings brimming with anticipations of a day's pleasure. The country through which they passed is as uninteresting as can well be imagined; but still it is the country: and the screams of delight from the children, and the low laughs of pleasure from the parents, at every blossoming tree that trailed its wreath against some cottage wall, or at the tufts of late primroses which lingered in the cool depths of grass along the canal banks, the thorough relish of everything, as if dreading to let the least circumstance of this happy day pass over without its due appreciation, made the time seem all too short, although it took two hours to arrive at a place only eight miles from Manchester. Even Franky, with all his impatience to see Dunham woods (which I think he confused with London, believing both to be paved with gold), enjoyed the easy motion of the boat so much, floating along, while pictures moved before him, that he regretted when the time came for landing among the soft, green meadows, that came sloping down to the dancing water's brim. His fellow-passengers carried him to the park, and refused all payment, although his mother had laid by sixpence on purpose, as a recompense for this service.

"Oh, Libbie, how beautiful! Oh, mother, mother! is the whole world out of Manchester as beautiful as this? I did not know trees were like this! Such green homes for birds! Look, Peter! would not you like to be there, up among those boughs? But I can't let you go, you know, because you're my little bird brother, and I should be quite lost without you."

They spread a shawl upon the fine mossy turf, at the root of a beech-tree, which made a sort of natural couch, and there they laid him, and bade him rest, in spite of the delight which made him believe himself capable of any exertion. Where he lay,—always holding Jupiter's cage, and often talking to him as to a playfellow,—he was on the verge of a green area, shut in by magnificent trees, in all the glory of their early foliage, before the summer heats had deepened their verdure into one rich, monotonous tint. And hither came party after party; old men and maidens, young men and children,—whole families trooped along after the guiding fathers, who bore the youngest in their arms, or astride upon their backs, while they turned round occasionally to the wives, with whom they shared some fond local remembrance. For years has Dunham Park been the favourite resort of the Manchester work-people; for more years than I can tell; probably ever since "the Duke," by his canals, opened out the system of cheap travelling. Its scenery, too, which presents such a complete contrast to the whirl and turmoil of Manchester; so thoroughly woodland, with its ancestral trees (here and there lightning blanched); its "verdurous walls;" its grassy walks, leading far away into some glade, where you start at the rabbit rustling among the last year's fern, and where the wood-pigeon's call seems the only fitting and accordant sound. Depend upon it, this complete sylvan repose, this accessible quiet, this lapping the soul in green images of the country, forms the most complete contrast to a town's-person, and consequently has over such the greatest power to charm.

Presently Libbie found out she was very hungry. Now they were but provided with dinner, which was, of course, to be eaten as near twelve o'clock as might be; and Margaret Hall, in her prudence, asked a working-man near to tell her what o'clock it was.

"Nay," said he, "I'll ne'er look at clock or watch to-day. I'll not spoil my pleasure by finding out how fast it's going away. If thou'rt hungry, eat. I make my own dinner hour, and I have eaten mine an hour ago."

So they had their veal pies, and then found out it was only about half-past ten o'clock; by so many pleasurable events had that morning been marked. But such was their buoyancy of spirits, that they only enjoyed their mistake, and joined in the general laugh against the man who had eaten his dinner somewhere about nine. He laughed most heartily of all, till, suddenly stopping, he said,—

"I must not go on at this rate; laughing gives one such an appetite."

"Oh! if that's all," said a merry-looking man, lying at full length, and brushing the fresh scent out of the grass, while two or three little children tumbled over him, and crept about him, as kittens or puppies frolic with their parents, "if that's all, we'll have a subscription of eatables for them improvident folk as have eaten their dinner for their breakfast. Here's a sausage pasty and a handful of nuts for my share. Bring round a hat, Bob, and see what the company will give."

Bob carried out the joke, much to little Franky's amusement; and no one was so churlish as to refuse, although the contributions varied from a peppermint drop up to a veal pie and a sausage pasty.

"It's a thriving trade," said Bob, as he emptied his hatful of provisions on the grass by Libbie's side. "Besides, it's tiptop, too, to live on the public. Hark! what is that?"

The laughter and the chat were suddenly hushed, and mothers told their little ones to listen,—as, far away in the distance, now sinking and falling, now swelling and clear, came a ringing peal of children's voices, blended together in one of those psalm tunes which we are all of us familiar with, and which bring to mind the old, old days, when we, as wondering children, were first led to worship "Our Father," by those beloved ones who have since gone to the more perfect worship. Holy was that distant choral praise, even to the most thoughtless; and when it, in fact, was ended, in the instant's pause, during which the ear awaits the repetition of the air, they caught the noontide hum and buzz of the myriads of insects who danced away their lives in the glorious day; they heard the swaying of the mighty woods in the soft but resistless breeze, and then again once more burst forth the merry jests and the shouts of childhood; and again the elder ones resumed their happy talk, as they lay or sat "under the greenwood tree." Fresh parties came dropping in; some laden with wild flowers—almost with branches of hawthorn, indeed; while one or two had made prizes of the earliest dog-roses, and had cast away campion, stitchwort, ragged robin, all to keep the lady of the hedges from being obscured or hidden by the community.

One after another drew near to Franky, and looked on with interest as he lay sorting the flowers given to him. Happy parents stood by, with their household bands around them, in health and comeliness, and felt the sad prophecy of those shrivelled limbs, those wasted fingers, those lamp-like eyes, with their bright, dark lustre. His mother was too eagerly watching his happiness to read the meaning of those grave looks, but Libbie saw them and understood them; and a chill shudder went through her, even on that day, as she thought on the future.

"Ay! I thought we should give you a start!"

A start they did give, with their terrible slap on Libbie's back, as she sat idly grouping flowers, and following out her sorrowful thoughts. It was the Dixons. Instead of keeping their holiday by lying in bed, they and their children had roused themselves, and had come by the omnibus to the nearest point. For an instant the meeting was an awkward one, on account of the feud between Margaret Hall and Mrs. Dixon, but there was no long resisting of kindly mother Nature's soothings, at that holiday time, and in that lonely tranquil spot; or if they could have been unheeded, the sight of Franky would have awed every angry feeling into rest, so changed was he since the Dixons had last seen him; and since he had been the Puck or Robin Goodfellow of the neighbourhood, whose marbles were always rolling under other people's feet, and whose top-strings were always hanging in nooses to catch the unwary. Yes, he, the feeble, mild, almost girlish-looking lad, had once been a merry, happy rogue, and as such often cuffed by Mrs. Dixon, the very Mrs. Dixon who now stood gazing with the tears in her eyes. Could she, in sight of him, the changed, the fading, keep up a quarrel with his mother?

"How long hast thou been here?" asked Dixon.

"Welly on for all day," answered Libbie.

"Hast never been to see the deer, or the king and queen oaks? Lord, how stupid."

His wife pinched his arm, to remind him of Franky's helpless condition, which of course tethered the otherwise willing feet. But Dixon had a remedy. He called Bob, and one or two others, and each taking a corner of the strong plaid shawl, they slung Franky as in a hammock, and thus carried him merrily along, down the wood paths, over the smooth, grassy turf, while the glimmering shine and shadow fell on his upturned face. The women walked behind, talking, loitering along, always in sight of the hammock; now picking up some green treasure from the ground, now catching at the low hanging branches of the horse-chestnut. The soul grew much on this day, and in these woods, and all unconsciously, as souls do grow. They followed Franky's hammock-bearers up a grassy knoll, on the top of which stood a group of pine trees, whose stems looked like dark red gold in the sunbeams. They had taken Franky there to show him Manchester, far away in the blue plain, against which the woodland foreground cut with a soft clear line. Far, far away in the distance on that flat plain, you might see the motionless cloud of smoke hanging over a great town, and that was Manchester,—ugly, smoky Manchester, dear, busy, earnest, noble-working Manchester; where their children had been born, and where, perhaps, some lay buried; where their homes were, and where God had cast their lives, and told them to work out their destiny.

"Hurrah! for oud smoke-jack!" cried Bob, putting Franky softly down on the grass, before he whirled his hat round, preparatory to a shout. "Hurrah! hurrah!" from all the men. "There's the rim of my hat lying like a quoit yonder," observed Bob quietly, as he replaced his brimless hat on his head with the gravity of a judge.

"Here's the Sunday-school children a-coming to sit on this shady side, and have their buns and milk. Hark! they're singing the infant-school grace."

They sat close at hand, so that Franky could hear the words they sang, in rings of children, making, in their gay summer prints, newly donned for that week, garlands of little faces, all happy and bright upon that green hill-side. One little "Dot" of a girl came shily behind Franky, whom she had long been watching, and threw her half-bun at his side, and then ran away and hid herself, in very shame at the boldness of her own sweet impulse. She kept peeping from her screen at Franky all the time; and he meanwhile was almost too much pleased and happy to eat; the world was so beautiful, and men, women, and children all so tender and kind; so softened, in fact, by the beauty of this earth, so unconsciously touched by the spirit of love, which was the Creator of this lovely earth. But the day drew to an end; the heat declined; the birds once more began their warblings; the fresh scents again hung about plant, and tree, and grass, betokening the fragrant presence of the reviving dew, and—the boat time was near. As they trod the meadow-path once more, they were joined by many a party they had encountered during the day, all abounding in happiness, all full of the day's adventures. Long-cherished quarrels had been forgotten, new friendships formed. Fresh tastes and higher delights had been imparted that day. We have all of us our look, now and then, called up by some noble or loving thought (our highest on earth), which will be our likeness in heaven. I can catch the glance on many a face, the glancing light of the cloud of glory from heaven, "which is our home." That look was present on many a hard-worked, wrinkled countenance, as they turned backwards to catch a longing, lingering look at Dunham woods, fast deepening into blackness of night, but whose memory was to haunt, in greenness and freshness, many a loom, and workshop, and factory, with images of peace and beauty.

That night, as Libbie lay awake, revolving the incidents of the day, she caught Franky's voice through the open windows. Instead of the frequent moan of pain, he was trying to recall the burden of one of the children's hymns,—

Here we suffer grief and pain,
 Here we meet to part again;
In Heaven we part no more.
 Oh! that will be joyful, &c.

She recalled his question, the whispered question, to her, in the happiest part of the day. He asked Libbie, "Is Dunham like heaven? the people here are as kind as angels, and I don't want heaven to be more beautiful than this place. If you and mother would but die with me, I should like to die, and live always there!" She had checked him, for she feared he was impious; but now the young child's craving for some definite idea of the land to which his inner wisdom told him he was hastening, had nothing in it wrong, or even sorrowful, for—

In Heaven we part no more.

ERA III

MICHAELMAS

The church clocks had struck three; the crowds of gentlemen returning to business, after their early dinners, had disappeared within offices and warehouses; the streets were clear and quiet, and ladies were venturing to sally forth for their afternoon shoppings and their afternoon calls.

Slowly, slowly, along the streets, elbowed by life at every turn, a little funeral wound its quiet way. Four men bore along a child's coffin; two women with bowed heads followed meekly.

I need not tell you whose coffin it was, or who were those two mourners. All was now over with little Frank Hall: his romps, his games, his sickening, his suffering, his death. All was now over, but the Resurrection and the Life.

His mother walked as in a stupor. Could it be that he was dead! If he had been less of an object of her thoughts, less of a motive for her labours, she could sooner have realized it. As it was, she followed his poor, cast-off, worn-out body as if she were borne along by some oppressive dream. If he were really dead, how could she be still alive?

Libbie's mind was far less stunned, and consequently far more active, than Margaret Hall's. Visions, as in a phantasmagoria, came rapidly passing before her—recollections of the time (which seemed now so long ago) when the shadow of the feebly-waving arm first caught her attention; of the bright, strangely isolated day at Dunham Park, where the world had seemed so full of enjoyment, and beauty, and life; of the long-continued heat, through which poor Franky had panted away his strength in the little close room, where there was no escaping the hot rays of the afternoon sun; of the long nights when his mother and she had watched by his side, as he moaned continually, whether awake or asleep; of the fevered moaning slumber of exhaustion; of the pitiful little self-upbraidings for his own impatience of suffering, only impatient in his own eyes—most true and holy patience in the sight of others; and then the fading away of life, the loss of power, the increased unconsciousness, the lovely look of angelic peace, which followed the dark shadow on the countenance, where was he—what was he now?

And so they laid him in his grave, and heard the solemn funeral words; but far off in the distance, as if not addressed to them.

Margaret Hall bent over the grave to catch one last glance—she had not spoken, nor sobbed, nor done aught but shiver now and then, since the morning; but now her weight bore more heavily on Libbie's arm, and without sigh or sound she fell an unconscious heap on the piled-up gravel. They helped Libbie to bring her round; but long after her half-opened eyes and altered breathing showed that her senses were restored, she lay, speechless and motionless, without attempting to rise from her strange bed, as if the earth contained nothing worth even that trifling exertion.

At last Libbie and she left that holy, consecrated spot, and bent their steps back to the only place more consecrated still; where he had rendered up his spirit; and where memories of him haunted each common, rude piece of furniture that their eyes fell upon. As the woman of the house opened the door, she pulled Libbie on one side, and said—

"Anne Dixon has been across to see you; she wants to have a word with you."

"I cannot go now," replied Libbie, as she pushed hastily along, in order to enter the room (his room), at the same time with the childless mother: for, as she had anticipated, the sight of that empty spot, the glance at the uncurtained open window, letting in the fresh air, and the broad, rejoicing light of day, where all had so long been darkened and subdued, unlocked the waters of the fountain, and long and shrill were the cries for her boy that the poor woman uttered.

"Oh! dear Mrs. Hall," said Libbie, herself drenched in tears, "do not take on so badly; I'm sure it would grieve him sore if he were alive, and you know he is—Bible tells us so; and may be he's here watching how we go on without him, and hoping we don't fret over much."

Mrs. Hall's sobs grew worse and more hysterical.

"Oh! listen," said Libbie, once more struggling against her own increasing agitation. "Listen! there's Peter chirping as he always does when he's put about, frightened like; and you know he that's gone could never abide to hear the canary chirp in that shrill way."

Margaret Hall did check herself, and curb her expressions of agony, in order not to frighten the little creature he had loved; and as her outward grief subsided, Libbie took up the large old Bible, which fell open at the never-failing comfort of the fourteenth chapter of St. John's Gospel.

How often these large family Bibles do open at that chapter! as if, unused in more joyous and prosperous times, the soul went home to its words of loving sympathy when weary and sorrowful, just as the little child seeks the tender comfort of its mother in all its griefs and cares.

And Margaret put back her wet, ruffled, grey hair from her heated, tear-stained, woeful face, and listened with such earnest eyes, trying to form some idea of the "Father's house," where her boy had gone to dwell.

They were interrupted by a low tap at the door. Libbie went. "Anne Dixon has watched you home, and wants to have a word with you," said the woman of the house, in a whisper. Libbie went back and closed the book, with a word of explanation to Margaret Hall, and then ran downstairs, to learn the reason of Anne's anxiety to see her.

"Oh, Libbie!" she burst out with, and then, checking herself with the remembrance of Libbie's last solemn duty, "how's Margaret Hall? But, of course, poor thing, she'll fret a bit at first; she'll be some time coming round, mother says, seeing it's as well that poor lad is taken; for he'd always ha' been a cripple, and a trouble to her—he was a fine lad once, too."

She had come full of another and a different subject; but the sight of Libbie's sad, weeping face, and the quiet, subdued tone of her manner, made her feel it awkward to begin on any other theme than the one which filled up her companion's mind. To her last speech Libbie answered sorrowfully—

"No doubt, Anne, it's ordered for the best; but oh! don't call him, don't think he could ever ha' been, a trouble to his mother, though he were a cripple. She loved him all the more for each thing she had to do for him—I am sure I did." Libbie cried a little behind her apron. Anne Dixon felt still more awkward in introducing the discordant subject.

"Well! 'flesh is grass,' Bible says," and having fulfilled the etiquette of quoting a text if possible, if not of making a moral observation on the fleeting nature of earthly things, she thought she was at liberty to pass on to her real errand.

"You must not go on moping yourself, Libbie Marsh. What I wanted special for to see you this afternoon, was to tell you, you must come to my wedding to-morrow. Nanny Dawson has fallen sick, and there's none as I should like to have bridesmaid in her place as well as you."

"To-morrow! Oh, I cannot!—indeed I cannot!"

"Why not?"

Libbie did not answer, and Anne Dixon grew impatient.

"Surely, in the name o' goodness, you're never going to baulk yourself of a day's pleasure for the sake of yon little cripple that's dead and gone!"

"No,—it's not baulking myself of—don't be angry, Anne Dixon, with him, please; but I don't think it would be a pleasure to me,—I don't feel as if I could enjoy it; thank you all the same. But I did love that little lad very dearly—I did," sobbing a little, "and I can't forget him and make merry so soon."

"Well—I never!" exclaimed Anne, almost angrily.

"Indeed, Anne, I feel your kindness, and you and Bob have my best wishes,—that's what you have; but even if I went, I should be thinking all day of him, and of his poor, poor mother, and they say it's bad to think very much on them that's dead, at a wedding."

"Nonsense," said Anne, "I'll take the risk of the ill-luck. After all, what is marrying? Just a spree, Bob says. He often says he does not think I shall make him a good wife, for I know nought about house matters, wi' working in a factory; but he says he'd rather be uneasy wi' me than easy wi' anybody else. There's love for you! And I tell him I'd rather have him tipsy than any one else sober."

"Oh! Anne Dixon, hush! you don't know yet what it is to have a drunken husband. I have seen something of it: father used to get fuddled, and, in the long run, it killed mother, let alone—oh! Anne, God above only knows what the wife of a drunken man has to bear. Don't tell," said she, lowering her voice, "but father killed our little baby in one of his bouts; mother never looked up again, nor father either, for that matter, only his was in a different way. Mother will have gotten to little Jemmie now, and they'll be so happy together,—and perhaps Franky too. Oh!" said she, recovering herself from her train of thought, "never say aught lightly of the wife's lot whose husband is given to drink!"

"Dear, what a preachment. I tell you what, Libbie, you're as born an old maid as ever I saw. You'll never be married to either drunken or sober."

Libbie's face went rather red, but without losing its meek expression.

"I know that as well as you can tell me; and more reason, therefore, as God has seen fit to keep me out of woman's natural work, I should try and find work for myself. I mean," seeing Anne Dixon's puzzled look, "that as I know I'm never likely to have a home of my own, or a husband that would look to me to make all straight, or children to watch over or care for, all which I take to be woman's natural work, I must not lose time in fretting and fidgetting after marriage, but just look about me for somewhat else to do. I can see many a one misses it in this. They will hanker after what is ne'er likely to be theirs, instead of facing it out, and settling down to be old maids; and, as old maids, just looking round for the odd jobs God leaves in the world for such as old maids to do. There's plenty of such work, and there's the blessing of God on them as does it." Libbie was almost out of breath at this outpouring of what had long been her inner thoughts.

"That's all very true, I make no doubt, for them as is to be old maids; but as I'm not, please God to-morrow comes, you might have spared your breath to cool your porridge. What I want to know is, whether you'll be bridesmaid to-morrow or not. Come, now do; it will do you good, after all your working, and watching, and slaving yourself for that poor Franky Hall."

"It was one of my odd jobs," said Libbie, smiling, though her eyes were brimming over with tears; "but, dear Anne," said she, recovering itself, "I could not do it to-morrow, indeed I could not."

"And I can't wait," said Anne Dixon, almost sulkily, "Bob and I put it off from to-day, because of the funeral, and Bob had set his heart on its being on Michaelmas-day; and mother says the goose won't keep beyond to-morrow. Do come: father finds eatables, and Bob finds drink, and we shall be so jolly! and after we've been to church, we're to walk round the town in pairs, white satin ribbon in our bonnets, and refreshments at any public-house we like, Bob says. And after dinner there's to be a dance. Don't be a fool; you can do no good by staying. Margaret Hall will have to go out washing, I'll be bound."

"Yes, she must go to Mrs. Wilkinson's, and, for that matter, I must go working too. Mrs. Williams has been after me to make her girl's winter things ready; only I could not leave Franky, he clung so to me."

"Then you won't be bridesmaid! is that your last word?"

"It is; you must not be angry with me, Anne Dixon," said Libbie, deprecatingly.

But Anne was gone without a reply.

With a heavy heart Libbie mounted the little staircase, for she felt how ungracious her refusal of Anne's kindness must appear, to one who understood so little the feelings which rendered her acceptance of it a moral impossibility.

On opening the door she saw Margaret Hall, with the Bible open on the table before her. For she had puzzled out the place where Libbie was reading, and, with her finger under the line, was spelling out the words of consolation, piecing the syllables together aloud, with the earnest anxiety of comprehension with which a child first learns to read. So Libbie took the stool by her side, before she was aware that any one had entered the room.

"What did she want you for?" asked Margaret. "But I can guess; she wanted you to be at th' wedding that is to come off this week, they say. Ay, they'll marry, and laugh, and dance, all as one as if my boy was alive," said she, bitterly. "Well, he was neither kith nor kin of yours, so I maun try and be thankful for what you've done for him, and not wonder at your forgetting him afore he's well settled in his grave."

"I never can forget him, and I'm not going to the wedding," said Libbie, quietly, for she understood the mother's jealousy of her dead child's claims.

"I must go work at Mrs. Williams' to-morrow," she said, in explanation, for she was unwilling to boast of her tender, fond regret, which had been her principal motive for declining Anne's invitation.

"And I mun go washing, just as if nothing had happened," sighed forth Mrs. Hall, "and I mun come home at night, and find his place empty, and all still where I used to be sure of hearing his voice ere ever I got up the stair: no one will ever call me mother again." She fell crying pitifully, and Libbie could not speak for her own emotion for some time. But during this silence she put the keystone in the arch of thoughts she had been building up for many days; and when Margaret was again calm in her sorrow, Libbie said, "Mrs. Hall, I should like—would you like me to come for to live here altogether?"

Margaret Hall looked up with a sudden light in her countenance, which encouraged Libbie to go on.

"I could sleep with you, and pay half, you know; and we should be together in the evenings; and her as was home first would watch for the other, and" (dropping her voice) "we could talk of him at nights, you know."

She was going on, but Mrs. Hall interrupted her.

"Oh, Libbie Marsh! and can you really think of coming to live wi' me. I should like it above—but no! it must not be; you've no notion on what a creature I am, at times; more like a mad one when I'm in a rage, and I cannot keep it down. I seem to get out of bed wrong side in the morning, and I must have my passion out with the first person I meet. Why, Libbie," said she, with a doleful look of agony on her face, "I even used to fly out on him, poor sick lad as he was, and you may judge how little you can keep it down frae that. No, you must not come. I must live alone now," sinking her voice into the low tones of despair.

But Libbie's resolution was brave and strong. "I'm not afraid," said she, smiling. "I know you better than you know yourself, Mrs. Hall. I've seen you try of late to keep it down, when you've been boiling over, and I think you'll go on a-doing so. And at any rate, when you've had your fit out, you're very kind, and I can forget if you've been a bit put out. But I'll try not to put you out. Do let me come: I think he would like us to keep together. I'll do my very best to make you comfortable."

"It's me! it's me as will be making your life miserable with my temper; or else, God knows, how my heart clings to you. You and me is folk alone in the world, for we both loved one who is dead, and who had none else to love him. If you will live with me, Libbie, I'll try as I never did afore to be gentle and quiet-tempered. Oh! will you try me, Libbie Marsh?" So out of the little grave there sprang a hope and a resolution, which made life an object to each of the two.

When Elizabeth Marsh returned home the next evening from her day's labours, Anne (Dixon no longer) crossed over, all in her bridal finery, to endeavour to induce her to join the dance going on in her father's house.

"Dear Anne, this is good of you, a-thinking of me to-night," said Libbie, kissing her, "and though I cannot come,—I've promised Mrs. Hall to be with her,—I shall think on you, and I trust you'll be happy. I have got a little needle-case I have looked out for you; stay, here it is,—I wish it were more—only—"

"Only, I know what. You've been a-spending all your money in nice things for poor Franky. Thou'rt a real good un, Libbie, and I'll keep your needle-book to my dying day, that I will." Seeing Anne in such a friendly mood, emboldened Libbie to tell her of her change of place; of her intention of lodging henceforward with Margaret Hall.

"Thou never will! Why father and mother are as fond of thee as can be; they'll lower thy rent if that's what it is—and thou knowst they never grudge thee bit or drop. And Margaret Hall, of all folk, to lodge wi'! She's such a Tartar! Sooner than not have a quarrel, she'd fight right hand against left. Thou'lt have no peace of thy life. What on earth can make you think of such a thing, Libbie Marsh?"

"She'll be so lonely without me," pleaded Libbie. "I'm sure I could make her happier, even if she did scold me a bit now and then, than she'd be a living alone, and I'm not afraid of her; and I mean to do my best not to vex her: and it will ease her heart, maybe, to talk to me at times about Franky. I shall often see your father and mother, and I shall always thank them for their kindness to me. But they have you and little Mary, and poor Mrs. Hall has no one."

Anne could only repeat, "Well, I never!" and hurry off to tell the news at home.

But Libbie was right. Margaret Hall is a different woman to the scold of the neighbourhood she once was; touched and softened by the two purifying angels, Sorrow and Love. And it is beautiful to see her affection, her reverence, for Libbie Marsh. Her dead mother could hardly have cared for her more tenderly than does the hard-hearted washerwoman, not long ago so fierce and unwomanly. Libbie, herself, has such peace shining on her countenance, as almost makes it beautiful, as she tenders the services of a daughter to Franky's mother, no longer the desolate lonely orphan, a stranger on the earth.

Do you ever read the moral, concluding sentence of a story? I never do, but I once (in the year 1811, I think) heard of a deaf old lady, living by herself, who did; and as she may have left some descendants with the same amiable peculiarity, I will put in, for their benefit, what I believe to be the secret of Libbie's peace of mind, the real reason why she no longer feels oppressed at her own loneliness in the world,—

She has a purpose in life; and that purpose is a holy one.

CHRISTMAS STORMS AND SUNSHINE

In the town of — (no matter where) there circulated two local newspapers (no matter when). Now the Flying Post was long established and respectable—alias bigoted and Tory; the Examiner was spirited and intelligent—alias new-fangled and democratic. Every week these newspapers contained articles abusing each other; as cross and peppery as articles could be, and evidently the production of irritated minds, although they seemed to have one stereotyped commencement,—"Though the article appearing in last week's Post (or Examiner) is below contempt, yet we have been induced," &c., &c., and every Saturday the Radical shopkeepers shook hands together, and agreed that the Post was done for, by the slashing, clever Examiner; while the more dignified Tories began by regretting that Johnson should think that low paper, only read by a few of the vulgar, worth wasting his wit upon; however the Examiner was at its last gasp.

It was not though. It lived and flourished; at least it paid its way, as one of the heroes of my story could tell. He was chief compositor, or whatever title may be given to the head-man of the mechanical part of a newspaper. He hardly confined himself to that department. Once or twice, unknown to the editor, when the manuscript had fallen short, he had filled up the vacant space by compositions of his own; announcements of a forthcoming crop of green peas in December; a grey thrush having been seen, or a white hare, or such interesting phenomena; invented for the occasion, I must confess; but what of that? His wife always knew when to expect a little specimen of her husband's literary talent by a peculiar cough, which served as prelude; and, judging from this encouraging sign, and the high-pitched and emphatic voice in which he read them, she was inclined to think, that an "Ode to an early Rose-bud," in the corner devoted to original poetry, and a letter in the correspondence department, signed "Pro Bono Publico," were her husband's writing, and to hold up her head accordingly.

I never could find out what it was that occasioned the Hodgsons to lodge in the same house as the Jenkinses. Jenkins held the same office in the Tory paper as Hodgson did in the Examiner, and, as I said before, I leave you to give it a name. But Jenkins had a proper sense of his position, and a proper reverence for all in authority, from the king down to the editor and sub-editor. He would as soon have thought of borrowing the king's crown for a nightcap, or the king's sceptre for a walking-stick, as he would have thought of filling up any spare corner with any production of his own; and I think it would have even added to his contempt of Hodgson (if that were possible), had he known of the "productions of his brain," as the latter fondly alluded to the paragraphs he inserted, when speaking to his wife.

Jenkins had his wife too. Wives were wanting to finish the completeness of the quarrel, which existed one memorable Christmas week, some dozen years ago, between the two neighbours, the two compositors. And with wives, it was a very pretty, a very complete quarrel. To make the opposing parties still more equal, still more well-matched, if the Hodgsons had a baby ("such a baby!—a poor, puny little thing"), Mrs. Jenkins had a cat ("such a cat! a great, nasty, miowling tom-cat, that was always stealing the milk put by for little Angel's supper"). And now, having matched Greek with Greek, I must proceed to the tug of war. It was the day before Christmas; such a cold east wind! such an inky sky! such a blue-black look in people's faces, as they were driven out more than usual, to complete their purchases for the next day's festival.

Before leaving home that morning, Jenkins had given some money to his wife to buy the next day's dinner.

"My dear, I wish for turkey and sausages. It may be a weakness, but I own I am partial to sausages. My deceased mother was. Such tastes are hereditary. As to the sweets—whether plum-pudding or mince-pies—I leave such considerations to you; I only beg you not to mind expense. Christmas comes but once a year."

And again he had called out from the bottom of the first flight of stairs, just close to the Hodgsons' door ("such ostentatiousness," as Mrs. Hodgson observed), "You will not forget the sausages, my dear?"

"I should have liked to have had something above common, Mary," said Hodgson, as they too made their plans for the next day, "but I think roast beef must do for us. You see, love, we've a family."

"Only one, Jem! I don't want more than roast beef, though, I'm sure. Before I went to service, mother and me would have thought roast beef a very fine dinner."

"Well, let's settle it then, roast beef and a plum-pudding; and now, good-by. Mind and take care of little Tom. I thought he was a bit hoarse this morning."

And off he went to his work.

Now, it was a good while since Mrs. Jenkins and Mrs. Hodgson had spoken to each other, although they were quite as much in possession of the knowledge of events and opinions as though they did. Mary knew that Mrs. Jenkins despised her for not having a real lace cap, which Mrs. Jenkins had; and for having been a servant, which Mrs. Jenkins had not; and the little occasional pinchings which the Hodgsons were obliged to resort to, to make both ends meet, would have been very patiently endured by Mary, if she had not winced under Mrs. Jenkins's knowledge of such economy. But she had her revenge. She had a child, and Mrs. Jenkins had none. To have had a child, even such a puny baby as little

Tom, Mrs. Jenkins would have worn commonest caps, and cleaned grates, and drudged her fingers to the bone. The great unspoken disappointment of her life soured her temper, and turned her thoughts inward, and made her morbid and selfish.

"Hang that cat! he's been stealing again! he's gnawed the cold mutton in his nasty mouth till it's not fit to set before a Christian; and I've nothing else for Jem's dinner. But I'll give it him now I've caught him, that I will!"

So saying, Mary Hodgson caught up her husband's Sunday cane, and despite pussy's cries and scratches, she gave him such a beating as she hoped might cure him of his thievish propensities; when lo! and behold, Mrs. Jenkins stood at the door with a face of bitter wrath.

"Aren't you ashamed of yourself, ma'am, to abuse a poor dumb animal, ma'am, as knows no better than to take food when he sees it, ma'am? He only follows the nature which God has given, ma'am; and it's a pity your nature, ma'am, which I've heard, is of the stingy saving species, does not make you shut your cupboard-door a little closer. There is such a thing as law for brute animals. I'll ask Mr. Jenkins, but I don't think them Radicals has done away with that law yet, for all their Reform Bill, ma'am. My poor precious love of a Tommy, is he hurt? and is his leg broke for taking a mouthful of scraps, as most people would give away to a beggar,—if he'd take 'em?" wound up Mrs. Jenkins, casting a contemptuous look on the remnant of a scrag end of mutton.

Mary felt very angry and very guilty. For she really pitied the poor limping animal as he crept up to his mistress, and there lay down to bemoan himself; she wished she had not beaten him so hard, for it certainly was her own careless way of never shutting the cupboard-door that had tempted him to his fault. But the sneer at her little bit of mutton turned her penitence to fresh wrath, and she shut the door in Mrs. Jenkins's face, as she stood caressing her cat in the lobby, with such a bang, that it wakened little Tom, and he began to cry.

Everything was to go wrong with Mary to-day. Now baby was awake, who was to take her husband's dinner to the office? She took the child in her arms, and tried to hush him off to sleep again, and as she sung she cried, she could hardly tell why,—a sort of reaction from her violent angry feelings. She wished she had never beaten the poor cat; she wondered if his leg was really broken. What would her mother say if she knew how cross and cruel her little Mary was getting? If she should live to beat her child in one of her angry fits?

It was of no use lullabying while she sobbed so; it must be given up, and she must just carry her baby in her arms, and take him with her to the office, for it was long past dinner-time. So she pared the mutton carefully, although by so doing she reduced the meat to an infinitesimal quantity, and taking the baked potatoes out of the oven, she popped them piping hot into her basket with the et-cæteras of plate, butter, salt, and knife and fork.

It was, indeed, a bitter wind. She bent against it as she ran, and the flakes of snow were sharp and cutting as ice. Baby cried all the way, though she cuddled him up in her shawl. Then her husband had made his appetite up for a potato pie, and (literary man as he was) his body got so much the better of his mind, that he looked rather black at the cold mutton. Mary had no appetite for her own dinner when she arrived at home again. So, after she had tried to feed baby, and he had fretfully refused to take his bread and milk, she laid him down as usual on his quilt, surrounded by playthings, while she sided away, and chopped suet for the next day's pudding. Early in the afternoon a parcel came, done up first in brown paper, then in such a white, grass-bleached, sweet-smelling towel, and a note from her dear, dear mother; in which quaint writing she endeavoured to tell her daughter that she was not forgotten at Christmas time; but that learning that Farmer Burton was killing his pig, she had made interest for some of his famous pork, out of which she had manufactured some sausages, and flavoured them just as Mary used to like when she lived at home.

"Dear, dear mother!" said Mary to herself. "There never was any one like her for remembering other folk. What rare sausages she used to make! Home things have a smack with 'em, no bought things can ever have. Set them up with their sausages! I've a notion if Mrs. Jenkins had ever tasted mother's she'd have no fancy for them town-made things Fanny took in just now."

And so she went on thinking about home, till the smiles and the dimples came out again at the remembrance of that pretty cottage, which would look green even now in the depth of winter, with its pyracanthus, and its holly-bushes, and the great Portugal laurel that was her mother's pride. And the back path through the orchard to Farmer Burton's; how well she remembered it. The bushels of unripe apples she had picked up there, and distributed among his pigs, till he had scolded her for giving them so much green trash.

She was interrupted—her baby (I call him a baby, because his father and mother did, and because he was so little of his age, but I rather think he was eighteen months old,) had fallen asleep some time before among his playthings; an uneasy, restless sleep; but of which Mary had been thankful, as his morning's nap had been too short, and as she was so busy. But now he began to make such a strange crowing noise, just like a chair drawn heavily and gratingly along a kitchen-floor! His eyes was open, but expressive of nothing but pain.

"Mother's darling!" said Mary, in terror, lifting him up. "Baby, try not to make that noise. Hush, hush, darling; what hurts him?" But the noise came worse and worse.

"Fanny! Fanny!" Mary called in mortal fright, for her baby was almost black with his gasping breath, and she had no one to ask for aid or sympathy but her landlady's daughter, a little girl of twelve or thirteen, who attended to the house in her mother's absence, as daily cook in gentlemen's families. Fanny was more especially considered the attendant of the upstairs lodgers (who paid for the use of the kitchin, "for Jenkins could not abide the smell of meat cooking"), but just now she was fortunately sitting at her afternoon's work of darning stockings, and hearing Mrs. Hodgson's cry of terror, she ran to her sitting-room, and understood the case at a glance.

"He's got the croup! Oh, Mrs. Hodgson, he'll die as sure as fate. Little brother had it, and he died in no time. The doctor said he could do nothing for him—it had gone too far. He said if we'd put him in a warm bath at first, it might have saved him; but, bless you! he was never half so bad as your baby." Unconsciously there mingled in her statement some of a child's love of producing an effect; but the increasing danger was clear enough.

"Oh, my baby! my baby! Oh, love, love! don't look so ill; I cannot bear it. And my fire so low! There, I was thinking of home, and picking currants, and never minding the fire. Oh, Fanny! what is the fire like in the kitchen? Speak."

"Mother told me to screw it up, and throw some slack on as soon as Mrs. Jenkins had done with it, and so I did. It's very low and black. But, oh, Mrs. Hodgson! let me run for the doctor—I cannot abear to hear him, it's so like little brother."

Through her streaming tears Mary motioned her to go; and trembling, sinking, sick at heart, she laid her boy in his cradle, and ran to fill her kettle.

Mrs. Jenkins, having cooked her husband's snug little dinner, to which he came home; having told him her story of pussy's beating, at which he was justly and dignifiedly indignant, saying it was all of a piece with that abusive Examiner; having received the sausages, and turkey, and mince pies, which her husband had ordered; and cleaned up the room, and prepared everything for tea, and coaxed and duly bemoaned her cat (who had pretty nearly forgotten his beating, but very much enjoyed the petting), having done all these and many other things, Mrs. Jenkins sate down to get up the real lace cap. Every thread was pulled out separately, and carefully stretched: when, what was that? Outside, in the street, a chorus of piping children's voices sang the old carol she had heard a hundred times in the days of her youth:—

"As Joseph was a walking he heard an angel sing, 'This night shall be born our heavenly King. He neither shall be born in housen nor in hall, Nor in the place of Paradise, but in an ox's stall. He neither shall be clothed in purple nor in pall, But all in fair linen, as were babies all: He neither shall be rocked in silver nor in gold, But in a wooden cradle that rocks on the mould,'" &c.

She got up and went to the window. There, below, stood the group of grey black little figures, relieved against the snow, which now enveloped everything. "For old sake's sake," as she phrased it, she counted out a halfpenny apiece for the singers, out of the copper bag, and threw them down below.

The room had become chilly while she had been counting out and throwing down her money, so she stirred her already glowing fire, and sat down right before it—but not to stretch her lace; like Mary Hodgson, she began to think over long-past days, on softening remembrances of the dead and gone, on words long forgotten, on holy stories heard at her mother's knee.

"I cannot think what's come over me to-night," said she, half aloud, recovering herself by the sound of her own voice from her train of thought—"My head goes wandering on them old times. I'm sure more texts have come into my head with thinking on my mother within this last half hour, than I've thought on for years and years. I hope I'm not going to die. Folks say, thinking too much on the dead betokens we're going to join 'em; I should be loth to go just yet—such a fine turkey as we've got for dinner to-morrow, too!"

Knock, knock, knock, at the door, as fast as knuckles could go. And then, as if the comer could not wait, the door was opened, and Mary Hodgson stood there as white as death.

"Mrs. Jenkins!—oh, your kettle is boiling, thank God! Let me have the water for my baby, for the love of God! He's got croup, and is dying!"

Mrs. Jenkins turned on her chair with a wooden inflexible look on her face, that (between ourselves) her husband knew and dreaded for all his pompous dignity.

"I'm sorry I can't oblige you, ma'am; my kettle is wanted for my husband's tea. Don't be afeared, Tommy, Mrs. Hodgson won't venture to intrude herself where she's not desired. You'd better send for the doctor, ma'am, instead of wasting your time in wringing your hands, ma'am—my kettle is engaged."

Mary clasped her hands together with passionate force, but spoke no word of entreaty to that wooden face—that sharp, determined voice; but, as she turned away, she prayed for strength to bear the coming trial, and strength to forgive Mrs. Jenkins.

Mrs. Jenkins watched her go away meekly, as one who has no hope, and then she turned upon herself as sharply as she ever did on any one else.

"What a brute I am, Lord forgive me! What's my husband's tea to a baby's life? In croup, too, where time is everything. You crabbed old vixen, you!—any one may know you never had a child!"

She was down stairs (kettle in hand) before she had finished her self-upbraiding; and when in Mrs. Hodgson's room, she rejected all thanks (Mary had not the voice for many words), saying, stiffly, "I do it for the poor babby's sake, ma'am, hoping he may live to have mercy to poor dumb beasts, if he does forget to lock his cupboards."

But she did everything, and more than Mary, with her young inexperience, could have thought of. She prepared the warm bath, and tried it with her husband's own thermometer (Mr. Jenkins was as punctual as clockwork in noting down the temperature of every day). She let his mother place her baby in the tub, still preserving the same rigid, affronted aspect, and then she went upstairs without a word. Mary longed to ask her to stay, but dared not; though, when she left the room, the tears chased each other down her cheeks faster than ever. Poor young mother! how she counted the minutes till the doctor should come. But, before he came, down again stalked Mrs. Jenkins, with something in her hand.

"I've seen many of these croup-fits, which, I take it, you've not, ma'am. Mustard plaisters is very sovereign, put on the throat; I've been up and made one, ma'am, and, by your leave, I'll put it on the poor little fellow."

Mary could not speak, but she signed her grateful assent.

It began to smart while they still kept silence; and he looked up to his mother as if seeking courage from her looks to bear the stinging pain; but she was softly crying, to see him suffer, and her want of courage reacted upon him, and he began to sob aloud. Instantly Mrs. Jenkins's apron was up, hiding her face: "Peep-bo, baby," said she, as merrily as she could. His little face brightened, and his mother having once got the cue, the two women kept the little fellow amused, until his plaister had taken effect.

"He's better,—oh, Mrs. Jenkins, look at his eyes! how different! And he breathes quite softly—"

As Mary spoke thus, the doctor entered. He examined his patient. Baby was really better.

"It has been a sharp attack, but the remedies you have applied have been worth all the Pharmacopoeia an hour later.—I shall send a powder," &c. &c.

Mrs. Jenkins stayed to hear this opinion; and (her heart wonderfully more easy) was going to leave the room, when Mary seized her hand and kissed it; she could not speak her gratitude.

Mrs. Jenkins looked affronted and awkward, and as if she must go upstairs and wash her hand directly.

But, in spite of these sour looks, she came softly down an hour or so afterwards to see how baby was.

The little gentleman slept well after the fright he had given his friends; and on Christmas morning, when Mary awoke and looked at the sweet little pale face lying on her arm, she could hardly realize the danger he had been in.

When she came down (later than usual), she found the household in a commotion. What do you think had happened? Why, pussy had been a traitor to his best friend, and eaten up some of Mr. Jenkins's own especial sausages; and gnawed and tumbled the rest so, that they were not fit to be eaten! There were no bounds to that cat's appetite! he would have eaten his own father if he had been tender enough. And now Mrs. Jenkins stormed and cried—"Hang the cat!"

Christmas Day, too! and all the shops shut! "What was turkey without sausages?" gruffly asked Mr. Jenkins.

"Oh, Jem!" whispered Mary, "hearken what a piece of work he's making about sausages,—I should like to take Mrs. Jenkins up some of mother's; they're twice as good as bought sausages."

"I see no objection, my dear. Sausages do not involve intimacies, else his politics are what I can no ways respect."

"But, oh, Jem, if you had seen her last night about baby! I'm sure she may scold me for ever, and I'll not answer. I'd even make her cat welcome to the sausages." The tears gathered to Mary's eyes as she kissed her boy.

"Better take 'em upstairs, my dear, and give them to the cat's mistress." And Jem chuckled at his saying.

Mary put them on a plate, but still she loitered.

"What must I say, Jem? I never know."

"Say—I hope you'll accept of these sausages, as my mother—no, that's not grammar;—say what comes uppermost, Mary, it will be sure to be right."

So Mary carried them upstairs and knocked at the door; and when told to "come in," she looked very red, but went up to Mrs. Jenkins, saying, "Please take these. Mother made them." And was away before an answer could be given.

Just as Hodgson was ready to go to church, Mrs. Jenkins came downstairs, and called Fanny. In a minute, the latter entered the Hodgsons' room, and delivered Mr. and Mrs. Jenkins's compliments, and they would be particular glad if Mr. and Mrs. Hodgson would eat their dinner with them.

"And carry baby upstairs in a shawl, be sure," added Mrs. Jenkins's voice in the passage, close to the door, whither she had followed her messenger. There was no discussing the matter, with the certainty of every word being overheard.

Mary looked anxiously at her husband. She remembered his saying he did not approve of Mr. Jenkins's politics.

"Do you think it would do for baby?" asked he.

"Oh, yes," answered she, eagerly; "I would wrap him up so warm."

"And I've got our room up to sixty-five already, for all it's so frosty," added the voice outside.

Now, how do you think they settled the matter? The very best way in the world. Mr. and Mrs. Jenkins came down into the Hodgsons' room, and dined there. Turkey at the top, roast beef at the bottom, sausages at one side, potatoes at the other. Second course, plum-pudding at the top, and mince pies at the bottom.

And after dinner, Mrs. Jenkins would have baby on her knee; and he seemed quite to take to her; she declared he was admiring the real lace on her cap, but Mary thought (though she did not say so) that he was pleased by her kind looks and coaxing words. Then he was wrapped up and carried carefully upstairs to tea, in Mrs. Jenkins's room. And after tea, Mrs. Jenkins, and Mary, and her husband, found out each other's mutual liking for music, and sat singing old glees and catches, till I don't know what o'clock, without one word of politics or newspapers.

Before they parted, Mary had coaxed pussy on to her knee; for Mrs. Jenkins would not part with baby, who was sleeping on her lap.

"When you're busy, bring him to me. Do, now, it will be a real favour. I know you must have a deal to do, with another coming; let him come up to me. I'll take the greatest of cares of him; pretty darling, how sweet he looks when he's asleep!"

When the couples were once more alone, the husbands unburdened their minds to their wives.

Mr. Jenkins said to his—"Do you know, Burgess tried to make me believe Hodgson was such a fool as to put paragraphs into the Examiner now and then; but I see he knows his place, and has got too much sense to do any such thing."

Hodgson said—"Mary, love, I almost fancy from Jenkins's way of speaking (so much civiler than I expected), he guesses I wrote that 'Pro Bono' and the 'Rose-bud,'—at any rate, I've no objection to your naming it, if the subject should come uppermost; I should like him to know I'm a literary man."

Well! I've ended my tale; I hope you don't think it too long; but, before I go, just let me say one thing.

If any of you have any quarrels, or misunderstandings, or coolnesses, or cold shoulders, or shynesses, or tiffs, or miffs, or huffs, with any one else, just make friends before Christmas,—you will be so much merrier if you do.

I ask it of you for the sake of that old angelic song, heard so many years ago by the shepherds, keeping watch by night, on Bethlehem Heights.

"Mother, I should so like to have a great deal of money," said little Tom Fletcher one evening, as he sat on a low stool by his mother's knee. His mother was knitting busily by the firelight, and they had both been silent for some time.

"What would you do with a great deal of money if you had it?"

"Oh! I don't know—I would do a great many things. But should not you like to have a great deal of money, mother?" persisted he.

"Perhaps I should," answered Mrs. Fletcher. "I am like you sometimes, dear, and think that I should be very glad of a little more money. But then I don't think I am like you in one thing, for I have always some little plan in my mind, for which I should want the money. I never wish for it just for its own sake."

"Why, mother! there are so many things we could do if we had but money;—real good, wise things I mean."

"And if we have real good, wise things in our head to do, which cannot be done without money, I can quite enter into the wish for money. But you know, my little boy, you did not tell me of any good or wise thing."

"No! I believe I was not thinking of good or wise things just then, but only how much I should like money to do what I liked," answered little Tom ingenuously, looking up in his mother's face. She smiled down upon him, and stroked his head. He knew she was pleased with him for having told her openly what was passing in his mind. Presently he began again.

"Mother, if you wanted to do something very good and wise, and if you could not do it without money, what should you do?"

"There are two ways of obtaining money for such wants; one is by earning; and the other is by saving. Now both are good, because both imply self-denial. Do you understand me, Tom? If you have to earn money, you must steadily go on doing what you do not like perhaps; such as working when you would like to be playing, or in bed, or sitting talking with me over the fire. You deny yourself these little pleasures; and that is a good habit in itself, to say nothing of the industry and energy you have to exert in working. If you save money, you can easily see how you exercise self-denial. You do without something you wish for in order to possess the money it would have cost. Inasmuch as self-denial, energy, and industry are all good things, you do well either to earn or to save. But you see the purpose for which you want the money must be taken into consideration. You say, for 'something wise and good.' Either earning or saving becomes holy in this case. I must then think which will be most consistent with my other duties, before I decide whether I will earn or save money."

"I don't quite know what you mean, mother."

"I will try and explain myself. You know I have to keep a little shop, and to try and get employment in knitting stockings, and to clean my house, and to mend our clothes, and many other things. Now, do you think I should be doing my duty if I left you in the evenings, when you come home from school, to go out as a waiter at ladies' parties? I could earn a good deal of money by it, and I could spend it well among those who are poorer than I am (such as lame Harry), but then I should be leaving you alone in the little time that we have to be together; I do not think I should be doing right even for our 'good and wise purpose' to earn money, if it took me away from you at nights: do you, Tom?"

"No, indeed; you never mean to do it, do you, mother?"

"No," said she, smiling; "at any rate not till you are older. You see at present then, I cannot earn money, if I want a little more than usual to help a sick neighbour. I must then try and save money. Nearly every one can do that."

"Can we, mother? We are so careful of everything. Ned Dixon calls us stingy: what could we save?"

"Oh, many and many a little thing. We use many things which are luxuries; which we do not want, but only use them for pleasure. Tea and sugar—butter—our Sunday's dinner of bacon or meat—the grey ribbon I bought for my bonnet, because you thought it prettier than the black, which was cheaper; all these are luxuries. We use very little tea or sugar, it is true; but we might do without any."

"You did do without any, mother, for a long, long time, you know, to help widow Black; it was only for your bad head-aches."

"Well! but you see we can save money; a penny, a halfpenny a day, or even a penny a week, would in time make a little store ready to be applied to the 'good and wise' purpose, when the time comes. But do you know, my little boy, I think we may be considering money too much as the only thing required if we want to do a kindness."

"If it is not the only thing, it is the chief thing, at any rate."

"No, love, it is not the chief thing. I should think very poorly of that beggar who liked sixpence given with a curse (as I have sometimes heard it), better than the kind and gentle words some people use in refusing to give. The curse sinks deep into the heart; or if it does not, it is a proof that the poor creature has been made hard before by harsh treatment. And mere money can do little to cheer a sore heart. It is kindness only that can do this. Now we have all of us kindness in our power. The little child of two years old, who can only just totter about, can show kindness?"

"Can I, mother?"

"To be sure, dear; and you often do, only perhaps not quite so often as you might do. Neither do I. But instead of wishing for money (of which I don't think either you or I are ever likely to have much), suppose you try to-morrow how you can make people happier, by thinking of little loving actions of help. Let us try and take for our text, 'Silver and gold I have none, but such as I have give I unto thee.'"

"Ay, mother, we will."

Must I tell you about little Tom's "to-morrow."

I do not know if little Tom dreamed of what his mother and he had been talking about, but I do know that the first thing he thought about, when he awoke in the morning, was his mother's saying that he might try how many kind actions he could do that day without money; and he was so impatient to begin, that he jumped up and dressed himself, although it was more than an hour before his usual time of getting up. All the time he kept wondering what a little boy like him, only eight years old, could do for other people; till at last he grew so puzzled with inventing occasions for showing kindness, that he very wisely determined to think no more about it, but learn his lessons very perfectly; that was the first thing he had to do; and then he would try, without too much planning beforehand, to keep himself ready to lend a helping hand, or to give a kind word, when the right time came. So he screwed himself into a corner, out of the way of his mother's sweeping and dusting, and tucked his feet up on the rail of the chair, turned his face to the wall, and in about half an hour's time, he could turn round with a light heart, feeling he had learnt his lesson well, and might employ his time as he liked till breakfast was ready. He looked round the room; his mother had arranged all neatly, and was now gone to the bedroom; but the coal-scuttle and the can for water were empty, and Tom ran away to fill them; and as he came back with the latter from the pump, he saw Ann Jones (the scold of the neighbourhood) hanging out her clothes on a line stretched across from side to side of the little court, and speaking very angrily and loudly to her little girl, who was getting into some mischief in the house-place, as her mother perceived through the open door.

"There never were such plagues as my children are, to be sure," said Ann Jones, as she went into her house, looking very red and passionate. Directly after, Tom heard the sound of a slap, and then a little child's cry of pain.

"I wonder," thought he, "if I durst go and offer to nurse and play with little Hester. Ann Jones is fearful cross, and just as likely to take me wrong as right; but she won't box me for mother's sake; mother nursed Jemmy many a day through the fever, so she won't slap me, I think. Any rate, I'll try." But it was with a beating heart he said to the fierce-looking Mrs. Jones, "Please, may I go and play with Hester. May be I could keep her quiet while you're busy hanging out clothes."

"What! and let you go slopping about, I suppose, just when I'd made all ready for my master's breakfast. Thank you, but my own children's mischief is as much as I reckon on; I'll have none of strange lads in my house."

"I did not mean to do mischief or slop," said Tom, a little sadly at being misunderstood in his good intentions. "I only wanted to help."

"If you want to help, lift me up those clothes' pegs, and save me stooping; my back's broken with it."

Tom would much rather have gone to play with and amuse little Hester; but it was true enough that giving Mrs. Jones the clothes' pegs as she wanted them would help her as much; and perhaps keep her from being so cross with her children if they did anything to hinder her. Besides, little Hester's cry had died away, and she was evidently occupied in some new pursuit (Tom could only hope that it was not in mischief this time); so he began to give Ann the pegs as she wanted them, and she, soothed by his kind help, opened her heart a little to him.

"I wonder how it is your mother has trained you up to be so handy, Tom; you're as good as a girl—better than many a girl. I don't think Hester in three years' time will be as thoughtful as you. There!" (as a fresh scream reached them from the little ones inside the house), "they are at some mischief again; but I'll teach 'em," said she, getting down from her stool in a fresh access of passion.

"Let me go," said Tom, in a begging voice, for he dreaded the cruel sound of another slap. "I'll lift the basket of pegs on to a stool, so that you need not stoop; and I'll keep the little ones safe out of mischief till you're done. Do let me go, missus."

With some grumblings at losing his help, she let him go into the house-place. He found Hester, a little girl of five, and two younger ones. They had been fighting for a knife, and in the struggle, the second, Johnnie, had cut his finger—not very badly, but he was frightened at the sight of the blood; and Hester, who might have helped, and who was really sorry, stood sullenly aloof, dreading the scolding her mother always gave her if either of the little ones hurt themselves while under her care.

"Hester," said Tom, "will you get me some cold water, please? it will stop the bleeding better than anything. I daresay you can find me a basin to hold it."

Hester trotted off, pleased at Tom's confidence in her power. When the bleeding was partly stopped, he asked her to find him a bit of rag, and she scrambled under the dresser for a little piece she had hidden there the day before. Meanwhile, Johnny ceased crying, he was so interested in all the preparation for dressing his little wound, and so much pleased to find himself an object of so much attention and consequence. The baby, too, sat on the floor, gravely wondering at the commotion; and thus busily occupied, they were quiet and out of mischief till Ann Jones came in, and, having hung out her clothes, and finished that morning's piece of work, she was ready to attend to her children in her rough, hasty kind of way.

[Illustration p. 220: The Cut Finger.]

"Well! I'm sure, Tom, you've tied it up as neatly as I could have done. I wish I'd always such an one as you to see after the children; but you must run off now, lad, your mother was calling you as I came in, and I said I'd send you—good-by, and thank you."

As Tom was going away, the baby, sitting in square gravity on the floor, but somehow conscious of Tom's gentle helpful ways, put up her mouth to be kissed; and he stooped down in answer to the little gesture, feeling very happy, and very full of love and kindliness.

After breakfast, his mother told him it was school time, and he must set off, as she did not like him to run in out of breath and flurried, just when the schoolmaster was going to begin; but she wished him to come in decently and in order, with quiet decorum, and thoughtfulness as to what he was going to do. So Tom got his cap and his bag, and went off with a light heart, which I suppose made his footsteps light, for he found himself above half way to school while it wanted yet a quarter to the time. So he slackened his pace, and looked about him a little more than he had been doing. There was a little girl on the other side of the street carrying a great big basket, and lugging along a little child just able to walk; but who, I suppose, was tired, for he was crying pitifully, and sitting down every two or three steps. Tom ran across the street, for, as perhaps you have found out, he was very fond of babies, and could not bear to hear them cry.

"Little girl, what is he crying about? Does he want to be carried? I'll take him up, and carry him as far as I go alongside of you."

So saying, Tom was going to suit the action to the word; but the baby did not choose that any one should carry him but his sister, and refused Tom's kindness. Still he could carry the heavy basket of potatoes for the little girl, which he did as far as their road lay together, when she thanked him, and bade him good-by, and said she could manage very well now, her home was so near. So Tom went into school very happy and peaceful; and had a good character to take home to his mother for that morning's lesson.

It happened that this very day was the weekly half-holiday, so that Tom had many hours unoccupied that afternoon. Of course, his first employment after dinner was to learn his lessons for the next day; and then, when he had put his books away, he began to wonder what he should do next.

He stood lounging against the door wishing all manner of idle wishes; a habit he was apt to fall into. He wished he were the little boy who lived opposite, who had three brothers ready to play with him on half-holidays; he wished he were Sam Harrison, whose father had taken him one day a trip by the railroad; he wished he were the little boy who always went with the omnibuses,—it must be so pleasant to go riding about on the step, and to see so many people; he wished he were a sailor, to sail away to the countries where grapes grew wild, and monkeys and parrots were to be had for the catching. Just as he was wishing himself the little Prince of Wales, to drive about in a goat-carriage, and wondering if he should not feel very shy with the three great ostrich-feathers always niddle-noddling on his head, for people to know him by, his mother came from washing up the dishes, and saw him deep in the reveries little boys and girls are apt to fall into when they are the only children in a house.

"My dear Tom," said she, "why don't you go out, and make the most of this fine afternoon?"

"Oh, mother," answered he (suddenly recalled to the fact that he was little Tom Fletcher, instead of the Prince of Wales, and consequently feeling a little bit flat), "it is so dull going out by myself. I have no one to play with. Can't you go with me, mother—just this once, into the fields?"

Poor Mrs. Fletcher heartily wished she could gratify this very natural desire of her little boy; but she had the shop to mind, and many a little thing besides to do; it was impossible. But however much she might regret a thing, she was too faithful to repine. So, after a moment's thought, she said, cheerfully, "Go into the fields for a walk, and see how many wild flowers you can bring me home, and I'll get down father's jug for you to put them in when you come back."

"But, mother, there are so few pretty flowers near a town," said Tom, a little unwillingly, for it was a coming down from being Prince of Wales, and he was not yet quite reconciled to it.

"Oh dear! there are a great many if you'll only look for them. I dare say you'll make me up as many as twenty different kinds."

"Will you reckon daisies, mother?"

"To be sure; they are just as pretty as any."

"Oh, if you'll reckon such as them, I dare say I can bring you more than twenty."

So off he ran; his mother watching him till he was out of sight, and then she returned to her work. In about two hours he came back, his pale cheeks looking quite rosy, and his eyes quite bright. His country walk, taken with cheerful spirits, had done him all the good his mother desired, and had restored his usually even, happy temper.

"Look, mother! here are three-and-twenty different kinds; you said I might count all, so I have even counted this thing like a nettle with lilac flowers, and this little common blue thing."

"Robin-run-in-the-hedge is its name," said his mother. "It's very pretty if you look at it close. One, two, three"—she counted them all over, and there really were three-and-twenty. She went to reach down the best jug.

"Mother," said little Tom, "do you like them very much?"

"Yes, very much," said she, not understanding his meaning. He was silent, and gave a little sigh. "Why, my dear?"

"Oh, only—it does not signify if you like them very much; but I thought how nice it would be to take them to lame Harry, who can never walk so far as the fields, and can hardly know what summer is like, I think."

"Oh, that will be very nice; I am glad you thought of it."

Lame Harry was sitting by himself, very patiently, in a neighbouring cellar. He was supported by his daughter's earnings; but as she worked in a factory, he was much alone.

If the bunch of flowers had looked pretty in the fields, they looked ten times as pretty in the cellar to which they were now carried. Lame Harry's eyes brightened up with pleasure at the sight; and he began to talk of the times long ago, when he was a little boy in the country, and had a corner of his father's garden to call his own, and grow lad's-love and wall-flower in. Little Tom put them in water for him, and put the jug on the table by him; on which his daughter had placed the old Bible, worn with much reading, although treated with careful reverence. It was lying open, with Harry's horn spectacles put in to mark the place.

"I reckon my spectacles are getting worn out; they are not so clear as they used to be; they are dim-like before my eyes, and it hurts me to read long together," said Harry. "It's a sad miss to me. I never thought the time long when I could read; but now I keep wearying for the day to be over, though the nights, when I cannot sleep for my legs paining me, are almost as bad. However, it's the Lord's will."

"Would you like me—I cannot read very well aloud, but I'd do my best, if you'd like me to read a bit to you. I'll just run home and get my tea, and be back directly." And off Tom ran.

He found it very pleasant reading aloud to lame Harry, for the old man had so much to say that was worth listening to, and was so glad of a listener, that I think there was as much talking as reading done that evening. But the Bible served as a text-book to their conversation; for in a long life old Harry had seen and heard so much, which he had connected with events, or promises, or precepts contained in the Scriptures, that it was quite curious to find how everything was brought in and dove-tailed, as an illustration of what they were reading.

When Tom got up to go away, lame Harry gave him many thanks, and told him he would not sleep the worse for having made an old man's evening so pleasant. Tom came home in high self-satisfaction. "Mother," said he, "it's all very true what you said about the good that may be done without money: I've done many pieces of good to-day without a farthing. First," said he, taking hold of his little finger, "I helped Ann Jones with hanging out her clothes when she was"—

His mother had been listening while she turned over the pages of the New Testament which lay by her, and now having found what she wanted, she put her arm gently round his waist, and drew him fondly towards her. He saw her finger put under one passage, and read,—

"Let not thy left hand know what thy right hand doeth."

He was silent in a moment.

Then his mother spoke in her soft low voice:—"Dearest Tom, though I don't want us to talk about it, as if you had been doing more than just what you ought, I am glad you have seen the truth of what I said; how far more may be done by the loving heart than by mere money-giving; and every one may have the loving heart."

I have told you of one day of little Tom's life, when he was eight years old, and lived with his mother. I must now pass over a year, and tell you of a very different kind of life he had then to lead. His mother had never been very strong, and had had a good deal of anxiety; at last she was taken ill, and soon felt that there was no hope for her recovery. For a long time the thought of leaving her little boy was a great distress to her, and a great trial to her faith. But God strengthened her, and sent his peace into her soul, and before her death she was content to leave her precious child in his hands, who is a Father to the fatherless, and defendeth the cause of the widow.

When she felt that she had not many more days to live, she sent for her husband's brother, who lived in a town not many miles off; and gave her little Tom in charge to him to bring up.

"There are a few pounds in the savings-bank—I don't know how many exactly—and the furniture and bit of stock in the shop; perhaps they would be enough to bring him up to be a joiner, like his father before him."

She spoke feebly, and with many pauses. Her brother-in-law, though a rough kind of man, wished to do all he could to make her feel easy in her last moments, and touched with the reference to his dead brother, promised all she required.

"I'll take him back with me after"—the funeral, he was going to say, but he stopped. She smiled gently, fully understanding his meaning.

"We shall, may be, not be so tender with him as you've been; but I'll see he comes to no harm. It will be a good thing for him to rough it a bit with other children,—he's too nesh for a boy; but I'll pay them if they aren't kind to him in the long run, never fear."

Though this speech was not exactly what she liked, there was quite enough of good feeling in it to make her thankful for such a protector and friend for her boy. And so, thankful for the joys she had had, and thankful for the sorrows which had taught her meekness, thankful for life, and thankful for death, she died.

Her brother-in-law arranged all as she had wished. After the quiet simple funeral was over, he took Tom by the hand, and set off on the six-mile walk to his home. Tom had cried till he could cry no more, but sobs came quivering up from his heart every now and then, as he passed some well-remembered cottage, or thorn-bush, or tree on the road. His uncle was very sorry for him, but did not know what to say, or how to comfort him.

"Now mind, lad, thou com'st to me if thy cousins are o'er hard upon thee. Let me hear if they misuse thee, and I'll give it them."

Tom shrunk from the idea that this gave him of the cousins, whose companionship he had, until then, been looking forward to as a pleasure. He was not reassured when, after threading several streets and by-ways, they came into a court of dingy-looking houses, and his uncle opened the door of one, from which the noise of loud, if not angry voices was heard.

A tall large woman was whirling one child out of her way with a rough movement of her arm; while she was scolding a boy a little older than Tom, who stood listening sullenly to her angry words.

"I'll tell father of thee, I will," said she; and turning to uncle John, she began to pour out her complaints against Jack, without taking any notice of little Tom, who clung to his uncle's hand as to a protector in the scene of violence into which he had entered.

"Well, well, wife!—I'll leather Jack the next time I catch him letting the water out of the pipe; but now get this lad and me some tea, for we're weary and tired."

His aunt seemed to wish Jack might be leathered now, and to be angry with her husband for not revenging her injuries; for an injury it was that the boy had done her in letting the water all run off, and that on the very eve of the washing day. The mother grumbled as she left off mopping the wet floor, and went to the fire to stir it up ready for the kettle, without a word of greeting to her little nephew, or of welcome to her husband. On the contrary, she complained of the trouble of getting tea ready afresh, just when she had put slack on the fire, and had no water in the house to fill the kettle with. Her husband grew angry, and Tom was frightened to hear his uncle speaking sharply.

"If I can't have a cup of tea in my own house without all this ado, I'll go to the Spread Eagle, and take Tom with me. They've a bright fire there at all times, choose how they manage it; and no scolding wives. Come, Tom, let's be off."

Jack had been trying to scrape acquaintance with his cousin by winks and grimaces behind his mother's back, and now made a sign of drinking out of an imaginary glass. But Tom clung to his uncle, and softly pulled him down again on his chair, from which he had risen to go to the public-house.

"If you please, ma'am," said he, sadly frightened of his aunt, "I think I could find the pump, if you'd let me try."

She muttered something like an acquiescence; so Tom took up the kettle, and, tired as he was, went out to the pump. Jack, who had done nothing but mischief all day, stood amazed, but at last settled that his cousin was a "softy."

When Tom came back, he tried to blow the fire with the broken bellows, and at last the water boiled, and the tea was made. "Thou'rt a rare lad, Tom," said his uncle. "I wonder when our Jack will be of as much use."

This comparison did not please either Jack or his mother, who liked to keep to herself the privilege of directing their father's dissatisfaction with his children. Tom felt their want of kindliness towards him; and now that he had nothing to do but rest and eat, he began to feel very sad, and his eyes kept filling with tears, which he brushed away with the back of his hand, not wishing to have them seen. But his uncle noticed him.

"Thou had'st better have had a glass at the Spread Eagle," said he, compassionately.

"No; I only am rather tired. May I go to bed?" said he, longing for a good cry unobserved under the bed-clothes.

"Where's he to sleep?" asked the husband of the wife.

"Nay," said she, still offended on Jack's account, "that's thy look-out. He's thy flesh and blood, not mine."

"Come, wife," said uncle John, "he's an orphan, poor chap. An orphan is kin to every one."

She was softened directly, for she had much kindness in her, although this evening she had been so much put out.

"There's no place for him but with Jack and Dick. We've the baby, and the other three are packed close enough."

She took Tom up to the little back room, and stopped to talk with him for a minute or two, for her husband's words had smitten her heart, and she was sorry for the ungracious reception she had given Tom at first.

"Jack and Dick are never in bed till we come, and it's work enough to catch them then on fine evenings," said she, as she took the candle away.

Tom tried to speak to God as his mother had taught him, out of the fulness of his little heart, which was heavy enough that night. He tried to think how she would have wished him to speak and to do, and when he felt puzzled with the remembrance of the scene of disorder and anger which he had seen, he earnestly prayed God would make and keep clear his path before him. And then he fell asleep.

He had had a long dream of other and happier days, and had thought he was once more taking a Sunday evening walk with his mother, when he was roughly wakened up by his cousins.

"I say, lad, you're lying right across the bed. You must get up, and let Dick and me come in, and then creep into the space that's left."

Tom got up dizzy and half awake. His cousins got into bed, and then squabbled about the largest share. It ended in a kicking match, during which Tom stood shivering by the bedside.

"I'm sure we're pinched enough as it is," said Dick at last. "And why they've put Tom in with us I can't think. But I'll not stand it. Tom shan't sleep with us. He may lie on the floor, if he likes. I'll not hinder him."

He expected an opposition from Tom, and was rather surprised when he heard the little fellow quietly lie down, and cover himself as well as he could with his clothes. After some more quarrelling, Jack and Dick fell asleep. But in the middle of the night Dick awoke, and heard by Tom's breathing that he was still awake, and was crying gently.

"What! molly-coddle, crying for a softer bed?" asked Dick.

"Oh, no—I don't care for that—if—oh! if mother were but alive," little Tom sobbed aloud.

"I say," said Dick, after a pause. "There's room at my back, if you'll creep in. There! don't be afraid—why, how cold you are, lad."

Dick was sorry for his cousin's loss, but could not speak about it. However, his kind tone sank into Tom's heart, and he fell asleep once more.

The three boys all got up at the same time in the morning, but were not inclined to talk. Jack and Dick put on their clothes as fast as possible, and ran downstairs; but this was quite a different way of going on to what Tom had been accustomed. He looked about for some kind of basin or mug to wash in; there was none—not even a jug of water in the room. He slipped on a few necessary clothes, and went downstairs, found a pitcher, and went off to the pump. His cousins, who were playing in the court, laughed at him, and would not tell him where the soap was kept: he had to look some minutes before he could find it. Then he went back to the bedroom; but on entering it from the fresh air, the smell was so oppressive that he could not endure it. Three people had been breathing the air all night, and had used up every particle many times over and over again; and each time that it had been sent out from the lungs, it was less fit than before to be breathed again. They had not felt how poisonous it was while they stayed in it; they had only felt tired and unrefreshed, with a dull headache; but now that Tom came back again into it, he could not mistake its oppressive nature. He went to the window to try and open it. It was what people call a "Yorkshire light," where you know one-half has to be pushed on one side. It was very stiff, for it had not been opened for a long time. Tom pushed against it with all his might; at length it gave way with a jerk; and the shake sent out a cracked pane, which fell on the floor in a hundred little bits. Tom was sadly frightened when he saw what he had done. He would have been sorry to have done mischief at any time, but he had seen enough of his aunt the evening before to find out that she was sharp, and hasty, and cross; and it was hard to have to begin the first day in his new home by getting into a scrape. He sat down on the bedside, and began to cry. But the morning air blowing in upon him, refreshed him, and made him feel stronger. He grew braver as he washed himself in the pure, cold water. "She can't be cross with me longer than a day; by to-night it will be all over; I can bear it for a day."

Dick came running upstairs for something he had forgotten.

"My word, Tom! but you'll catch it!" exclaimed he, when he saw the broken window. He was half pleased at the event, and half sorry for Tom. "Mother did so beat Jack last week for throwing a stone right through the window downstairs. He kept out of the way till night, but she was on the look-out for him, and as soon as she saw him, she caught hold of him and gave it him. Eh! Tom, I would not be you for a deal!"

Tom began to cry again at this account of his aunt's anger; Dick became more and more sorry for him.

"I'll tell thee what; we'll go down and say it was a lad in yon back-yard throwing stones, and that one went smack through the window. I've got one in my pocket that will just do to show."

"No," said Tom, suddenly stopping crying. "I dare not do that."

"Daren't! Why you'll have to dare much more if you go down and face mother without some such story."

"No! I shan't. I shan't have to dare God's anger. Mother taught me to fear that; she said I need never be really afraid of aught else. Just be quiet, Dick, while I say my prayers."

Dick watched his little cousin kneel down by the bed, and bury his face in the clothes; he did not say any set prayer (which Dick was accustomed to think was the only way of praying), but Tom seemed, by the low murmuring which Dick heard, to be talking to a dear friend; and though at first he sobbed and cried, as he asked for help and strength, yet when he got up, his face looked calm and bright, and he spoke quietly as he said to Dick, "Now I'm ready to go and tell aunt."

"Aunt" meanwhile had missed her pitcher and her soap, and was in no good-tempered mood when Tom came to make his confession. She had been hindered in her morning's work by his taking her things away; and now he was come to tell her of the pane being broken and that it must be mended, and money must go all for a child's nonsense.

She gave him (as he had been led to expect) one or two very sharp blows. Jack and Dick looked on with curiosity, to see how he would take it; Jack, at any rate, expecting a hearty crying from "softy" (Jack himself had cried loudly at his last beating), but Tom never shed a tear, though his face did go very red, and his mouth did grow set with the pain. But what struck the boys more even than his being "hard" in bearing such blows, was his quietness afterwards. He did not grumble loudly, as Jack would have done, nor did he turn sullen, as was Dick's custom; but the minute afterwards he was ready to run an errand for his aunt; nor did he make any mention of the hard blows, when his uncle came in to breakfast, as his aunt had rather expected he would. She was glad he did not, for she knew her husband would have been displeased to know how early she had begun to beat his orphan nephew. So she almost felt grateful to Tom for his silence, and certainly began to be sorry she had struck him so hard.

Poor Tom! he did not know that his cousins were beginning to respect him, nor that his aunt was learning to like him; and he felt very lonely and desolate that first morning. He had nothing to do. Jack went to work at the factory; and Dick went grumbling to school. Tom wondered if he was to go to school again, but he did not like to ask. He sat on a little stool, as much out of his terrible aunt's way as he could. She had her youngest child, a little girl of about a year and a half old, crawling about on the floor.

Tom longed to play with her; but he was not sure how far his aunt would like it. But he kept smiling at her, and doing every little thing he could to attract her attention and make her come to him. At last she was coaxed to come upon his knee. His aunt saw it, and though she did not speak, she did not look displeased. He did everything he could think of to amuse little Annie; and her mother was very glad to have her attended to. When Annie grew sleepy, she still kept fast hold of one of Tom's fingers in her little, round, soft hand, and he began to know the happy feeling of loving somebody again. Only the night before, when his cousins had made him get out of bed, he had wondered if he should live to be an old man, and never have anybody to love all that long time; but now his heart felt quite warm to the little thing that lay on his lap.

"She'll tire you, Tom," said her mother, "you'd better let me put her down in the cot."

"Oh, no!" said he, "please don't! I like so much to have her here." He never moved, though she lay very heavy on his arm, for fear of wakening her.

When she did rouse up, his aunt said, "Thank you, Tom. I've got my work done rarely with you for a nurse. Now take a run in the yard, and play yourself a bit."

His aunt was learning something, and Tom was teaching, though they would both have been very much surprised to hear it. Whenever, in a family, every one is selfish, and (as it is called) "stands up for his own rights," there are no feelings of gratitude; the gracefulness of "thanks" is never called for; nor can there be any occasion for thoughtfulness for others when those others are sure to get the start in thinking for themselves, and taking care of number one. Tom's aunt had never had to remind Jack or Dick to go out to play. They were ready enough to see after their own pleasures.

Well! dinner-time came, and all the family gathered to the meal. It seemed to be a scramble who should be helped first, and cry out for the best pieces. Tom looked very red. His aunt in her new-born liking for him, helped him early to what she thought he would like. But he did not begin to eat. It had been his mother's custom to teach her little son to say a simple "grace" with her before they began their dinner. He expected his uncle to follow the same observance; and waited. Then he felt very hot and shy; but, thinking that it was right to say it, he put away his shyness, and very quietly, but very solemnly said the old accustomed sentence of thanksgiving. Jack burst out laughing when he had done; for which Jack's father gave him a sharp rap and a sharp word, which made him silent through the rest of the dinner. But, excepting Jack, who was angry, I think all the family were the happier for having listened reverently (if with some surprise) to Tom's thanksgiving. They were not an ill-disposed set of people, but wanted thoughtfulness in their every-day life; that sort of thoughtfulness which gives order to a home, and makes a wise and holy spirit of love the groundwork of order.

From that first day Tom never went back in the regard he began then to win. He was useful to his aunt, and patiently bore her hasty ways, until for very shame she left off being hasty with one who was always so meek and mild. His uncle sometimes said he was more like a girl than a boy, as was to be looked for from being brought up for so many years by a woman; but that was the greatest fault he ever had to find with him; and in spite of it, he really respected him for the very qualities which are most truly "manly;" for the courage with which he dared to do what was right, and the quiet firmness with which he bore many kinds of pain. As for little Annie, her friendship and favour and love were the delight of Tom's heart. He did not know how much the others were growing to like him, but Annie showed it in every way, and he loved her in return most dearly. Dick soon found out how useful Tom could be to him in his lessons; for though older than his cousin, Master Dick was a regular dunce, and had never even wished to learn till Tom came; and long before Jack could be brought to acknowledge it, Dick maintained that "Tom had a great deal of pluck in him, though it was not of Jack's kind."

Now I shall jump another year, and tell you a very little about the household twelve months after Tom had entered it. I said above that his aunt had learned to speak less crossly to one who was always gentle after her scoldings. By-and-by her ways to all became less hasty and passionate, for she grew ashamed of speaking to any one in an angry way before Tom; he always looked so sad and sorry to hear her. She has also spoken to him sometimes about his mother; at first because she thought he would like it; but latterly because she became really interested to hear of her ways; and Tom being an only child, and his mother's friend and companion, has been able to tell her of many household arts of comfort, which coming quite unconscious of any purpose, from the lips of a child, have taught her many things which she would have been too proud to learn from an older person. Her husband is softened by the additional cleanliness and peace of his home. He does not now occasionally take refuge in a public-house, to get out of the way of noisy children, an unswept hearth, and a scolding wife. Once when Tom was ill for a day or two, his uncle missed the accustomed grace, and began to say it himself. He is now the person to say "Silence, boys;" and then to ask the blessing on the meal. It makes them gather round the table, instead of sitting down here and there in the comfortless, unsociable way they used to do. Tom and Dick go to school together now, and Dick is getting on famously, and will soon be able to help his next brother over his lessons, as Tom has helped him.

Even Jack has been heard to acknowledge that Tom has "pluck" in him; and as "pluck" in Jack's mind is a short way of summing up all the virtues, he has lately become very fond of his cousin. Tom does not think about happiness, but is happy; and I think we may hope that he, and the household among whom he is adopted, will go "from strength to strength."

Now do you not see how much happier this family are from the one circumstance of a little child's coming among them? Could money have made one-tenth part of this real and increasing happiness? I think you will all say no. And yet Tom was no powerful person; he was not clever; he was very friendless at first; but he was loving and good; and on those two qualities, which any of us may have if we try, the blessing of God lies in rich abundance.

BESSY'S TROUBLES AT HOME

"Well, mother, I've got you a Southport ticket," said Bessy Lee, as she burst into a room where a pale, sick woman lay dressed on the outside of a bed. "Aren't you glad?" asked she, as her mother moved uneasily, but did not speak.

"Yes, dear, I'm very thankful to you; but your sudden coming in has made my heart flutter so, I'm ready to choke."

Poor Bessy's eyes filled with tears: but, it must be owned, they were tears half of anger. She had taken such pains, ever since the doctor said that Southport was the only thing for her mother, to get her an order from some subscriber to the charity; and she had rushed to her, in the full glow of success, and now her mother seemed more put out by the noise she had made on coming in, than glad to receive the news she had brought.

Mrs. Lee took her hand and tried to speak, but, as she said, she was almost choked with the palpitation at her heart.

"You think it very silly in me, dear, to be so easily startled; but it is not altogether silliness; it is I am so weak that every little noise gives me quite a fright. I shall be better, love, please God, when I come back from Southport. I am so glad you've got the order, for you've taken a deal of pains about it." Mrs. Lee sighed.

"Don't you want to go?" asked Bessy, rather sadly. "You always seem so sorrowful and anxious when we talk about it."

"It's partly my being ailing that makes me anxious, I know," said Mrs. Lee. "But it seems as if so many things might happen while I was away."

Bessy felt a little impatient. Young people in strong health can hardly understand the fears that beset invalids. Bessy was a kind-hearted girl, but rather headstrong, and just now a little disappointed. She forgot that her mother had had to struggle hard with many cares ever since she had been left a widow, and that her illness now had made her nervous.

"What nonsense, mother! What can happen? I can take care of the house and the little ones, and Tom and Jem can take care of themselves. What is to happen?"

"Jenny may fall into the fire," murmured Mrs. Lee, who found little comfort in being talked to in this way. "Or your father's watch may be stolen while you are in, talking with the neighbours, or—"

"Now come, mother, you know I've had the charge of Jenny ever since father died, and you began to go out washing—and I'll lock father's watch up in the box in our room."

"Then Tom and Jem won't know at what time to go to the factory. Besides, Bessy," said she, raising herself up, "they're are but young lads, and there's a deal of temptation to take them away from their homes, if their homes are not comfortable and pleasant to them. It's that, more than anything, I've been fretting about all the time I've been ill,—that I've lost the power of making this house the cleanest and brightest place they know. But it's no use fretting," said she, falling back weakly upon the bed and sighing. "I must leave it in God's hands. He raiseth up and He bringeth low."

Bessy stood silent for a minute or two. Then she said, "Well, mother, I will try to make home comfortable for the lads, if you'll but keep your mind easy, and go off to Southport quiet and cheerful."

"I'll try," said Mrs. Lee, taking hold of Bessy's hand, and looking up thankfully in her face.

The next Wednesday she set off, leaving home with a heavy heart, which, however, she struggled against, and tried to make more faithful. But she wished her three weeks at Southport were over.

Tom and Jem were both older than Bessy, and she was fifteen. Then came Bill and Mary and little Jenny. They were all good children, and all had faults. Tom and Jem helped to support the family by their earnings at the factory, and gave up their wages very cheerfully for this purpose, to their mother, who, however, insisted on a little being put by every week in the savings' bank. It was one of her griefs now that, when the doctor ordered her some expensive delicacy in the way of diet during her illness (a thing which she persisted in thinking she could have done without), her boys had gone and taken their money out in order to procure it for her. The article in question did not cost one quarter of the amount of their savings, but they had put off returning the remainder into the bank, saying the doctor's bill had yet to be paid, and that it seemed so silly to be always taking money in and out. But meanwhile Mrs. Lee feared lest it should be spent, and begged them to restore it to the savings' bank. This had not been done when she left for Southport. Bill and Mary went to school. Little Jenny was the darling of all, and toddled about at home, having been her sister Bessy's especial charge when all went on well, and the mother used to go out to wash.

Mrs. Lee, however, had always made a point of giving all her children who were at home a comfortable breakfast at seven, before she set out to her day's work; and she prepared the boys' dinner ready for Bessy to warm for them. At night, too, she was anxious to be at home as soon after her boys as she could; and many of her employers respected her wish, and, finding her hard-working and conscientious, took care to set her at liberty early in the evening.

Bessy felt very proud and womanly when she returned home from seeing her mother off by the railway. She looked round the house with a new feeling of proprietorship, and then went to claim little Jenny from the neighbour's where she had been left while Bessy had gone to the station. They asked her to stay and have a bit of chat; but she replied that she could not, for that it was near dinner-time, and she refused the invitation that was then given her to go in some evening. She was full of good plans and resolutions.

That afternoon she took Jenny and went to her teacher's to borrow a book, which she meant to ask one of her brothers to read to her in the evenings while she worked. She knew that it was a book which Jem would like, for though she had never read it, one of her school-fellows had told her it was all about the sea, and desert islands, and cocoanut-trees, just the things that Jem liked to hear about. How happy they would all be this evening.

She hurried Jenny off to bed before her brothers came home; Jenny did not like to go so early, and had to be bribed and coaxed to give up the pleasure of sitting on brother Tom's knee; and when she was in bed, she could not go to sleep, and kept up a little whimper of distress. Bessy kept calling out to her, now in gentle, now in sharp tones, as she made the hearth clean and bright against her brothers' return, as she settled Bill and Mary to their next day's lessons, and got her work ready for a happy evening.

Presently the elder boys came in.

"Where's Jenny?" asked Tom, the first thing.

"I've put her to bed," said Bessy. "I've borrowed a book for you to read to me while I darn the stockings; and it was time for Jenny to go."

"Mother never puts her to bed so soon," said Tom, dissatisfied.

"But she'd be so in the way of any quietness over our reading," said Bessy.

"I don't want to read," said Tom; "I want Jenny to sit on my knee, as she always does, while I eat my supper."

"Tom, Tom, dear Tom!" called out little Jenny, who had heard his voice, and, perhaps, a little of the conversation.

Tom made but two steps upstairs, and re-appeared with Jenny in his arms, in her night-clothes. The little girl looked at Bessy half triumphant and half afraid. Bessy did not speak, but she was evidently very much displeased. Tom began to eat his porridge with Jenny on his knee. Bessy sat in sullen silence; she was vexed with Tom, vexed with Jenny, and vexed with Jem, to gratify whose taste for reading travels she had especially borrowed this book, which he seemed to care so little about. She brooded over her fancied wrongs, ready to fall upon the first person who might give the slightest occasion for anger. It happened to be poor little Jenny, who, by some awkward movement, knocked over the jug of milk, and made a great splash on Bessy's clean white floor.

"Never mind!" said Tom, as Jenny began to cry. "I like my porridge as well without milk as with it."

"Oh, never mind!" said Bessy, her colour rising, and her breath growing shorter. "Never mind dirtying anything, Jenny; it's only giving trouble to Bessy! But I'll make you mind," continued she, as she caught a glance of intelligence peep from Jem's eyes to Tom; and she slapped Jenny's head. The moment she had done it she was sorry for it; she could have beaten herself now with the greatest pleasure for having given way to passion; for she loved little Jenny dearly, and she saw that she really had hurt her. But Jem, with his loud, deep, "For shame, Bessy!" and Tom, with his excess of sympathy with his little sister's wrongs, checked back any expression which Bessy might have uttered of sorrow and regret. She sat there ten times more unhappy than she had been before the accident, hardening her heart to the reproaches of her conscience, yet feeling most keenly that she had been acting wrongly. No one seemed to notice her; this was the evening she had planned and arranged for so busily; and the others, who never thought about it at all, were all quiet and happy, at least in outward appearance, while she was so wretched. By-and-by, she felt the touch of a little soft hand stealing into her own. She looked to see who it was; it was Mary, who till now had been busy learning her lessons, but uncomfortably conscious of the discordant spirit prevailing in the room; and who had at last ventured up to Bessy, as the one who looked the most unhappy, to express, in her own little gentle way, her sympathy in sorrow. Mary was not a quick child; she was plain and awkward in her ways, and did not seem to have many words in which to tell her feelings, but she was very tender and loving, and submitted meekly and humbly to the little slights and rebuffs she often met with for her stupidity.

"Dear Bessy! good night!" said she, kissing her sister; and, at the soft kiss, Bessy's eyes filled with tears, and her heart began to melt.

"Jenny," continued Mary, going to the little spoilt, wilful girl, "will you come to bed with me, and I'll tell you stories about school, and sing you my songs as I undress? Come, little one!" said she, holding out her arms. Jenny was tempted by this speech, and went off to bed in a more reasonable frame of mind than any one had dared to hope.

And now all seemed clear and open for the reading, but each was too proud to propose it. Jem, indeed, seemed to have forgotten the book altogether, he was so busy whittling away at a piece of wood. At last Tom, by a strong effort, said, "Bessy, mayn't we have the book now?"

"No!" said Jem, "don't begin reading, for I must go out and try and make Ned Bates give me a piece of ash-wood—deal is just good for nothing."

"Oh!" said Bessy, "I don't want any one to read this book who does not like it. But I know mother would be better pleased if you were stopping at home quiet, rather than rambling to Ned Bates's at this time of night."

"I know what mother would like as well as you, and I'm not going to be preached to by a girl," said Jem, taking up his cap and going out. Tom yawned and went up to bed. Bessy sat brooding over the evening.

"So much as I thought and I planned! I'm sure I tried to do what was right, and make the boys happy at home. And yet nothing has happened as I wanted it to do. Every one has been so cross and contrary. Tom would take Jenny up when she ought to have been in bed. Jem did not care a straw for this book that I borrowed on purpose for him, but sat laughing. I saw, though he did not think I did, when all was going provoking and vexatious. Mary—no! Mary was a help and a comfort, as she always is, I think, though she is so stupid over her book. Mary always contrives to get people right, and to have her own way somehow; and yet I'm sure she does not take half the trouble I do to please people."

Jem came back soon, disappointed because Ned Bates was out, and could not give him any ash-wood. Bessy said it served him right for going at that time of night, and the brother and sister spoke angrily to each other all the way upstairs, and parted without even saying good-night. Jenny was asleep when Bessy entered the bedroom which she shared with her sisters and her mother; but she saw Mary's wakeful eyes looking at her as she came in.

"Oh, Mary," said she, "I wish mother was back. The lads would mind her, and now I see they'll just go and get into mischief to spite and plague me."

"I don't think it's for that," said Mary, softly. "Jem did want that ash-wood, I know, for he told me in the morning he didn't think that deal would do. He wants to make a wedge to keep the window from rattling so on windy nights; you know how that fidgets mother."

The next day, little Mary, on her way to school, went round by Ned Bates's to beg a piece of wood for her brother Jem; she brought it home to him at dinner-time, and asked him to be so good as to have everything ready for a quiet whittling at night, while Tom or Bessy read aloud. She told Jenny she would make haste with her lessons, so as to be ready to come to bed early, and talk to her about school (a grand, wonderful place, in Jenny's eyes), and thus Mary quietly and gently prepared for a happy evening, by attending to the kind of happiness for which every one wished.

While Mary had thus been busy preparing for a happy evening, Bessy had been spending part of the afternoon at a Mrs. Foster's, a neighbour of her mother's, and a very tidy, industrious old widow. Mrs. Foster earned part of her livelihood by working for the shops where knitted work of all kinds is to be sold; and Bessy's attention was caught, almost as soon as she went in, by a very gay piece of wool-knitting, in a new stitch, that was to be used as a warm covering for the feet. After admiring its pretty looks, Bessy thought how useful it might be to her mother; and when Mrs. Foster heard this, she offered to teach Bessy how to do it. But where were the wools to come from? Those which Mrs. Foster used were provided her by the shop; and she was a very poor woman—too poor to make presents, though rich enough (as we all are) to give help of many other kinds, and willing too to do what she could (which some of us are not).

The two sat perplexed. "How much did you say it would cost?" said Bessy at last; as if the article was likely to have become cheaper, since she asked the question before.

"Well! it's sure to be more than two shillings if it's German wool. You might get it for eighteenpence if you could be content with English."

"But I've not got eighteenpence," said Bessy, gloomily.

"I could lend it you," said Mrs. Foster, "if I was sure of having it back before Monday. But it's part of my rent-money. Could you make sure, do you think?"

"Oh, yes!" said Bessy, eagerly. "At least I'd try. But perhaps I had better not take it, for after all I don't know where I could get it. What Tom and Jem earn is little enough for the house, now that mother's washing is cut off."

"They are good, dutiful lads, to give it to their mother," said Mrs. Foster, sighing: for she thought of her own boys, that had left her in her old age to toil on, with faded eyesight and weakened strength.

"Oh! but mother makes them each keep a shilling out of it for themselves," said Bessy, in a complaining tone, for she wanted money, and was inclined to envy any one who possessed it.

"That's right enough," said Mrs. Foster. "They that earn it should have some of the power over it."

"But about this wool; this eighteenpence! I wish I was a boy and could earn money. I wish mother would have let me go to work in the factory."

"Come now, Bessy, I can have none of that nonsense. Thy mother knows what's best for thee; and I'm not going to hear thee complain of what she has thought right. But may be, I can help you to a way of gaining eighteenpence. Mrs. Scott at the worsted shop told me that she should want some one to clean on Saturday; now you're a good strong girl, and can do a woman's work if you've a mind. Shall I say you will go? and then I don't mind if I lend you my eighteenpence. You'll pay me before I want my rent on Monday."

"Oh! thank you, dear Mrs. Foster," said Bessy. "I can scour as well as any woman, mother often says so; and I'll do my best on Saturday; they shan't blame you for having spoken up for me."

"No, Bessy, they won't, I'm sure, if you do your best. You're a good sharp girl for your years."

Bessy lingered for some time, hoping that Mrs. Foster would remember her offer of lending her the money; but finding that she had quite forgotten it, she ventured to remind the kind old woman. That it was nothing but forgetfulness, was evident from the haste with which Mrs. Foster bustled up to her tea-pot and took from it the money required.

"You're as welcome to it as can be, Bessy, as long as I'm sure of its being repaid by Monday. But you're in a mighty hurry about this coverlet," continued she, as she saw Bessy put on her bonnet and prepare to go out. "Stay, you must take patterns, and go to the right shop in St. Mary's Gate. Why, your mother won't be back this three weeks, child."

"No. But I can't abide waiting, and I want to set to it before it is dark; and you'll teach me the stitch, won't you, when I come back with the wools? I won't be half an hour away."

But Mary and Bill had to "abide waiting" that afternoon; for though the neighbour at whose house the key was left could let them into the house, there was no supper ready for them on their return from school; even Jenny was away spending the afternoon with a playfellow; the fire was nearly out, the milk had been left at a neighbour's; altogether home was very comfortless to the poor tired children, and Bill grumbled terribly; Mary's head ached, and the very tones of her brother's voice, as he complained, gave her pain; and for a minute she felt inclined to sit down and cry. But then she thought of many little sayings which she had heard from her teacher—such as "Never complain of what you can cure," "Bear and forbear," and several other short sentences of a similar description. So she began to make up the fire, and asked Bill to fetch some chips; and when he gave her the gruff answer, that he did not see any use in making a fire when there was nothing to cook by it, she went herself and brought the wood without a word of complaint.

Presently Bill said, "Here! you lend me those bellows; you're not blowing it in the right way; girls never do!" He found out that Mary was wise in making a bright fire ready; for before the blowing was ended, the neighbour with whom the milk had been left brought it in, and little handy Mary prepared the porridge as well as the mother herself could have done. They had just ended when Bessy came in almost breathless; for she had suddenly remembered, in the middle of her knitting-lesson, that Bill and Mary must be at home from school.

"Oh!" she said, "that's right. I have so hurried myself! I was afraid the fire would be out. Where's Jenny? You were to have called for her, you know, as you came from school. Dear! how stupid you are, Mary. I am sure I told you over and over again. Now don't cry, silly child. The best thing you can do is to run off back again for her."

"But my lessons, Bessy. They are so bad to learn. It's tables day to-morrow," pleaded Mary.

"Nonsense; tables are as easy as can be. I can say up to sixteen times sixteen in no time."

"But you know, Bessy, I'm very stupid, and my head aches so to-night!"

"Well! the air will do it good. Really, Mary, I would go myself, only I'm so busy; and you know Bill is too careless, mother says, to fetch Jenny through the streets; and besides they would quarrel, and you can always manage Jenny."

Mary sighed, and went away to bring her sister home. Bessy sat down to her knitting. Presently Bill came up to her with some question about his lesson. She told him the answer without looking at the book; it was all wrong, and made nonsense; but Bill did not care to understand what he learnt, and went on saying, "Twelve inches make one shilling," as contentedly as if it were right.

Mary brought Jenny home quite safely. Indeed, Mary always did succeed in everything, except learning her lessons well; and sometimes, if the teacher could have known how many tasks fell upon the willing, gentle girl at home, she would not have thought that poor Mary was slow or a dunce; and such thoughts would come into the teacher's mind sometimes, although she fully appreciated Mary's sweetness and humility of disposition.

To-night she tried hard at her tables, and all to no use. Her head ached so, she could not remember them, do what she would. She longed to go to her mother, whose cool hands around her forehead always seemed to do her so much good, and whose soft, loving words were such a help to her when she had to bear pain. She had arranged so many plans for to-night, and now all were deranged by Bessy's new fancy for knitting. But Mary did not see this in the plain, clear light in which I have put it before you. She only was sorry that she could not make haste with her lessons, as she had promised Jenny, who was now upbraiding her with the non-fulfilment of her words. Jenny was still up when Tom and Jem came in. They spoke sharply to Bessy for not having their porridge ready; and while she was defending herself, Mary, even at the risk of imperfect lessons, began to prepare the supper for her brothers. She did it all so quietly, that, almost before they were aware, it was ready for them; and Bessy, suddenly ashamed of herself, and touched by Mary's quiet helpfulness, bent down and kissed her, as once more she settled to the never-ending difficulty of her lesson.

Mary threw her arms round Bessy's neck, and began to cry, for this little mark of affection went to her heart; she had been so longing for a word or a sign of love in her suffering.

"Come, Molly," said Jem, "don't cry like a baby;" but he spoke very kindly. "What's the matter? the old headache come back? Never mind. Go to bed, and it will be better in the morning."

"But I can't go to bed. I don't know my lesson!" Mary looked happier, though the tears were in her eyes.

"I know mine," said Bill, triumphantly.

"Come here," said Jem. "There! I've time enough to whittle away at this before mother comes back. Now let's see this difficult lesson."

Jem's help soon enabled Mary to conquer her lesson; but, meanwhile, Jenny and Bill had taken to quarrelling in spite of Bessy's scolding, administered in small sharp doses, as she looked up from her all-absorbing knitting.

"Well," said Tom, "with this riot on one side, and this dull lesson on the other, and Bessy as cross as can be in the midst, I can understand what makes a man go out to spend his evenings from home."

Bessy looked up, suddenly wakened up to a sense of the danger which her mother had dreaded.

Bessy thought it was very fortunate that it fell on a Saturday, of all days in the week, that Mrs. Scott wanted her; for Mary would be at home, who could attend to the household wants of everybody; and so she satisfied her conscience at leaving the post of duty that her mother had assigned to her, and that she had promised to fulfil. She was so eager about her own plans that she did not consider this; she did not consider at all, or else I think she would have seen many things to which she seemed to be blind now. When were Mary's lessons for Monday to be learnt? Bessy knew as well as we do, that lesson-learning was hard work to Mary. If Mary worked as hard as she could after morning school she could hardly get the house cleaned up bright and comfortable before her brothers came home from the factory, which "loosed" early on the Saturday afternoon; and if pails of water, chairs heaped up one on the other, and tables put topsy-turvy on the dresser, were the most prominent objects in the house-place, there would be no temptation for the lads to stay at home; besides which, Mary, tired and weary (however gentle she might be), would not be able to give the life to the evening that Bessy, a clever, spirited girl, near their own age, could easily do, if she chose to be interested and sympathising in what they had to tell. But Bessy did not think of all this. What she did think about was the pleasant surprise she should give her mother by the warm and pretty covering for her feet, which she hoped to present her with on her return home. And if she had done the duties she was pledged to on her mother's departure first, if they had been compatible with her plan of being a whole day absent from home, in order to earn the money for the wools, the project of the surprise would have been innocent and praiseworthy.

Bessy prepared everything for dinner before she left home that Saturday morning. She made a potato-pie all ready for putting in the oven; she was very particular in telling Mary what was to be cleaned, and how it was all to be cleaned; and then she kissed the children, and ran off to Mrs. Scott's. Mary was rather afraid of the responsibility thrust upon her; but still she was pleased that Bessy could trust her to do so much. She took Jenny to the ever-useful neighbour, as she and Bill went to school; but she was rather frightened when Mrs. Jones began to grumble about these frequent visits of the child.

"I was ready enough to take care of the wench when thy mother was ill; there was reason for that. And the child is a nice child enough, when she is not cross; but still there are some folks, it seems, who, if you give them an inch, will take an ell. Where's Bessy, that she can't mind her own sister?"

"Gone out charing," said Mary, clasping the little hand in hers tighter, for she was afraid of Mrs. Jones's anger.

"I could go out charing every day in the week if I'd the face to trouble other folks with my children," said Mrs. Jones, in a surly tone.

"Shall I take her back, ma'am?" said Mary, timidly, though she knew this would involve her staying away from school, and being blamed by the dear teacher. But Mrs. Jones growled worse than she bit, this time at least.

"No," said she, "you may leave her with me. I suppose she's had her breakfast?"

"Yes; and I'll fetch her away as soon as ever I can after twelve."

If Mary had been one to consider the hardships of her little lot, she might have felt this morning's occurrence as one;—that she, who dreaded giving trouble to anybody, and was painfully averse from asking any little favour for herself, should be the very one on whom it fell to presume upon another person's kindness. But Mary never did think of any hardships; they seemed the natural events of life, and as if it was fitting and proper that she, who managed things badly, and was such a dunce, should be blamed. Still she was rather flurried by Mrs. Jones's scolding; and almost wished that she had taken Jenny home again. Her lessons were not well said, owing to the distraction of her mind.

When she went for Jenny she found that Mrs. Jones, repenting of her sharp words, had given the little girl bread and treacle, and made her very comfortable; so much so that Jenny was not all at once ready to leave her little playmates, and when once she had set out on the road, she was in no humour to make haste. Mary thought of the potato-pie and her brothers, and could almost have cried, as Jenny, heedless of her sister's entreaties, would linger at the picture-shops.

"I shall be obliged to go and leave you, Jenny! I must get dinner ready."

"I don't care," said Jenny. "I don't want any dinner, and I can come home quite well by myself."

Mary half longed to give her a fright, it was so provoking. But she thought of her mother, who was so anxious always about Jenny, and she did not do it. She kept patiently trying to attract her onwards, and at last they were at home. Mary stirred up the fire, which was to all appearance quite black; it blazed up, but the oven was cold. She put the pie in, and blew the fire; but the paste was quite white and soft when her brothers came home, eager and hungry.

"Oh! Mary, what a manager you are!" said Tom. "Any one else would have remembered and put the pie in in time."

Mary's eyes filled full of tears; but she did not try to justify herself. She went on blowing, till Jem took the bellows, and kindly told her to take off her bonnet, and lay the cloth. Jem was always kind. He gave Tom the best baked side of the pie, and quietly took the side himself where the paste was little better than dough, and the potatoes quite hard; and when he caught Mary's little anxious face watching him, as he had to leave part of his dinner untasted, he said, "Mary, I should like this pie warmed up for supper; there is nothing so good as potato-pie made hot the second time."

Tom went off saying, "Mary, I would not have you for a wife on any account. Why, my dinner would never be ready, and your sad face would take away my appetite if it were."

But Jem kissed her and said, "Never mind, Mary! you and I will live together, old maid and old bachelor."

So she could set to with spirit to her cleaning, thinking there never was such a good brother as Jem; and as she dwelt upon his perfections, she thought who it was who had given her such a good, kind brother, and felt her heart full of gratitude to Him. She scoured and cleaned in right-down earnest. Jenny helped her for some time, delighted to be allowed to touch and lift things. But then she grew tired; and Bill was out of doors; so Mary had to do all by herself, and grew very nervous and frightened, lest all should not be finished and tidy against Tom came home. And the more frightened she grew, the worse she got on. Her hands trembled, and things slipped out of them; and she shook so, she could not lift heavy pieces of furniture quickly and sharply; and in the middle the clock struck the hour for her brothers' return, when all ought to have been tidy and ready for tea. She gave it up in despair, and began to cry.

"Oh, Bessy, Bessy! why did you go away? I have tried hard, and I cannot do it," said she aloud, as if Bessy could hear.

"Dear Mary, don't cry," said Jenny, suddenly coming away from her play. "I'll help you. I am very strong. I can do anything. I can lift that pan off the fire."

The pan was full of boiling water, ready for Mary. Jenny took hold of the handle, and dragged it along the bar over the fire. Mary sprung forwards in terror to stop the little girl. She never knew how it was, but the next moment her arm and side were full of burning pain, which turned her sick and dizzy, and Jenny was crying passionately beside her.

"Oh, Mary! Mary! Mary! my hand is so scalded. What shall I do? I cannot bear it. It's all about my feet on the ground." She kept shaking her hand to cool it by the action of the air. Mary thought that she herself was dying, so acute and terrible was the pain; she could hardly keep from screaming out aloud; but she felt that if she once began she could not stop herself, so she sat still, moaning, and the tears running down her face like rain. "Go, Jenny," said she, "and tell some one to come."

"I can't, I can't, my hand hurts so," said Jenny. But she flew wildly out of the house the next minute, crying out, "Mary is dead. Come, come, come!" For Mary could bear it no longer; but had fainted away, and looked, indeed, like one that was dead. Neighbours flocked in; and one ran for a doctor. In five minutes Tom and Jem came home. What a home it seems! People they hardly knew standing in the house-place, which looked as if it had never been cleaned—all was so wet, and in such disorder, and dirty with the trampling of many feet; Jenny still crying passionately, but half comforted at being at present the only authority as to how the affair happened; and faint moans from the room upstairs, where some women were cutting the clothes off poor Mary, preparatory for the doctor's inspection. Jem said directly, "Some one go straight to Mrs. Scott's, and fetch our Bessy. Her place is here, with Mary."

And then he civilly, but quietly, dismissed all the unnecessary and useless people, feeling sure that in case of any kind of illness, quiet was the best thing. Then he went upstairs.

Mary's face was scarlet now with violent pain; but she smiled a little through her tears at seeing Jem. As for him, he cried outright.

"I don't think it was anybody's fault, Jem," said she, softly. "It was very heavy to lift."

"Are you in great pain, dear?" asked Jem, in a whisper.

"I think I'm killed, Jem. I do think I am. And I did so want to see mother again."

"Nonsense!" said the woman who had been helping Mary. For, as she said afterwards, whether Mary died or lived, crying was a bad thing for her; and she saw the girl was ready to cry when she thought of her mother, though she had borne up bravely all the time the clothes were cut off.

Bessy's face, which had been red with hard running, faded to a dead white when she saw Mary; she looked so shocked and ill that Jem had not the heart to blame her, although the minute before she came in, he had been feeling very angry with her. Bessy stood quite still at the foot of Mary's bed, never speaking a word, while the doctor examined her side and felt her pulse; only great round tears gathered in her eyes, and rolled down her cheeks, as she saw Mary quiver with pain. Jem followed the doctor downstairs. Then Bessy went and knelt beside Mary, and wiped away the tears that were trickling down the little face.

"Is it very bad, Mary?" asked Bessy.

"Oh yes! yes! if I speak, I shall scream."

Then Bessy covered her head in the bed-clothes and cried outright.

"I was not cross, was I? I did not mean to be—but I hardly know what I am saying," moaned out little Mary. "Please forgive me, Bessy, if I was cross."

"God forgive me!" said Bessy, very low. They were the first words she had spoken since she came home. But there could be no more talking between the sisters, for now the woman returned who had at first been assisting Mary. Presently Jem came to the door, and beckoned. Bessy rose up, and went with, him below. Jem looked very grave, yet not so sad as he had done before the doctor came. "He says she must go into the infirmary. He will see about getting her in."

"Oh, Jem! I did so want to nurse her myself!" said Bessy, imploringly. "It was all my own fault," (she choked with crying); "and I thought I might do that for her, to make up."

"My dear Bessy,"—before he had seen Bessy, he had thought he could never call her "dear" again, but now he began—"My dear Bessy, we both want Mary to get better, don't we? I am sure we do. And we want to take the best way of making her so, whatever that is; well, then, I think we must not be considering what we should like best just for ourselves, but what people, who know as well as doctors do, say is the right way. I can't remember all that he said; but I'm clear that he told me, all wounds on the skin required more and better air to heal in than Mary could have here: and there the doctor will see her twice a day, if need be."

Bessy shook her head, but could not speak at first. At last she said, "Jem, I did so want to do something for her. No one could nurse her as I should."

Jem was silent. At last he took Bessy's hand, for he wanted to say something to her that he was afraid might vex her, and yet that he thought he ought to say.

"Bessy!" said he, "when mother went away, you planned to do all things right at home, and to make us all happy. I know you did. Now may I tell you how I think you went wrong? Don't be angry, Bessy."

"I think I shall never have spirit enough in me to be angry again," said Bessy, humbly and sadly.

"So much the better, dear. But don't over-fret about Mary. The doctor has good hopes of her, if he can get her into the infirmary. Now, I'm going on to tell you how I think you got wrong after mother left. You see, Bessy, you wanted to make us all happy your way—as you liked; just as you are wanting now to nurse Mary in your way, and as you like. Now, as far as I can make out, those folks who make home the happiest, are people who try and find out how others think they could be happy, and then, if it's not wrong, help them on with their wishes as far as they can. You know, you wanted us all to listen to your book; and very kind it was in you to think of it; only, you see, one wanted to whittle, and another wanted to do this or that, and then you were vexed with us all. I don't say but what I should have been if I had been in your place, and planned such a deal for others; only lookers-on always see a deal; and I saw that if you'd done what poor little Mary did next day, we should all have been far happier. She thought how she could forward us in our plans, instead of trying to force a plan of her own on us. She got me my right sort of wood for whittling, and arranged all nicely to get the little ones off to bed, so as to get the house quiet, if you wanted some reading, as she thought you did. And that's the way, I notice, some folks have of making a happy home. Others may mean just as well, but they don't hit the thing."

"I dare say it's true," said Bessy. "But sometimes you all hang about as if you did not know what to do. And I thought reading travels would just please you all."

Jem was touched by Bessy's humble way of speaking, so different from her usual cheerful, self-confident manner. He answered, "I know you did, dear. And many a time we should have been glad enough of it, when we had nothing to do, as you say."

"I had promised mother to try and make you all happy, and this is the end of it!" said Bessy, beginning to cry afresh.

"But, Bessy! I think you were not thinking of your promise, when you fixed to go out and char."

"I thought of earning money."

"Earning money would not make us happy. We have enough, with care and management. If you were to have made us happy, you should have been at home, with a bright face, ready to welcome us; don't you think so, dear Bessy?"

"I did not want the money for home. I wanted to make mother a present of such a pretty thing!"

"Poor mother! I am afraid we must send for her home now. And she has only been three days at Southport!"

"Oh!" said Bessy, startled by this notion of Jem's; "don't, don't send for mother. The doctor did say so much about her going to Southport being the only thing for her, and I did so try to get her an order! It will kill her, Jem! indeed it will; you don't know how weak and frightened she is,—oh, Jem, Jem!"

Jem felt the truth of what his sister was saying. At last, he resolved to leave the matter for the doctor to decide, as he had attended his mother, and now knew exactly how much danger there was about Mary. He proposed to Bessy that they should go and relieve the kind neighbour who had charge of Mary.

"But you won't send for mother," pleaded Bessy; "if it's the best thing for Mary, I'll wash up her things to-night, all ready for her to go into the infirmary. I won't think of myself, Jem."

"Well! I must speak to the doctor," said Jem. "I must not try and fix any way just because we wish it, but because it is right."

All night long, Bessy washed and ironed, and yet was always ready to attend to Mary when Jem called her. She took Jenny's scalded hand in charge as well, and bathed it with the lotion the doctor sent; and all was done so meekly and patiently that even Tom was struck with it, and admired the change. The doctor came very early. He had prepared everything for Mary's admission into the infirmary. And Jem consulted him about sending for his mother home. Bessy sat trembling, awaiting his answer.

"I am very unwilling to sanction any concealment. And yet, as you say, your mother is in a very delicate state. It might do her serious harm if she had any shock. Well! suppose for this once, I take it on myself. If Mary goes on as I hope, why—well! well! we'll see. Mind that your mother is told all when she comes home. And if our poor Mary grows worse—but I'm not afraid of that, with infirmary care and nursing—but if she does, I'll write to your mother myself, and arrange with a kind friend I have at Southport all about sending her home. And now," said he, turning suddenly to Bessy, "tell me what you were doing from home when this happened. Did not your mother leave you in charge of all at home?"

"Yes, sir!" said Bessy, trembling. "But, sir, I thought I could earn money to make mother a present!"

"Thought! fiddle-de-dee. I'll tell you what; never you neglect the work clearly laid out for you by either God or man, to go making work for yourself, according to your own fancies. God knows what you are most fit for. Do that. And then wait; if you don't see your next duty clearly. You will not long be idle in this world, if you are ready for a summons. Now let me see that you send Mary all clean and tidy to the infirmary."

Jem was holding Bessy's hand. "She has washed everything and made it fit for a queen. Our Bessy worked all night long, and was content to let me be with Mary (where she wished sore to be), because I could lift her better, being the stronger."

"That's right. Even when you want to be of service to others, don't think how to please yourself."

I have not much more to tell you about Bessy. This sad accident of Mary's did her a great deal of good, although it cost her so much sorrow at first. It taught her several lessons, which it is good for every woman to learn, whether she is called upon, as daughter, sister, wife, or mother, to contribute to the happiness of a home. And Mary herself was hardly more thoughtful and careful to make others happy in their own way, provided that way was innocent, than was Bessy hereafter. It was a struggle between her and Mary which could be the least selfish, and do the duties nearest to them with the most faithfulness and zeal. The mother stayed at Southport her full time, and came home well and strong. Then Bessy put her arms round her mother's neck, and told her all—and far more severely against herself than either the doctor or Jem did, when they related the same story afterwards.

DISAPPEARANCES

I am not in the habit of seeing the Household Words regularly; but a friend, who lately sent me some of the back numbers, recommended me to read "all the papers relating to the Detective and Protective Police," which I accordingly did—not as the generality of readers have done, as they appeared week by week, or with pauses between, but consecutively, as a popular history of the Metropolitan Police; and, as I suppose it may also be considered, a history of the police force in every large town in England. When I had ended these papers, I did not feel disposed to read any others at that time, but preferred falling into a train of reverie and recollection.

First of all I remembered, with a smile, the unexpected manner in which a relation of mine was discovered by an acquaintance, who had mislaid or forgotten Mr. B.'s address. Now my dear cousin, Mr. B., charming as he is in many points, has the little peculiarity of liking to change his lodgings once every three months on an average, which occasions some bewilderment to his country friends, who have no sooner learnt the 19, Belle Vue Road, Hampstead, than they have to take pains to forget that address, and to remember the 27½, Upper Brown Street, Camberwell; and so on, till I would rather learn a page of Walker's Pronouncing Dictionary, than try to remember the variety of directions which I have had to put on my letters to Mr. B. during the last three years. Last summer it pleased him to remove to a beautiful village not ten miles out of London, where there is a railway station. Thither his friend sought him. (I do not now speak of the following scent there had been through three or four different lodgings, where Mr. B. had been residing, before his country friend ascertained that he was now lodging at R—.) He spent the morning in making inquiries as to Mr. B.'s whereabouts in the village; but many gentlemen were lodging there for the summer, and neither butcher nor baker could inform him where Mr. B. was staying; his letters were unknown at the post-office, which was accounted for by the circumstance of their always being directed to his office in town. At last the country friend sauntered back to the railway-office, and while he waited for the train he made inquiry, as a last resource, of the book-keeper at the station. "No, sir, I cannot tell you where Mr. B. lodges—so many gentlemen go by the trains; but I have no doubt but that the person standing by that pillar can inform you." The individual to whom he directed the inquirer's attention had the appearance of a tradesman—respectable enough, yet with no pretensions to "gentility," and had, apparently, no more urgent employment than lazily watching the passengers who came dropping in to the station. However, when he was spoken to, he answered civilly and promptly. "Mr. B.? tall gentleman, with light hair? Yes, sir, I know Mr. B. He lodges at No. 8, Morton Villas—has done these three weeks or more; but you'll not find him there, sir, now. He went to town by the eleven o'clock train, and does not usually return until the half-past four train."

The country friend had no time to lose in returning to the village, to ascertain the truth of this statement. He thanked his informant, and said he would call on Mr. B. at his office in town; but before he left R—station, he asked the book-keeper who the person was to whom he had referred him for information as to his friend's place of residence. "One of the Detective Police, sir," was the answer. I need hardly say that Mr. B., not without a little surprise, confirmed the accuracy of the policeman's report in every particular.

When I heard this anecdote of my cousin and his friend, I thought that there could be no more romances written on the same kind of plot as Caleb Williams; the principal interest of which, to the superficial reader, consists in the alternation of hope and fear, that the hero may, or may not, escape his pursuer. It is long since I have read the story, and I forget the name of the offended and injured gentleman, whose privacy Caleb has invaded; but I know that his pursuit of Caleb—his detection of the various hiding-places of the latter—his following up of slight clues—all, in fact, depended upon his own energy, sagacity, and perseverance. The interest was caused by the struggle of man against man; and the uncertainty as to which would ultimately be successful in his object; the unrelenting pursuer, or the ingenious Caleb, who seeks by every device to conceal himself. Now, in 1851, the offended master would set the Detective Police to work; there would be no doubt as to their success; the only question would be as to the time that would elapse before the hiding-place could be detected, and that could not be a question long. It is no longer a struggle between man and man, but between a vast organized machinery, and a weak, solitary individual; we have no hopes, no fears—only certainty. But if the materials of pursuit and evasion, as long as the chase is confined to England, are taken away from the store-house of the romancer, at any rate we can no more be haunted by the idea of the possibility of mysterious disappearances; and any one who has associated much with those who were alive at the end of the last century, can testify that there was some reason for such fears.

When I was a child, I was sometimes permitted to accompany a relation to drink tea with a very clever old lady, of one hundred and twenty—or, so I thought then; I now think she, perhaps, was only about seventy. She was lively, and intelligent, and had seen and known much that was worth narrating. She was a cousin of the Sneyds, the family whence Mr. Edgeworth took two of his wives; had known Major André; had mixed in the Old Whig Society that the beautiful Duchess of Devonshire and "Buff and Blue Mrs. Crewe" gathered round them; her father had been one of the early patrons of the lovely Miss Linley. I name these facts to show that she was too intelligent and cultivated by association, as well as by natural powers, to lend an over-easy credence to the marvellous; and yet I have heard her relate stories of disappearances which haunted my imagination longer than any tale of wonder. One of her stories was this:—Her father's estate lay in Shropshire, and his park-gates opened right on to a scattered village of which he was landlord. The houses formed a straggling irregular street—here a garden, next a gable-end of a farm, there a row of cottages, and so on. Now, at the end house or cottage lived a very respectable man and his wife. They were well known in the village, and were esteemed for the patient attention which they paid to the husband's father, a paralytic old man. In winter, his chair was near the fire; in summer, they carried him out into the open space in front of the house to bask in the sunshine, and to receive what placid amusement he could from watching the little passings to and fro of the villagers. He could not move from his bed to his chair without help. One hot and sultry June day, all the village turned out to the hay-fields. Only the very old and the very young remained.

The old father of whom I have spoken was carried out to bask in the sunshine that afternoon as usual, and his son and daughter-in-law went to the hay-making. But when they came home in the early evening, their paralysed father had disappeared—was gone! and from that day forwards, nothing more was ever heard of him. The old lady, who told this story, said with the quietness that always marked the simplicity of her narration, that every inquiry which her father could make was made, and that it could never be accounted for. No one had observed any stranger in the village; no small household robbery, to which the old man might have been supposed an obstacle, had been committed in his son's dwelling that afternoon. The son and daughter-in-law (noted too for their attention to the helpless father) had been a-field among all the neighbours the whole of the time. In short, it never was accounted for; and left a painful impression on many minds.

I will answer for it, the Detective Police would have ascertained every fact relating to it in a week.

This story from its mystery was painful, but had no consequences to make it tragical. The next which I shall tell (and although traditionary, these anecdotes of disappearances which I relate in this paper are correctly repeated, and were believed by my informants to be strictly true), had consequences, and melancholy ones too. The scene of it is in a little country-town, surrounded by the estates of several gentlemen of large property. About a hundred years ago there lived in this small town an attorney, with his mother and sister. He was agent for one of the squires near, and received rents for him on stated days, which of course were well known. He went at these times to a small public-house, perhaps five miles from —, where the tenants met him, paid their rents, and were entertained at dinner afterwards. One night he did not return from this festivity. He never returned. The gentleman whose agent he was, employed the Dogberrys of the time to find him, and the missing cash; the mother, whose support and comfort he was, sought him with all the perseverance of faithful love. But he never returned; and by-and-by the rumour spread that he must have gone abroad with the money; his mother heard the whispers all around her, and could not disprove it; and so her heart broke, and she died. Years after, I think as many as fifty, the well-to-do butcher and grazier of — died; but, before his death, he confessed that he had waylaid Mr. — on the heath close to the town, almost within call of his own house, intending only to rob him, but meeting with more resistance than he anticipated, had been provoked to stab him; and had buried him that very night deep under the loose sand of the heath. There his skeleton was found; but too late for his poor mother to know that his fame was cleared. His sister, too, was dead, unmarried, for no one liked the possibilities which might arise from being connected with the family. None cared if he was guilty or innocent now.

If our Detective Police had only been in existence!

This last is hardly a story of unaccounted-for disappearance. It is only unaccounted for in one generation. But disappearances never to be accounted for on any supposition are not uncommon, among the traditions of the last century. I have heard (and I think I have read it in one of the earlier numbers of Chambers's Journal), of a marriage which took place in Lincolnshire about the year 1750. It was not then de rigueur that the happy couple should set out on a wedding journey; but instead, they and their friends had a merry jovial dinner at the house of either bride or groom; and in this instance the whole party adjourned to the bridegroom's residence, and dispersed, some to ramble in the garden, some to rest in the house until the dinner-hour. The bridegroom, it is to be supposed, was with his bride, when he was suddenly summoned away by a domestic, who said that a stranger wished to speak to him; and henceforward he was never seen more. The same tradition hangs about an old deserted Welsh Hall standing in a wood near Festiniog; there, too, the bridegroom was sent for to give audience to a stranger on his wedding-day, and disappeared from the face of the earth from that time; but there, they tell in addition, that the bride lived long,—that she passed her three-score years and ten, but that daily during all those years, while there was light of sun or moon to lighten the earth, she sat watching,—watching at one particular window which commanded a view of the approach to the house. Her whole faculties, her whole mental powers, became absorbed in that weary watching; long before she died, she was childish, and only conscious of one wish—to sit in that long high window, and watch the road, along which he might come. She was as faithful as Evangeline, if pensive and inglorious.

That these two similar stories of disappearance on a wedding-day "obtained," as the French say, shows us that anything which adds to our facility of communication, and organization of means, adds to our security of life. Only let a bridegroom try to disappear from an untamed Katherine of a bride, and he will soon be brought home, like a recreant coward, overtaken by the electric telegraph, and clutched back to his fate by a detective policeman.

Two more stories of disappearance, and I have done. I will give you the last in date first, because it is the most melancholy; and we will wind up cheerfully (after a fashion). Some time between 1820 and 1830, there lived in North Shields a respectable old woman, and her son, who was trying to struggle into sufficient knowledge of medicine, to go out as ship-surgeon in a Baltic vessel, and perhaps in this manner to earn money enough to spend a session in Edinburgh. He was furthered in all his plans by the late benevolent Dr. G—, of that town. I believe the usual premium was not required in his case; the young man did many useful errands and offices which a finer young gentleman would have considered beneath him; and he resided with his mother in one of the alleys (or "chares,") which lead down from the main street of North Shields to the river. Dr. G—had been with a patient all night, and left her very early on a winter's morning to return home to bed; but first he stepped down to his apprentice's home, and bade him get up, and follow him to his own house, where some medicine was to be mixed, and then taken to the lady. Accordingly the poor lad came, prepared the dose, and set off with it some time between five and six on a winter's morning. He was never seen again. Dr. G— waited, thinking he was at his mother's house; she waited, considering that he had gone to his day's work. And meanwhile, as people remembered afterwards, the small vessel bound to Edinburgh sailed out of port. The mother expected him back her whole life long; but some years afterwards occurred the discoveries of the Hare and Burke horrors, and people seemed to gain a dark glimpse at his fate; but I never heard that it was fully ascertained, or indeed more than surmised. I ought to add that all who knew him spoke emphatically as to his steadiness of purpose, and conduct, so as to render it improbable in the highest degree that he had run off to sea, or suddenly changed his plan of life in any way.

My last story is one of a disappearance which was accounted for after many years. There is a considerable street in Manchester leading from the centre of the town to some of the suburbs. This street is called at one part Garratt, and afterwards, where it emerges into gentility and, comparatively, country, Brook Street. It derives its former name from an old black-and-white hall of the time of Richard the Third, or thereabouts, to judge from the style of building; they have closed in what is left of the old hall now; but a few years since this old house was visible from the main road; it stood low on some vacant ground, and appeared to be half in ruins. I believe it was occupied by several poor families who rented tenements in the tumble-down dwelling. But formerly it was Gerard Hall, (what a difference between Gerard and Garratt!) and was surrounded by a park with a clear brook running through it, with pleasant fish-ponds, (the name of these was preserved until very lately, on a street near,) orchards, dovecotes, and similar appurtenances to the manor-houses of former days. I am almost sure that the family to whom it belonged were Mosleys, probably a branch of the tree of the lord of the Manor of Manchester. Any topographical work of the last century relating to their district would give the name of the last proprietor of the old stock, and it is to him that my story refers.

Many years ago there lived in Manchester two old maiden ladies, of high respectability. All their lives had been spent in the town, and they were fond of relating the changes which had taken place within their recollection, which extended back to seventy or eighty years from the present time. They knew much of its traditionary history from their father, as well; who, with his father before him, had been respectable attorneys in Manchester, during the greater part of the last century: they were, also, agents for several of the county families, who, driven from their old possessions by the enlargement of the town, found some compensation in the increased value of any land which they might choose to sell. Consequently the Messrs. S—, father and son, were conveyancers in good repute, and acquainted with several secret pieces of family history, one of which related to Garratt Hall.

The owner of this estate, some time in the first half of the last century, married young; he and his wife had several children, and lived together in a quiet state of happiness for many years. At last, business of some kind took the husband up to London; a week's journey in those days. He wrote and announced his arrival; I do not think he ever wrote again. He seemed to be swallowed up in the abyss of the metropolis, for no friend (and the lady had many and powerful friends) could ever ascertain for her what had become of him; the prevalent idea was that he had been attacked by some of the street-robbers who prowled about in those days, that he had resisted, and had been murdered. His wife gradually gave up all hopes of seeing him again, and devoted herself to the care of her children; and so they went on, tranquilly enough, until the heir came of age, when certain deeds were necessary before he could legally take possession of the property. These deeds Mr. S— (the family lawyer) stated had been given up by him into the missing gentleman's keeping just before the last mysterious journey to London, with which I think they were in some way concerned. It was possible that they were still in existence; some one in London might have them in possession, and be either conscious or unconscious of their importance. At any rate, Mr. S—'s advice to his client was that he should put an advertisement in the London papers, worded so skilfully that any one who might hold the important documents should understand to what it referred, and no one else. This was accordingly done; and although repeated at intervals for some time, it met with no success. But at last a mysterious answer was sent; to the effect that the deeds were in existence, and should be given up; but only on certain conditions, and to the heir himself. The young man, in consequence, went up to London, and adjourned, according to directions, to an old house in Barbican, where he was told by a man, apparently awaiting him, that he must submit to be blindfolded, and must follow his guidance. He was taken through several long passages before he left the house; at the termination of one of these he was put into a sedan-chair, and carried about for an hour or more; he always reported that there were many turnings, and that he imagined he was set down finally not very far from his starting point.

When his eyes were unbandaged, he was in a decent sitting-room, with tokens of family occupation lying about. A middle-aged gentleman entered, and told him that, until a certain time had elapsed (which should be indicated to him in a particular way, but of which the length was not then named), he must swear to secrecy as to the means by which he obtained possession of the deeds. This oath was taken; and then the gentleman, not without some emotion, acknowledged himself to be the missing father of the heir. It seems that he had fallen in love with a damsel, a friend of the person with whom he lodged. To this young woman he had represented himself as unmarried; she listened willingly to his wooing, and her father, who was a shopkeeper in the City, was not averse to the match, as the Lancashire squire had a goodly presence, and many similar qualities, which the shopkeeper thought might be acceptable to his customers. The bargain was struck; the descendant of a knightly race married the only daughter of the City shopkeeper, and became a junior partner in the business. He told his son that he had never repented the step he had taken; that his lowly-born wife was sweet, docile, and affectionate; that his family by her was large; and that he and they were thriving and happy. He inquired after his first (or rather, I should say, his true) wife with friendly affection; approved of what she had done with regard to his estate, and the education of his children; but said that he considered he was dead to her, as she was to him. When he really died he promised that a particular message, the nature of which he specified, should be sent to his son at Garrett; until then they would not hear more of each other; for it was of no use attempting to trace him under his incognito, even if the oath did not render such an attempt forbidden. I dare say the youth had no great desire to trace out the father, who had been one in name only. He returned to Lancashire; took possession of the property at Manchester; and many years elapsed before he received the mysterious intimation of his father's real death. After that, he named the particulars connected with the recovery of the title-deeds to Mr. S., and one or two intimate friends. When the family became extinct, or removed from Garratt, it became no longer any very closely kept secret, and I was told the tale of the disappearance by Miss S., the aged daughter of the family agent.

Once more, let me say I am thankful I live in the days of the Detective Police; if I am murdered, or commit bigamy, at any rate my friends will have the comfort of knowing all about it.

A correspondent has favoured us with the sequel of the disappearance of the pupil of Dr. G., who vanished from North Shields, in charge of certain potions he was entrusted with, very early one morning, to convey to a patient:—"Dr. G.'s son married my sister, and the young man who disappeared was a pupil in the house. When he went out with the medicine, he was hardly dressed, having merely thrown on some clothes; and he went in slippers—which incidents induced the belief that he was made away with. After some months his family put on mourning; and the G.'s (very timid people) were so sure that he was murdered, that they wrote verses to his memory, and became sadly worn by terror. But, after a long time (I fancy, but am not sure, about a year and a half), came a letter from the young man, who was doing well in America. His explanation was, that a vessel was lying at the wharf about to sail in the morning, and the youth, who had long meditated evasion, thought it a good opportunity, and stepped on board, after leaving the medicine at the proper door. I spent some weeks at Dr. G.'s after the occurrence; and very doleful we used to be about it. But the next time I went they were, naturally, very angry with the inconsiderate young man."

Elizabeth Gaskell – A Short Biography

Elizabeth Gaskell (1810-1865) is today remembered as one of the greatest female writers of the English tongue. She was born in Chelsea on September 29th, 1810, to William Stevenson, a Scottish Unitarian minister before becoming the keeper of the Treasury Records, and to Elizabeth Holland. Both parents inculcated their strong Unitarian beliefs into their children, including Elizabeth who was often reluctant to display her religious convictions, though. A number of her novels were highly controversial for dealing with delicate political and social issues of the Victorian Age such as the exploitation of the working class and the situation of women in society. These included *Mary Barton: A Tale of Manchester Life*, *Ruth* and *Cranford*. Due to their concentration on the observation of the Victorian society and the mechanisms that governed social classes, Gaskell's works are today of much interest not only to literary scholars and critics, but also to social historians.

The early death of Elizabeth Gaskell's mother represented a crucial turning point in the daughter's life. Indeed, her father decided to send her to be brought up by her maternal aunt in Knutsford, Cheshire. Such a crucial development left Gaskell deprived of the care of both her parents. Her father soon remarried and had other children from his new wife. Although Gaskell spent most of her childhood in Cheshire away from her father and his new family, she used to have a positive attitude towards her half-siblings.

Gaskell's aunt encouraged her to learn the rules of language and writing and to read books. In the beginning, Gaskell attended a school at Bradford House before she went to another school in Stratford-upon-Avon in 1824 where she was able to learn about the arts, literature and Victorian traditions and manners. In addition, and despite being separated from her family, her brother John and her father used to encourage her to read and write, often providing her with necessary books and writing material. After finishing school, Gaskell paid some visits to maternal relatives in London, Newcastle upon Tyne and Edinburgh. In 1828, her brother John, who worked in the merchant navy, disappeared definitively on a journey to India. This disastrous loss depressed her father and she had to go to his household to nurse him for the next year before he died.

In 1832, Elizabeth Gaskell, née Stevenson, fell in love with William Gaskell and married him. Like Elizabeth's father, William was a Unitarian minister and was equally fond of literature and the arts. Unitarianism, which was largely present in Elizabeth Gaskell's childhood and married life, is a Christian doctrine that believes in divine unity as opposed to Trinitarianism. Unitarianism is also a highly rationalistic belief that highlights the fundamental role of the human in the world. This set of beliefs greatly marked Elizabeth Gaskell's life and work whose professional career as a published writer actually started when she settled with her husband in Manchester. The industrial aspect of the city had a great impact on Gaskell who felt the need to speak about poor workers and their exploitation by large industrial companies. A collection of poems and short stories entitled "Sketches among the Poor" first appeared in 1837 in *The Blackwood Magazine*. The work, which was co-authored by her husband, was followed by the anonymously-published "Clopton Hall" and then by "Notes on Cheshire Customs" in 1840. Both short works were included in compilations. Gaskell later published "Libbie Marsh's Three Eras" and "Sexton's Hero." However, Gaskell's first major work, which did not bear her real name either, *was Mary Barton: A Tale of Manchester Life* published in 1848.

According to biographers, the decision to write *Mary Barton* came after Gaskell lost her nine-month son named William when her husband advised her to resort to writing in order to escape depression. The novel was an immediate success and many critics still believe it to be Gaskell's masterpiece. Set in the industrial city of Manchester, the novel displays the hardships of the working class. It centers on the eponymous character whose father is concerned with the state of the poor and who gets involved in trade-unionism. Mary, who has to choose between her two suitors, chooses the wealthier, Carson, in an attempt to help her father. However, she soon that she discovers that she committed a mistake by refusing Wilson, the man that she really loves. Apart from the events centering on Mary's life, the description of the poverty of workers was shocking to many. Manchester business owners felt offended by the novel which, they believed, was unfairly harsh on them.

On the other hand, literary critics and novelists of the time rather hailed Gaskell's refined writing style. These included renowned figures like William Makepeace Thackeray, Thomas Carlyle, John Ruskin, and mainly the great Victorian novelist Charles Dickens who soon invited Gaskell to publish her stories in his periodical *Household Words*. During this period, Gaskell was also busy being a mother and a minister's wife. She was also engaged along with her husband in numerous charitable activities. With Dickens, Gaskell first published *Lizzie Leigh* in 1850 which dealt with the taboo subject of prostitution, to be followed by *The Well of Pen Morfa* and *The Heart of John Middleton*.

Generally, Gaskell was not only an excellent writer whose stories and style impressed the greatest among her fellow Victorian literary figures, but also a social critic whose works often created a lot of polemics. After the polemic caused by Mary Barton among capitalist classes, she published another novel entitled *Ruth* in 1853 to cause much more uproar. *Ruth*'s plot follows the life of a young female who engages in a sensual relation and gives birth to an illegitimate child. The novel unveils Victorian social hypocrisy and focuses on the miserable state of women in society. The ensuing scandal might have caused embarrassment even to her husband as a copy of the book was burnt in his same church. Most critics of the book who declared the anathema missed the story's moral lesson and caused the book to be banned from libraries.

Four years later, another polemic rose after the publication of Gaskell's biography of her close friend Charlotte Bronte. It was right after the death of Bronte in 1855 that her father Patrick Bronte asked Gaskell to do the work and she accepted. *The Life of Charlotte Bronte* caused a great controversy and this was because many of the people portrayed in the work complained about being misrepresented. Some even threatened to sue Gaskell and the latter was forced to publish an apology in *The Times* and to make some revision and modifications for the final version. In the meantime, Gaskell continued publishing her stories in Dickens's *Household*

Words and later in his *All the Year Round* as other important novels of hers were gaining popularity such as *Cranford* (1853) and *North and South* (1854).

Many of Gaskell's short stories are today believed to have a great influence on the Gothic genre which witnessed a revival after her death with writers like Sheridan Le Fanu, Robert Louis Stevenson and Bram Stoker. Towards her twilight years, Elizabeth Gaskell started sending her stories to *The Cornhill Magazine* which was edited by another outstanding Victorian literary figure, William Makepeace Thackeray. Soon Gaskell started the serialization of the "saddest story [she] ever wrote," *Sylvia's Lovers* (1863). The story is set back in the late eighteenth-century at the time of the Napoleonic wars. It follows the character of young Sylvia Robson, her simple family life and her secret romantic relation with Charlie Kinraid. In 1864, Gaskell published her four-part novella *Cousin Phillis* which is considered by many critics as a crucial achievement. They also agree that the novella unintentionally fits as a prelude for Gaskell's final remarkable achievement *Wives and Daughters*.

Wives and Daughters (1864-1866) is Elizabeth Gaskell's last novel first serialized in *The Cornhill Magazine* and of which the last installment was completed posthumously by Frederick Greenwood. Nonetheless, the book is considered by many as Gaskell's finest achievement and masterpiece. It tells the story of Molly Gibson who is raised by her widowed father. As a middle-class woman, she knows that she is not suitable for the son of a gentry family, the Hamleys, with whom she falls in love. Her father marries again and Molly is far from appreciating her too ambitious stepmother who also wishes to match her own daughter to one of the Hamleys. By and large, the novel is a social investigation and a condemnation of social hypocrisy. It shows Gaskell's characterization skills at their best.

Elizabeth Gaskell's interest in social criticism is one of the most important features of her fiction. It made some critics compare her to Friedrich Engels and even to Carl Marx. Her novels are today used not only as literary references, but also as historical and sociological sources for researchers interested in the Victorian society. On November 12th, 1865, Elizabeth Gaskell died in Holybourne, Hampshire, after suffering from a heart attack a month earlier. A memorial dedicated to the Victorian novelist is located in The Poets' Corner in Westminster Abbey next to Britain's greatest writers and poets.

Elizabeth Gaskell – A Concise Bibliography

Novels
Mary Barton (1848)
Cranford (1851–53)

Ruth (1853)
North and South (1854–55)
Sylvia's Lovers (1863)
Wives and Daughters: An Everyday Story (1865)

Novellas and Collections
The Moorland Cottage (1850)
Mr. Harrison's Confessions (1851)
The Old Nurse's Story (1852)
Lizzie Leigh (1855)
My Lady Ludlow (1859)
Round the Sofa (1859)
Lois the Witch (1861)
A Dark Night's Work (1863)
Cousin Phillis (1864)

Short Stories
Libbie Marsh's Three Eras (1847)
The Sexton's Hero (1847)
Christmas Storms and Sunshine (1848)
Hand and Heart (1849)
The Well of Pen-Morfa (1850)
The Heart of John Middleton (1850)
Disappearances (1851)
Bessy's Troubles at Home (1852)
The Old Nurse's Story (1852)
Cumberland Sheep-Shearers (1853)
Morton Hall (1853)
Traits and Stories of the Huguenots (1853)
My French Master (1853)
The Squire's Story (1853)
Half a Life-time Ago (1855)
Company Manners (1854)
The Poor Clare (1856)
The Doom of the Griffiths (1858)
Right at Last (1858)
"The Manchester Marriage" (1858)[19]
The Haunted House (1859)[20]
The Crooked Branch (1859)
The Half-brothers (1859)
Curious If True (1860)
The Grey Woman (1861)

The Cage at Cranford (1863)
Crowley Castle (1863)

Non Fiction
Sketches Among the Poor (poems 1837)
An Accursed Race (1855)
The Life of Charlotte Brontë (1857)
French Life (1864)